D1756894

Fighting
FALLON
UNDERGROUND OMEGA SYNDICATE
SINCLAIR KELLY

Copyright © 2023 by Sinclair Kelly

All rights reserved.

No portion of this book may be reproduced in any form or by any electronic or mechanical means, including information storage and retrieval systems, without written permission from the publisher or author, except as permitted by U.S. copyright law.

Cover: JODIELOCKS Designs

Editor: Michelle Oberleiton

Formatting: Sinclair Kelly

DEDICATION

To Laura...
because without you I would've *glitched!*

To Elizabeth...
because you're a genius and saved me literal hours of formatting headaches!

To My Past Self...
because despite royally fucking up your schedule, you kept on swimming!

Contents

Chapter 1

Faking innocence gets harder with each tiny piece of my soul I give up. It's been so long—well over a decade—since I was that sweet, innocent teenage omega with hope in her heart and stars in her eyes.

Fuck. I can't even reconcile that image in my head with the reality I now face. Oh, sure, when I look in the mirror, I see the big, bright blue eyes and Cupid's bow lips that give the impression of a youthful sort of purity most can't see past. That couldn't be further from the truth. Didn't their mama tell them to never judge a book by its cover?

The alpha's breath is hot against my lips, bringing me back to the situation at hand. I suppose I should count myself lucky that he at least brushed his teeth because I'm getting intimately acquainted with *all* of his scents right now thanks to his large body boxing me against the on-call room wall. The smell of freshly mowed grass doused in antiseptic is especially displeasing.

I fight back a sneeze, barely managing to hide the disgust from my face when one of his hands lands beside my head. The other finds my hip, and I fight down the instinct to break his wrist for touching me.

"Well, aren't you a sweet little piece?"

Running his nose along my jaw and down my neck, he nuzzles into me, marking me with his scent. Any alpha should know better than to do that to an unbonded omega, but this shithead doesn't care. When he finally pulls back, his pupils are blown wide, and barely concealed lust drips out of damn near every pore in his body. His alpha pheromones fill the small space around us, the scent so thick it's almost suffocating. Good thing I can hold my breath for a *really* long time.

"It's time to give you the new intern orientation. You see, there are some rules that have to be followed at this hospital, Fallon, if you want to be successful. Would you like to hear what they are?"

I lick my lips, playing up my nervousness by glancing at the sole door in the room.

"Ah ah. No one will interrupt us while we're in here. They know the drill," he explains with a smarmy smirk plastered on his devilishly handsome face. "Which means your only job right now is to focus on me, and *only* me, do you understand?"

Nodding, I bow my head, being the good lil' omega by deferring to his natural alpha aggression.

"Good," he growls. "First rule—*I'm* the one in charge here. You do what I say, when I say it."

When his hand roughly grabs my breast through the scrubs, I try to look appropriately shocked, parting my lips and letting out a soft gasp. His grin grows wider.

"Second rule—what happens in the ER, stays in the ER."

He kneads and squeezes, his fingers finding my nipple through the fabric and pinching hard. His eyes have left mine, watching himself fondle me. The fact that I'm completely unwilling doesn't mean shit to him.

Sick fuck.

While he's not looking at my face, I drop the innocent act and very carefully reach into my back pocket where my little surprise is waiting oh so helpfully. I can feel my lips curving up and allow myself a second of smugness.

"God, you're fucking perfect. Where in the hell did they find you? They definitely got it right this time," he murmurs reverently.

Yes. Yes, they did. They chose very *well.*

The grin disappears just as he looks up.

"Now, third rule—if you ever open those pouty little lips of yours, I'll make sure you never get to do it again."

And there it is. The reason this emergency room can't seem to keep good nurses on staff for more than a week. This motherfucker uses them like a perpetually changing omega buffet provided solely for his pleasure.

But that stops tonight.

I tilt my head. "Are you done?"

A slow growl works itself up in his chest.

"Maybe you misheard me."

"Oh, I don't think so. You think you're hot shit, don't you, Phillip?"

He pulls back the slightest bit, which works to my advantage, his body vibrating with fury.

"Excuse me?"

"Big bad ER doctor who needs to rape innocent women just to get off."

His eyes narrow, anger drawing his mouth into a tight line. In seconds, I find myself spun around, my cheek hitting the textured wall with enough force to make me wince. If the fucker leaves a bruise, I'm going to be pissed. His arm is braced against my upper back, his mouth against my ear.

"Maybe I wasn't clear. You don't make the rules. I do. You're nothing but a weak omega, and I'm the alpha here. *Your* alpha until I decide I'm done with you. Got it?" he snarls.

That grassy smell of his has turned sharp, tickling my nose, but he's still aroused. I can feel the evidence pressing against my lower back. His free hand drops to the waistband of my scrubs, pushing the material down my hips.

Yeah. That's enough of that.

My hand is by my side, the syringe fisted in the perfect position. Swinging my arm back, I hit my target with unerring accuracy. The needle slips through his scrubs into the fatty tissue of his ass. In a motion so seamless I start singing Michael Jackson's "Smooth Criminal" in my head, my thumb presses down, injecting the good doctor with a combination of drugs that happens to be one of my faves.

He howls, knocking my arm out of the way as he stumbles back. The clear plastic is still protruding from his body, and he yanks it out, tossing it aside so he can focus his fury on me.

"You little bitch! What did you do?"

I casually lean back against the wall as if I don't have a care in the world. Crossing my arms over my chest, I purse my lips.

"Now, Phillip, I thought you were smarter than that. I injected you with something, silly. The better question is, what was in the syringe? It's a little concoction a friend came up with. Apparently, it induces heart attack symptoms within a minute to a minute and a half, which means..." I glance down at my watch. "Just about any time now."

Right as the last word slips out of my lips, his hand raises to his chest and his eyes go wide.

I straighten from the wall, walking up to the man who is smart enough to recognize the gravity of what he's now experiencing.

"It's a shame there isn't anything that will stop the cocktail from doing what it was made to do." I step into his space, noting how his breathing has become ragged as the drug works its magic. "And when they examine your body, it will look like you were on nothing more than a wicked combination of natural steroids and other shit that I don't understand and couldn't possibly pronounce."

He's gasping now, his skin pale and clammy, as he drops to his knees. I watch with morbid satisfaction, memories of another time and another man imposing themselves over the present. Except that girl suffered at the alpha's hands more times than she could count before finally finding the courage to do what needed to be done. Thankfully, that girl is long gone, replaced by one who knows her worth and works tirelessly to help others who require her particular set of skills.

"Such a pity no one will save you because, like you said, they know the drill and won't disturb us. Now you'll die at the hands of a *weak omega*. How ironic."

His body falls back onto the cold tile floor, his eyes blankly staring up at the ceiling as he struggles for every tiny breath of air. It won't be long now. His brand of evil will no longer taint the world in which we live. When his body goes still, I carefully lean forward and check for a pulse.

Nothing. He's gone.

I head over to the lockers in the corner and pull out the dark wig and glasses, putting them on and throwing the backpack over my shoulders. Without a care in the world, I walk out of the small room and down the hall until the bright lights of the lobby greet me. The large sliding doors open, and I slip out into the night, a smile on my face and a lightness in my heart that never lasts.

T he bar is blissfully quiet. Only a couple of tables are occupied by regulars who spend more time at the Thirsty Alpha than they do at home. I should know. I come here frequently myself.

A TV above the bar is playing the nightly news, the newscasters' voices battling the wind howling outside the windows. A nasty storm rolled in just as I arrived, and I'm not looking forward to trudging home in it when closing time comes. Somewhere along the lines, this became my ritual after every successful job. Maybe it's because Jimmy was my first paying client, or maybe it's because, despite how slimy it is, this bar provides just a little bit of normalcy that I struggle to find anywhere else. Socialization isn't exactly my strong suit. I'm too jaded and suspicious for small talk.

"It's getting nasty out there," an unfamiliar voice says from behind the bar.

I glance at the young, handsome man that's watching me. I haven't seen him in here before, and my omega senses begin to tingle.

"Where's Jimmy?"

He wipes the bar down with the rag in his hand while I do a quick, unobtrusive scan around me, noticing nothing else out of the norm.

"He has the night off. I'm Chance Donovan. Started a week ago." He holds out his hand, which I ignore.

I study him. Perfectly styled blond hair. Pretty blue eyes that sparkle under the dim lights above the bar. Muscles that flex as he cleans the mahogany wood a little more aggressively than is probably necessary. Ready smile and perfect teeth.

Yeah, something's definitely not right here. Men who look like him don't come into this place. *Ever.* I would know. I've been coming here longer than I've been a legal adult.

"You going to tell me your name, pretty girl?"

I blink. My instincts are telling me this beta isn't what he appears to be, but whether he's a danger or not is as clear as mud. Which, I'll admit, is unusual. Normally, I can judge a person's character within seconds. I might be more exhausted than I thought. Of course, I've also just watched a man die by my own hand, so maybe I'm just being paranoid.

"I'll take a Jack and Coke, hold the Jack."

His brow raises, but he reaches over to grab a glass, lifting the nozzle and filling it with the carbonated beverage. Then he slides it over to me.

"Here you go."

"Thank you."

I hear the reporter jump in with a breaking news update. Seems as though they've already gotten word on poor Phillip. My grin is hidden behind my glass as I take a sip of my drink.

Chance nods up at the TV. "Man, that's crazy stuff. The authorities believe the string of alpha deaths may not be accidental after all. They think there might be a killer on the loose targeting them. Not sure how I'd feel if I was an alpha right now, that's for sure," he murmurs.

When I glance at him, his eyes are watching me with a keen astuteness that doesn't go unnoticed.

"Well, *I'm* not sure how I feel about omegas being treated no better than blow-up dolls—like we're placed on this planet solely for an alpha's entertainment. That's what they're finding, right? All of the alphas seem to have some pretty nasty skeletons in their closets with victims coming out of the woodwork."

His lips quirk up. *Weirdo.* "I like you..."

He's giving me a pointed look that makes me sigh. What harm could giving him my name do? He'll no doubt learn it soon enough if he sticks around. Besides, I can handle a pretty boy like him, and if he decides to cause problems I'm not comfortable dealing with, I've got a contingency plan and money saved up for just such an emergency.

"Fallon."

"I like you, Fallon."

"Yeah, well, the jury's still out on *you*."

His smirk is just shy of cocky. "Beautiful *and* smart."

"Just so you're aware, flattery will get you nowhere with me. Just keep the sodas coming, and we'll be good."

He chuckles, shooting me a wink. "You got it."

The rest of the night goes much the same as they always do. A random ass grab or two when I walk to the restroom by Old Man Murphy who doesn't understand personal bubbles but is just as lonely as me, so I give him a pass, a chatty beta who doesn't seem to get the message that I'm not in the mood, and exhaustion that pulls me deeper and deeper into my head.

"Closing time, Fallon. Anything I can get you before you head out?"

"No. Thanks, Chance."

The place is empty as he cleans up behind the bar.

"Got any plans?" he asks.

"Sleep. Maybe for a solid week."

Fuck. My life is sad. Beyond sad, actually, but I don't want to dwell too hard on that right now.

"You sure you don't want one drink for the road?" Chance asks. "You look like you could use it."

"I don't drink."

"Doesn't like talking to strangers. Doesn't drink. Curves for days and that innocent look with those big blue eyes that don't even notice all the attention she attracts." His head tilts as he pours two fingers from an almost empty bottle into a whiskey glass and slides it to the edge of the counter. "What's a girl like you doing in a place like this, Fallon?"

Sighing, I shift on the old wooden barstool. My hands grip the glass, spinning it around and around while I stare at the amber liquid inside.

"I don't have anything else," I reply softly, the truth of it twisting my gut. Why I'm even telling him this, I have no idea. I don't even talk to Jimmy this much.

"How is that possible?" he asks.

"It's a long story."

"I've got nothing but time."

That's when I hear it—the song playing in the background of the latest news update. It's not like I live under a rock. I've heard their music before and know the rumors that the media talks about on repeat. Normally, I'm so much better at ignoring the emotions it always stirs inside, but right now, my belly flips, and tears threaten to spill for the first time in a long time. I blame the fatigue, and maybe even Chance for showing me kindness, for weakening my usually airtight defenses.

Don't look at the TV, Fallon. Don't look.

"The pop rock band, Feral Lyrics, is in town this weekend, drawing thousands to their sold-out shows..."

Needing a distraction, I lift the glass to my lips without thought, swallowing the whiskey in one gulp. The alcohol burns as it goes down, and I can't stop the shiver that wracks my body at the taste. The turmoil only gets worse when I hear a voice fill the space around me with the same raspy quality that used to soothe me to sleep every night.

"We're excited to be here in Chicago, the first stop on our *It Can Only Be Her* tour."

"Tell me a little more about that," the reporter suggests. "The theories your fans continue to come up with about this mystery girl in your songs seem to get wilder and wilder with each album."

"She was ours," another familiar voice says. It's low and gruff and riddled with emotions I fight to ignore. Fuck. I barely manage to swallow down the whine that wants to escape. "Then we lost her. Every song we write, every lyric we put down on paper, we dedicate to her in the hopes it might bring her back to us."

The reporter asks another question, but I can't seem to remember what she just said. I focus on the words, listening to her speak, and struggle to stay awake.

"You okay, pretty girl?" Chance whispers.

His words sound far away, and the room is beginning to blur.

"No, I..." I blink, forgetting what I was about to say.

With the last bit of energy I have, I glance up at the screen. The man staring down at me steals my breath away. His brown eyes are as intense and serious as I remember them. His black hair is long on top, carelessly combed back in a way that manages to look hip and edgy. With a tight white dress shirt that clings to his broad chest and thick arms, the black bow tie seems at odds with his worn jeans.

For the briefest second, it feels like if I just reached out my hand, I could run it over the stubble covering his jaw. Could feel his calloused fingers brushing against my cheek before his fingers tangle in my hair.

God, how long has it been since I've experienced anything close to what we shared? The answer is easy. I've never been close to anyone else. Our connection was the last time I felt safe. *Loved*—or at least what I thought was love. Now, I can't tolerate anyone else's hands on me. When I walked out of *that* house for the last time, I stopped yearning for them to find me and save me from the hell they left me in because I saved myself. For years, I cursed them for leaving me after they promised we'd be forever. Over a decade later, I've proven I can live without them. I don't need them. I don't *want* them...no matter how much they try to lure me back in with sweet words and voices that beg me to succumb to their call.

"If you're out there somewhere listening, we'll never give up. You're ours. Do you hear me? Come to us, sunshine. We need you."

His voice is so incredibly deep and sensuous, those words slipping from his lips as they have so many times before. *We need you.* It was a lie then, and it's a lie now. But then why does lust still bloom in my core at the same time my heart pounds in my chest?

"Felix?" I whisper before I can stop myself.

I know his words don't mean anything. They're all a ploy to draw in more unsuspecting, naive, vulnerable women...like me. Or at least who I used to be until I finally recognized my self-worth and gave them up for good.

The world begins to tilt, and the realization of what's happening breaks through the fog just as strong arms catch me, surrounding me with a fresh laundry scent that makes me want to cuddle in for comfort despite being responsible for my helplessness.

"Chance? Why?"

"Shhh. I've got you. It'll be okay."

Then the world goes black.

Chapter 2

M *otherfucker!* I'm going to kill him.

There's a very uncomfortable pressure building in my throat, and my eyes fly open. I'm pretty sure I'm about to be sick. The room is overly bright, sending piercing pain through my pounding head. Groaning, I sit up, out of sorts and confused, and scan the strange room around me. Thankfully, there's a trash can placed right next to the bed—*wasn't he thoughtful*—and I reach for it just as my stomach heaves.

Once I've emptied what little I had in my belly, I stand on weak legs and notice I'm still fully dressed. Chance has earned himself a small bit of mercy for that little gift. I'll make sure his death is quick and mostly painless.

Making my way to the bathroom, I clean myself up, rinse my mouth out, and stare in the mirror. I'm pale but otherwise okay. Taking stock of the rest of my body, I don't feel anything else out of sorts other than my gun and knife missing.

What the fuck is his game?

Looking around, I ascertain that I'm in a hotel room, and it isn't the cheap variety. The bed is way too comfortable, the sheets a thread count so high I damn near feel like royalty...if you forget the fact that I was abducted and placed here against my will. I'm obviously in some sort of suite, with the bedroom closed off from the rest of the space. I fully expect the door to be locked, but when my hand turns the knob, it opens. A quiet living room greets me. The air is still, and the blinds are wide open, letting in the mid-afternoon sun.

Fuck, how long was I out?

Walking over to the window, I see downtown Chicago laid out from high in the sky. There's a notepad on the desk in the corner with the emblem of a high-end hotel chain. Damn. *He spent a pretty penny putting me up here, but why?*

On the coffee table sits my gun and my knife, along with a small black cell phone next to one of those placecards you see at a wedding reception, featuring my name in big bold letters. I pick up the phone, and the screen illuminates, revealing a notification. My finger swipes up and taps on the text icon—the only one available on the home screen.

Hello, Ms. Parker, and welcome to the Underground Omega Syndicate.

You have been chosen for a very important project based on your particular set of unique skills and/or connections. We've taken the liberty of relocating you to the Omega Garden Suites, which will serve as the starting point for your new role within our organization.

There are three rules you must abide by:

> 1. **Keep this phone with you at all times. It is your sole source of funding and anything else you may need to**

be successful in your mission.

2. *Follow any orders given, within the time frame pro-*
   vided. If an issue arises, reach out to this number im-
   mediately.

3. *Never discuss the Syndicate or your affiliation with the*
   Syndicate.

Follow these instructions, and you will be able to earn your
freedom. Should you choose to ignore or deviate from these
guidelines, the penalties will be swift and severe. Any attempt to
expose our organization will immediately activate Termination
Protocol *which includes (but is not limited to) release of dam-*
aging evidence relating to your rather illicit business dealings,
immediate termination of funding and available resources,
and potential loss of life.

Further instructions will follow shortly. Remember, we are
always watching...for your safety and ours. For now, please
make use of the snacks and beverages provided. You'll need to
regain your strength for what lies ahead.

We are glad to have you here, helping to further our cause
of putting omegas in positions of power globally. Together, we
will strive for equality and a better, safer, more prosperous
tomorrow for all designations.

U.O.S.

"Is this a joke?" I mutter, reading through the note again.

If they wanted to hire me for a job, they definitely didn't have
to go through all this trouble. But this sounds like something else,
something that I'm most definitely *not* interested in. *Potential loss of*
life, my ass. Maybe theirs. Most definitely *not* mine.

The smell of freshly brewed coffee hits my nose, and I glance up to see a loaded cart placed just inside the door.

Snacks. Right.

Carrying the phone with me, my eyes scan over the options while my nose dips to sniff each one. Nothing obvious stands out, not that I have a good track record detecting that. Willing to take a risk in order to settle my stomach, I pour myself a cup of coffee and read the note again while I snag a piece of bacon from the covered plate. Their overall cause is something I can totally get behind, but that doesn't explain why they felt the need to start off our working relationship like this.

Grabbing one more piece of bacon, I make my way over to the chaise lounge placed conveniently in front of the window and stare out over the city that's been my home since my late teens. If I can survive this—whatever *this* is—maybe it's time to move on. Get outta dodge and start over somewhere fresh. If this *Syndicate* managed to find me so easily, that means others might be able to as well.

A ding has me lifting the phone to check the screen.

Ms. Parker - now that you've hopefully taken advantage of the food and beverage provided, we would like to give you more details on your upcoming assignment.

It has been brought to our attention that an omega sex trafficking ring has been established and is in full operating mode as of the time of this communication. Initial reports estimate at least two dozen cases of omega abductions reported in the last twenty-four months. We've found a potential connection to the trafficking ring between the record label, Theta Records, the manager, Mr. Sebastian Fuller, and their signed clients, Feral Lyrics.

My heart skips a beat. No. No way. The guys might be lying asshats, but they'd never hurt innocent omegas.

They hurt you, a little voice in my head reminds me. I ignore it and continue reading.

Tonight is the opening night of their world tour. We would like you to attend the concert and see if you can find anything that might lead to confirmation that the information we've been provided is accurate. If so, we'll send you the next set of instructions. A ticket will be sent to your phone shortly. Please send us a message of what you will require for tonight's mission, and we will ensure the necessary arrangements are made in a timely fashion.

Remember, you are not to discuss the Syndicate or your mission with anyone. Please provide regular updates on your progress. Due to your history with the band, we feel you are the perfect omega for this project. However, do not let that connection get in the way of your end goal.

We have faith in your skills, Ms. Parker, and look forward to a successful working relationship.

They're out of their goddamn minds. No way in hell am I facing the guys after all these years just because some mysterious organization tells me I have to. Looking out over the downtown skyline, I feel the hitch in my chest at the thought of seeing them again. It dredges up all of the hurt and pain from those early months after their departure. Drawing my knees up, I rest my chin on them and can't help but wonder how many other omegas out there right now are in trouble while I sit safely tucked away within the walls of this luxurious suite. Can I really leave them to struggle alone the way I had to? Isn't that what I fight against every damn day?

If the Syndicate is right, and omegas truly are being trafficked, then this is totally up my alley, though I don't like going in blind. I typically research my targets heavily before accepting a job in order to confirm the guilty verdict that's already been handed down. This time, I'm the one who will be responsible for providing the burden of proof.

But maybe I can utilize their resources to enact my own form of vengeance. Find the guilty party before anyone else has to get hurt. That would be unusual considering I'm usually hired after the fact. I don't even have to use my connection to the band at all. I can go undercover, take a peek at things behind the scenes, get cozy with the manager, and see if anything feels off. My gut tells me the guys aren't involved, and assuming that's true, I can do this while keeping them in the dark. There are thousands of fans at these things, and blending in is the nature of my business. I can totally do this.

With my mind made up and a little more confidence than is probably safe, I type out a list of what I'll need for potentially the most important job of my life and send up a silent prayer to whoever may be listening for some goddamn luck because I'm going to need it.

G roupies are a bunch of fucking bitches. They easily set womanly solidarity back at least five decades. Why do guys find this so damn attractive—a bunch of desperate, barely legal girls all shouting and shoving each other out of the way? I stand amongst them, my long black wig pulled into a tight ponytail that hangs to the middle of my back, my icy blues covered by brown contacts, and my lips a deep red. The skintight black designer dress hugs all of my curves in a way that naturally draws the eye. With one arm bare, the top of the dress curves behind my neck and over my shoulder to completely cover the other arm, leaving a narrow strip of skin visible above my right breast, giving the barest hint at the cleavage there. My four-inch stilettos add decent height to my otherwise short frame, so at least I won't get trampled when the groupies stampede.

I'm not too proud to admit I look hot. Probably another reason why I'm getting all sorts of dirty looks from the younger, less sophisticated competition who thought glitter and more glitter was the way to go. We're all stuck behind the metal barricades that separate us from the band's tour bus. I have no intentions of actually talking to them or even getting all that close for that matter. I'm only here to scope out their security and to try to catch a glimpse of their manager. While the other girls complain about their feet hurting and the length of the wait, I edge closer to the front of the line, peeking into the area behind the bus where SUVs and other vehicles park and begin to unload various people and equipment. A larger semi-trailer is parked further back, its doors open, making stage equipment visible from where I'm standing.

Taking it all in, I realize just how easy it would be to establish a trafficking system with this setup. A tour that makes stops all over the country. New crews added at each concert means a continual flow of people coming and going. It would be incredibly easy to snatch up an omega or two and squirrel them away on the trailer or in one of the many SUVs.

Without warning, the bus's door opens, and the crowd of girls around me goes wild. I try to slip back into the mix, but they're all pushing forward in order to get closer to the barricades.

My breath catches in my throat when Wren appears, talking to someone over his shoulder as he pauses on the top step. The girls scream his name, and my hips hit the metal when I'm roughly shoved forward. He's so damn tall, easily six-four, with his dark hair messily styled like he just rolled out of bed. His tight white t-shirt hugs a broad chest that flexes when he lifts his hand to run over his hair. There's a set of leather bands around his wrist, but I catch sight of a hint of silver tucked in between them, a charm that dangles with each movement.

The world around me goes silent. I bought him that bracelet when I was eleven after saving all of my allowance to get it for him that Christmas. He had seen it at the local drugstore and told me that he needed it because he was going to be a drummer one day.

He's still wearing it. My heart skips a beat. That doesn't mean anything though, right? My heart knows the answer to that question even though my brain fights to deny it.

His laugh draws me out of the memory, turning my attention to the man behind him that has to duck to get through the door. Anson steps out in a gray henley and worn jeans. He tops Wren by at least three inches, and his long sandy blond hair hangs loosely over his shoulders. I can see tattoos peeking out from his collar and his sleeves. Those are definitely new, and I begrudgingly acknowledge my approval of the way the cute boy I remember turned into inspiration for women who shebop their own happy buttons.

They descend the steps no more than thirty feet away, the two of them discussing something. There's this sort of restless anticipation in the crowd. We're all waiting, knowing who comes next. A soft breeze blows across the lot, and despite the sea of different scents, I can clearly make out Anson's summer rain and Wren's caramel apple. My body comes alive, and emotions rush forward so quickly that I have to close my eyes for a second to get myself under control.

Then the last man finally steps through the door. He's got on another tight dress shirt with the sleeves rolled up to his forearms along with another bow tie. His hair is combed up and back, making my fingers itch to mess it all up. The stubble has gotten thicker, outlining plush lips that are moving as he talks to the man in a suit beside him. I barely notice the manager because the alpha beside him draws all of my attention. Out of all of them, Felix has changed the most. Once the runt of the group, he's got to be at least as tall as Wren now, and he's definitely filled into his alpha designation. When his rich chocolate scent hits my nose over the scent of lilacs and oranges and spilled beer, I stifle a whine.

The group walks toward us, and panic grips me. I once again attempt to slip back into the crowd of desperation with no luck. Arms are reaching out beside me, hoping for even the smallest brush against one of the alphas that stops barely fifteen feet away.

"Fuck," Anson says, his nose in the air as he actively sniffs the breeze. "Do you smell that?"

My stomach pitches. No. There's absolutely no fucking way he can smell me in this perfume and lust haze.

Wren's eyes close as he inhales deeply. "Peaches. But..." His eyes fly open on a gasp. "It's so much stronger now. With a hint of vanilla."

"She's a fucking omega. And she's *here*," Felix growls. "Find her."

Their eyes drop to the crowd I'm currently trying to lose myself in. I try to stay calm, knowing I don't look anything like the girl they remember right now, but if they get close enough, they'll be able to figure it out. I see the man next to Felix snapping pictures of the group just as the guys surge forward, scanning the frenzy to find me. For one brief moment, Anson's eyes connect with mine, and they narrow in concentration just before I'm shoved to the back. For once, I'm thankful for the jealous nature of the crowd because they quickly push me out of the way in an attempt to catch the band's attention.

I slink further and further into anonymity, relief and disappointment warring inside.

You don't need them, Fallon. They lied and left you behind.

I repeat the mantra and slowly break off into a separate group who's making their way toward the venue. Risking one last glance over my shoulder, I see all three guys desperately searching the hoard of groupies, looking for *me*.

Too bad for them, I'm already gone. I'll head inside, watch the show, and try to gather details all while they're none the wiser. I'll have to be smarter now, though. I'll use the scent-block spray in my purse, so they won't be able to pick me out of the crowd. Pride got the better of me this time, but I won't let it happen again. I can still do this. I can finish this job and be out of here without ever having to face my past head on.

The Syndicate thinks my connection to the guys will work in my favor, but I know that my history with them will be my demise.

Chapter 3

Backstage is bustling with activity while the opening act plays to a sold-out crowd, but none of us even care. The scent of peaches and cream lingers in my nose, and I can think of nothing but the girl we've loved our entire lives.

She's an *omega*. No wonder our bond was so fucking strong even when we were too young to know what was up. Biology did. She was ours even then and will be ours again if I get my way.

"I'm telling you, man. It was her," Felix growls at Sebastian. "You were taking pictures outside. Let me see your phone. Maybe you caught her on camera."

Our manager sputters, unused to being told what to do. We're normally so easygoing. Growing up in the system taught us some harsh realities when it came to life, like knowing the difference between wants and needs and learning not to be too picky as long as the *needs* were taken care of. The wants would come later, when we could work for them ourselves. "I'll send you the pictures I took, but I'm not just going to hand over my phone. What the fuck, Felix?"

He pulls his phone out of his back pocket, and I share a look with the guys. We're all too riled up. Even the barest hint of her scent is damn near enough to send us into rut after all the years we've spent pining for the girl we lost. Now, after finding out she's an omega, our instincts have shifted into hyperdrive. We haven't been monks; in those early years, our desire to forget her drove us to find any warm hole available, but nothing worked. Eventually, we made a pact of celibacy until we could get her back because, at the end of the day, it's only her we want.

As our band's popularity rose, we knew it was the perfect platform to aid in our search, but we're no closer now than we were before, which means we've spent six years getting intimately acquainted with our hands during the long days and lonely nights without her. Of course, during the darkest moments, we've wondered if something happened to her. If... No, I won't let my mind go there. I have to believe the scent we caught outside was her, and she just hasn't found a way to make it back to us. Until now.

Our phones ding with notifications when Seb's photos come through. Pulling out my phone, I zoom in, trying to find the honey blonde hair and bright blue eyes I've never been able to forget. I see plenty of variations, sure, but even after a decade, I know the difference. I know *her*. My eyes snag on a woman in the front who looks conspicuously...blank. She's the one I made eye contact with. Her long, dark hair is pulled away from her face, highlighting her high cheekbones and Cupid's bow lips that stir something inside that no one else ever could. But her eyes are brown, not the icy hue that belongs to the only omega I've ever wanted. It doesn't make sense, but as I scan over her perfect fucking tits and down the curve of her waist,

I find myself fighting back a growl. This doesn't appear to be her, but my instincts tell me it is.

"Her," I hear Wren say, and when I glance up, I find him pointing someone out to Seb.

"Let me see," I murmur, walking over and glancing over our manager's shoulder. "Fuck. I saw her too, but I don't know, man. The eyes—"

"It has to be her, Anson. What are the chances all three of us pick out the same damn girl within seconds?" Felix's voice has gotten impossibly deeper, another sign of how close he is to the edge. With the prospect of finally having our mate back in our arms, need is batting at all of us.

"But why is she in a disguise?" I ask.

"Maybe she doesn't want us to know she's here," Wren whispers. "Maybe she doesn't want *us*."

My gut twists. If that's true, I wouldn't blame her. We left her, and even though we promised we'd be back for her, we took too long. By the time we made it back to the foster home, she was already gone—like dust in the wind, slipping right between our fingers, our hopes and dreams flying away with her.

I cross my arms over my chest. "Then why even show up in the first place? It doesn't make any sense."

The Fallon we knew would never go to such lengths for something she didn't *really* want to do. No, she's too headstrong and confident for that. If she's here, it's because some part of her—no matter how small—wants to be.

"If she doesn't want us, then she should have the fucking balls to tell us that," Felix demands, anger vibrating through his body. "Not hide behind a goddamn mask. We've spent years trying to find her, so she can at least say *fuck off* to our faces."

Wren anxiously paces back and forth, hands on top of his head and his anxiety skimming along our pack bond. My foot is tapping the concrete beneath my boot, nervous energy making me antsy. I have to tune out the others, or else I might say fuck the concert and go search for the woman myself.

"Look, we're going on in two minutes. We're going to play our set while Sebastian hunts that woman down." Felix turns to our manager. "Find her, Seb, and have her wait on our bus. I don't care if you have to lock her in and post guards around the perimeter. Make sure she doesn't leave. We'll get our answers and go from there. At least then we'll know and can start mending our broken fucking hearts."

He runs both hands down his face, tilting his head in each direction, as we prepare to go out and play our music—the songs we poured our souls into *for her*.

Thoughts of the sad little girl that needed a friend play through my mind. Even back then, the need to comfort and care for her were instincts I couldn't deny. As we got older, and our relationship began to change, I was always the one careful not to rock the boat. To be her ear when she needed someone to listen or offer a hug when she needed to know she wasn't alone. I played it safe. I was the good guy. The *nice* guy. Now, I'm wondering if I played it a little too safe. If I had pushed just a little harder, stood my ground a little firmer, then maybe we wouldn't have been forced to walk away without a solid plan in place.

"Are you guys ready?" he asks.

Wren and I share a look before we turn back to Felix with a nod.

"Let's do this. Play your fucking hearts out, boys, because this may be our only chance to convince her she's ours. Always has been. Always will be."

The stage goes dark, and the crowd begins to clap and cheer, shouting our names as we take our places on stage. The leather strap of my guitar slides over my head, the pick between my fingers feeling heavier than it has in a long time. Everything is on the line right now, so we can't fuck this up.

"Good evening, Chicago!" Felix growls, and the crowd goes wild. "We are Feral Lyrics. Welcome to the *It Can Only Be Her* Tour!"

The first strum of my guitar feels electric, and the opening chords of "It Can Only Be Her" echo through the amphitheater. The soft, steady beats of Wren's drums have the bass pounding in my chest and the energy in the room building around us.

"You're all we've ever wanted," Felix sings, his voice soft and deep, the emotion in that one line sparking through our pack bond—the desperation damn near enough to choke us all. "Our future set in stone."

My eyes try to scan the crowd, but the light shines down on us, making the audience appear as nothing more than faceless silhouettes. I know she's out there. I can feel her somewhere deep inside despite the years that separated us.

"Until the day we were forced to walk away," Felix croons, his voice smoother and more melodic than I've heard him in a long time, "leaving you all alone."

His voice cracks on that last note just before Wren cuts in with a heavier beat that has the crowd screaming and girls crying out for Felix to marry them. The lights raise as they flicker around the room.

In that split second, I see the attractive raven-haired woman from earlier. She's standing along the walkway between the lower sections, staring up at the stage with a stricken look on her face. She glances behind her and spots the three security guards heading her way. Turning, her eyes connect with mine, and for one brief moment, I swear I can see my pain reflected right back at me, but then it's lost when the lights drop back down. Felix heads into the next verse, but I don't even hear it. My focus is on the spot where I saw her last, my fingers strumming the strings as if, by some stroke of luck, I can make her feel what we feel every time we think of her through the notes of the music we've poured so much of ourselves into.

If she thinks I'm just going to let her walk away without a fight, she's got another damn thing coming. I have no intention of playing fair. For once in my life, I plan on getting dirty...and enjoying it.

Chapter 4

The music continues to play around me, songs that strike right at my withered up heart. Some of them I've heard before, but others I haven't, and I'm starting to think I've made a huge miscalculation in coming here. That fleeting moment with Anson on stage was enough to prove that the hurt I felt then is still very much alive inside me, right along with the intense need I feel for them despite it.

It doesn't make a damn bit of sense.

After a few close calls, I can finally breathe easy. Security is everywhere, and maybe I'm just being paranoid, but it feels like they're targeting me.

Glancing over my shoulder, I maneuver through the backstage area where I use the darkness to my advantage. Roadies hustle around, moving carts loaded with stuff I can't even begin to name. I notice the manager chatting up two young girls off in the corner, both of them in barely there dresses, no doubt trying to talk their way onto the bus, and my stomach rolls at the thought. I need to get his attention off the omegas and onto me—for their sake *and* mine.

I confidently walk by, watching his eyes snag on my ass at the sound of my heels on the pavement. Then I notice the two security guards heading straight for me. One says something into a walkie-talkie while the other one narrows his eyes.

"Stop right there! You're not supposed to be back here."

The shout catches Sebastian's attention, and his eyes fly up from my ass to my face.

Well, that's one way to do it, I suppose.

He steps toward me just as I take a few steps back, coming up short thanks to the huge speaker blocking my retreat.

"Well, hello there." His smirk is instantaneous. "We've been looking all over for you."

Looking for me? I hide my surprise and decide not to point out the fact that he had his face all up in some cleavage not more than ten seconds ago.

"Me? You must be thinking of someone else. I think I just got turned around trying to find the restroom."

"Well, lucky for you, I'll lead you straight to one. Now, I'll have to politely ask that you come with us. "

He steps closer, motioning for me to follow along. Sebastian Fuller is not at all what I expected. A little smarmy and a whole lot of fake—fake teeth, fake smile, and fake politeness. How could any omega in their right mind fall for what he's offering? But I'm not your average omega, and I have no interest in giving some overzealous alpha head just to *meet the band*. I'm here with a job to do, which makes my decision to go along *willingly* a lot easier to stomach. I'll play the eager groupie...for now.

His scent—like cigarettes and leather—sits heavy in my nose. He's on the short side for an alpha, maybe a few inches taller than my five-five frame. In his designer suit, he cuts an attractive figure, though he's far removed from my taste.

"Where are you taking me?"

"The band's tour bus."

My brain balks at going anywhere near their personal space.

I shake my head. "I'm not interested."

"Your interest or lack thereof doesn't concern me."

My eyes narrow. That's another mark against Sebastian Fuller.

"Listen, you've got the wrong girl. I'm not into the band. I prefer my alphas…" I force myself to bite my lip and scan his entire body. "…a little more mature."

"Sadly, I'll have to insist. The band has requested your presence, and as their manager, I like to keep them happy and provide what they ask for whenever possible."

I curse myself and my stupid scent. That has to be what this is about.

"There must be some mistake—"

"There's no mistake. They picked you out from a photo, and now that we've found you, I'll need to ask you—once again—to come with me. Don't make this any harder than it needs to be."

The warning is clear. That's two points against me. Being too cocky to cover my scent and allowing a photo to be taken of me. *Get yourself together, Fallon.*

By this point, we've attracted quite a crowd, with another security guard and a large portion of the set crew watching on. Not to mention the very angry faces of the two girls whose night I've just fucked up. Of course, they're not aware I just saved them from potentially being trafficked. My job is so fucking thankless.

Straightening my shoulders, I nod and fall into step behind him, noticing the three security guards trailing closely behind. We weave our way through the crowd of people and out a side door backstage which leads directly to the back lot where the bus is parked. It's dark now, and the temperature has dropped enough that I fight off a shiver as my mind begins to work through all the ways I can get out of this. I try to make small talk with Sebastian, but he ignores me.

The closer I get to the bus, the more my nerves begin to make themselves known—internally at least. Externally, I'm as cool as a cucumber. I hate them. I do...or that's what I need to keep believing. But my control has always been threadbare where they're concerned, so it doesn't take much to have it snapping in two.

Sebastian opens the door, never once looking back, expecting me to follow without question. I ignore him and the beefy security guards that are surely on some sort of beta-roids because there's no way that amount of muscle is natural. Instead, I survey the surprisingly cozy interior of the bus as we ascend the dark granite steps that lead to the raised living space. With tones of creams, dark wood, and splashes of turquoise, it's comfortable and warm—welcoming in a way I hadn't anticipated. Their combined scents are everywhere, making this all feel surprisingly familiar, right along with the drumsticks placed on the counter, the books stacked on the table, and the sheets of paper with hastily scrawled words scattered along the cushions.

The security guards wait by the door, but Sebastian turns to me, giving me a onceover from head to toe. I try not to fidget, assessing him the same way he's assessing me.

"Now, Miss..."

He eyes me pointedly, waiting for me to provide my name.

I don't. Can't make it *too* easy on him.

His smile is kind and understanding despite the antagonizing aura I'm clearly giving off.

"Look, I know this is outside of the norm, but I assure you, the band just wants to have a quick word."

"And if I don't want to talk with them? You'll...what? Hold me here against my will until I do?"

He shakes his head. "No, my dear. Just hear them out. If you aren't interested in what they have to say, you'll be free to go. I'll be right outside the door if you need anything. In the meantime, make yourself at home."

Well, okay then. Maybe this will work out in my favor after all. I can snoop through their shit, confirm that they truly aren't involved in anything as abhorrent as omega trafficking, and get the hell outta dodge before they get back.

With one last glance over his shoulder, Sebastian gives me a kind smile that throws me off and exits the bus. I could swear that smile was real, and maybe even a little hopeful. The loud click of the lock engaging doesn't escape my notice, but surely there's a window or something that opens enough for me to slip out.

Quickly I get to work, searching through all the cabinets, nooks and crannies, drawers, and hidden pockets I can find. It takes longer than it should because each and every time I turn around, I find some reminder of our time together on a table or displayed on a shelf. A picture of the group of us bundled up in our winter coats and hats, standing outside the skating rink in town. A horrible picture I drew for Anson when I was maybe ten. A CD I burned for Felix on an old laptop I was gifted, containing all of our favorite songs. Everywhere I turn, there's evidence of the relationship we used to have and the people we used to be. It's impossible not to get stuck walking down memory lane.

Small fissures begin to form in all the lies I've told myself about my feelings for them, creating tiny, irreparable pieces. I hopelessly try to hold them all together, but they crumble in my hands.

The sound of the lock disengaging sounds incredibly loud in the silence of the space, and my eyes dart up to the clock. Two hours have passed without me even realizing it. Fucking memories sucked me in and damn near dragged me under just as much as their damn scents that linger everywhere in here. That means that the concert is done. I'm about to come face to face with the alphas who broke my heart.

Said heart begins to beat rapidly in my chest as I claim a seat on the softest leather sofa I've ever felt and take a few calming breaths. I applied the spray scent blockers. No way will they know who I am. Everything will be okay.

I sit primly in the small living space, shoulders straight and legs crossed in front of me. My hands are resting on my knees, and I'm the picture of cool, calm, and collected. Inside, I'm a hot fucking mess.

Anson is the first one through the door, this energy trailing in along with him that has me discreetly squeezing my thighs together just a little bit harder. He smells like summer rain showers, and the long-forgotten memories of nights we spent camping in the backyard of the foster house we all shared hits me. The night he cuddled me close because I was afraid of an unexpected thunderstorm becomes as clear in my mind as if it happened yesterday. The wind howling, the rain pelting the tent, and me in Anson's lap shaking like a leaf while his big arms held me tight. His soothing voice hummed our favorite song, and to this day, I can't listen to it without thinking of him. I'm staring, I realize, so I let my eyes fall from the gentle giant that slayed all my nightmares as a young girl.

Their footsteps are loud, the door shutting softly behind them. When I'm finally brave enough to peek through my lashes, I find Felix staring down at me, his brows furrowed. I can't imagine what he's thinking, my serious, brooding alpha. He was always so introspective that others considered him aloof, unfriendly, but when it came to me, he softened up like chocolate melting in your hand. That's what he smells like. Rich, decadent chocolate.

Wren steps up beside him, a hopeful smile on his lips that makes the urge to kiss him spring to life inside me. I swallow down the whine I feel building in my throat, desperately trying to find my center despite his excitement making his sweet caramel apple scent turn just a little bit tart.

"Hello, Fallon," Felix purrs in a voice so deep I swear the bass of it vibrates against my clit. There's no denying the slick that trickles out between my thighs.

My head tilts as I cross my arms over my chest, which unintentionally pushes my boobs out, and three sets of hungry eyes immediately lock onto them.

Shit. That simple look sends my own desire into a frenzy. Mayday, mayday.

I blink slowly, feigning confusion. "I'm sorry. Who's Fallon?"

"Please. We just want to know that it's you," Anson pleads. "We've spent years wondering if you were okay."

I can feel my jaw clenching and my teeth grinding together, but I force my muscles to relax. "I think you've mistaken me for someone else."

"Have we, though?" Wren murmurs.

"You most definitely have."

"Then who are you?" Anson asks.

"Mia Carmichael, and I've got to say, this is *not* how I ever expected to meet the members of Feral Lyrics."

Felix stares me down. "You're lying."

"I can show you my ID if you don't believe me," I offer. "Although, I unfortunately left my purse back with my friends."

"There's another way you can prove it." Felix mimics my pose, his shirt straining against his biceps when they cross over each other.

"And that is...?" I play dumb for the moment, my brain frantically trying to come up with a way out of this.

"Our Fallon had a small birthmark shaped like a heart in a very...discreet place."

Shit. Shit, shit, shitty, shit, shit.

I can't show him my ass cheek because that mark is still very much present. I should've anticipated this. The fucker was always obsessed with it. At night, I'd often find him tracing the shape of it as we lay huddled together in bed.

"Am I expected to know where this *discreet place* is? Not that it matters because I have no such mark."

"You see, it was on her right ass cheek—"

That gives me an idea. Faking outrage, I abruptly stand, shoving my way through the line of alphas while purposely ignoring the way my body reacts to that brief touch.

"Your manager said I could leave if I wasn't interested in what you had to say, so this will be goodbye, boys," I say without looking back.

I try to twist the handle, but it doesn't budge, so I knock. Sebastian said he'd be right outside, but no one comes. Goosebumps break out along my skin when heat and the smell of warm chocolate rushes over me, his warm breath hitting my ear as he leans in close.

"I think you're scared."

Felix's words are like kryptonite to my damaged soul, so I close my eyes. I have to take control, but he's right. I *am* scared of the very real danger they represent. I'm not sure I'm strong enough to face him and tell him all the things I've thought about him and the others over the years. I don't think I can spew my honesty and remain guarded while their alpha pheromones fill up the enclosed space of the bus, creating the lust-filled fog that's becoming increasingly difficult to ignore. I seriously miscalculated their draw when factored in with my own overwhelmed instincts. Taking a deep breath and immediately regretting it, I turn around, coming face to crotch with Felix. My head tilts back until I meet his eyes. Wren and Anson are standing at the top of the stairs, looking at the two of us with uninterrupted focus.

"You think you know me?" I whisper.

I don't think I'm capable of doing more right now. The temptation to lean into him is strong, but I manage to hold myself back from making a fool of myself.

"We know we do, sunshine. Let us see you. We've fucking waited long enough."

And that's all it takes—that one little reminder that they walked out of my life and never looked back—to jumpstart my fury.

"Ten years isn't long enough as far as I'm concerned," I spit out, pushing past him and stomping up the stairs.

"Take it back," he whispers menacingly, following me and getting in my face.

"Not a chance, which also accurately represents any possibility you have of getting into my panties ever again, by the way."

His eyes narrow, then his hand reaches up, his fingers tangling in the synthetic hair of the wig. With a gentle tug, he manages to yank it off, along with the cap, sending blonde hair spilling out around my face.

"There you are..." he mutters sarcastically. "I wanna see your eyes, Fallon. Want to look into them while you tell me to go to hell. That you don't feel the connection that has always fucking existed between us. Tell me that we wasted all of these years on something that wasn't real. That you don't want us anymore. Don't want *me* anymore. Because the moment we picked up your scent outside, that tether sprang to life again whether you want to admit it or not. "

Angrily, I swipe the contacts out, letting them drop to the floor. One of the others gasps, getting a good look at my flushed face for the first time in a decade. I curse as tears unexpectedly spring to my eyes, and the words get stuck between my lips.

"Say it, sunshine. Say the words, and you can walk away."

"Fuck you, Felix," I whisper shout, the first drop trailing down my cheek.

Come on. Say it, Fallon. Tell them. You don't need them anymore. Go on. Do it.

"Baby girl..." Anson's reverent tone has a whine slipping out unbidden. "*Fuck.*"

"Sweetheart, please," Wren begs.

My eyes close, their scents suffocating me as I try to fight off the feelings I knew would come with this moment. Why am I so damn helpless where they're concerned? I'm strong on my own, fully capable of sending a grown man to his knees in excruciating pain, but when it comes to *these* men, I'm powerless.

My head shakes back and forth, and words fail me.

"It's okay, sunshine. We know," Felix whispers against my lips, wrapping an arm around my waist and pulling me into him.

I try to protest, try to pull back, but there's no real power behind it. Instead, I end up wrapped in his arms, his scent surrounding me. It provides the first real comfort I've experienced in way too long, and then I catch a hint of the others, who have closed ranks around us, creating one big cuddle pile so much like the ones from when we were innocent kids.

"Give us a chance, Fallon. Let us heal what we broke all those years ago. That's all we ask."

I pull my face out of Felix's neck, finding Anson's soft brown eyes staring into mine. His huge hand raises to my cheek, brushing away the tears still silently falling, then he tucks my chaotic hair behind my ear.

"I'm not sure I can, Anson." It's the only honesty I can give them right now.

His eyes narrow in determination. "And I'm not sure I can let you walk away without trying."

"So you'll...what? Hold me captive?"

"Stay here with us," Wren suggests, hooking a finger underneath my chin to pull my face toward his over Felix's other shoulder.

My nose scrunches up. "I'm not a groupie, Wren. Fucking the band is not on the agenda."

"Now, who said anything about fucking?" Felix purrs against my neck, sending shivers over my body.

Wetness is dripping down my thighs in exact opposition to my denial of moments ago. No doubt my perfume has washed away the spray, letting them know exactly how traitorous my body is.

"We can't..." But then I remember my objective. Remember the real reason I'm here. My connections—those very same ones he wanted me to deny. The Syndicate wanted me to use that to my advantage. Well, here I am. That's all this is. Me, doing my job.

I'm a pro at rationalization.

Felix's tongue chooses that moment to lick up my throat, and a real purr rattles deeply in his chest.

"Goddamn, she smells too good," Anson groans, sliding his hand behind my neck as my head tilts back to give Felix better access.

"Fuck, sweetheart," Wren pleads, his hazel eyes searching mine. "It's been too long. We're going out of our minds here."

"Too long?"

"Six years," Felix grunts out. His fingertips trail up my inner thigh, tracing circles in the slick he encounters.

"Six *years*?"

At this point, my brain is malfunctioning. All I'm capable of is repeating their words back at them.

"Six years of no pussy," Anson practically growls, pupils blown wide and nostrils flared.

Gone is the calm, steady man I remember. In his place is an alpha on the verge of going feral. My eyes fly back to Wren. I can see the struggle across his face as he fights his instincts. Fights his need...for *me*.

I want to deny them. Make them hurt the same way I hurt for so long. My head insists that's what I should do. My body, however, says fuck no.

I've got three hungry alphas staring at me like I'm the first offering of a five-course meal, and my omega instincts have taken notice.

I see your six and raise you ten, boys.

My hand reaches out, gripping Wren's neck to pull him closer.

"For the record, this doesn't change shit," I rasp against his lips.

"Like hell it doesn't, sunshine," Felix growls back just as my mouth crashes into Wren's.

Chapter 5

It's been six long fucking years, but every single one was worth it for this moment right here when her lips crash into mine and it feels like coming *home*. She tastes of peaches, tangy and sweet, and everything I've never forgotten.

Just as quickly as the fire sparks in my veins, this almost feral need—to have her, claim her, mark her—rears up, damn near taking over. She was always going to be ours. There was never a question in my mind about that, and despite her denials, I'm pretty sure she knows it too. But what's happening right now, this desire-fueled desperation and anger, is not the way I ever wanted it to happen. She means too much to us, and we've waited too long to start our second verse like that. We likely won't have a choice.

A low growl fills the room, followed by another, and I somehow manage to pull away from Fallon in time to see Felix and Anson standing chest to chest. Their eyes are narrowed, their breathing rapid. This is some crazy alpha shit right here, the pheromone fog so thick you can damn near swim in it. With our omega in the room, our instincts are raging out of control, and I have no idea what to do about it.

"Wren?" she whispers.

Much like my brothers, I can feel myself sinking deeper, need battering against my self-control until I have to shake my head to try to maintain even the smallest hint of civility. I'm not an aggressive guy, but right now, the things I want to do to her are fucking raw and nasty and so far from my norm that I'm starting to get a little worried.

She steps back, eyes wide and lips swollen. My nostrils flare when her scent hits my nose, and when I glance down, there's moisture dripping down her thick thighs. Now, it's my turn to growl.

"You have to be fucking kidding me right now," she mutters, slowly backing up, eyes nervously scanning the room. "I'm horny, but an alpha pissing contest? This... This is more than I bargained for."

I see it—the second she makes the decision to run—and I prepare to be the one to catch her. She slowly kicks off her heels, the move making her appear smaller than she already was. Why that's even more appealing, I can't say. Her eyes dart to each of us, with Anson and Felix now fully focused on her rather than on each other. When she turns, running down the short hall to the main bedroom at the back of the bus, I take off after her. Twin snarls sound off behind me, followed by the pounding of their footsteps. I catch the door with my foot just as she tries to slam it shut. Yeah, they're going to have to wait. I got here first, so she's mine.

"Wren, baby, let's talk about this," she croons softly, and for a split second, a small hint of protectiveness rises above the lust coursing through my veins.

My name off her lips is the sweetest song I've ever heard.

She backs up, her thighs hitting the large king mattress that takes up most of the space. She manages to climb up without ever taking her eyes off me, standing on the plush mattress and using that height advantage to peer down at me. All that does is put that dripping pussy of hers even closer to where I need it to be, and just like that, lust wins.

I step forward, pausing when she holds out one hand and reaches between her tits with the other, that small bare strip of skin above her breast giving her just enough room to dig into her cleavage. What she pulls out makes me hesitate. In her hand is a small switchblade that she flicks open with surprising dexterity.

"Y'all really know how to fuck up the mood, that's for sure."

"What are you doing, sweetheart?" I manage, my voice hoarse with everything I'm struggling to fight back.

"Have you seen your goddamn faces? No way in hell are you getting anywhere near this pussy acting like feral fucking beasts."

"Six years might as well be sixty, sunshine. " Felix comes up beside me. "We fucking *need* you."

"And I need a lot of things, Felix—like a year of sleep and some good fucking wine. Getting fucked raw is *not* on that list."

"No one said anything about—" Felix begins.

She points between the two of us. I can feel the blush working its way up my throat and into my cheeks at the very real way she just mirrored my darkest desires.

My brother's eyes turn to me, and in that brief second, I know I'm not the only one imagining her swollen and pink and so goddamn sore she can't walk straight for a week.

"Mine," Anson growls impatiently, shoving between Felix and me.

Fallon's eyes go wide as he basically charges her on his knees, one of his big ass hands gripping the wrist with the knife. She doesn't even have a chance to react. In a matter of seconds, he's taken control, his fingers digging into the collar of her dress as he carefully drags the knife down the middle.

"What the actual *fuck*?" Fallon whisper yells, her eyes darting up to ours. "Come get your boy."

At that very moment, the material slips off her body, revealing inch after inch of bare, creamy skin. Her breasts are round and fuller than I remember—definitely more than a handful—with pink nipples that pebble under our stares. The mole next to her belly button is still there, though I'm not sure why I'm suddenly so fascinated by that. Then my eyes drop to her completely smooth pussy.

"Felix," I rasp.

"Same, brother. Same," he grunts.

With the little control we have left, we start stripping out of our clothes while Anson leans in, swiping his tongue right through that fucking peach nectar between her thighs. She groans, her head falling back and hands gripping his head as he feasts on her.

"Okay. *Shit.* But this still doesn't change anything," she whimpers, and a growl leaves Anson's lips against her clit. "*Fuck.*"

"Keep telling yourself that, sweetheart," I murmur.

Felix and I stand, watching—naked, stroking our cocks to help ease the ache—while Anson grips her thighs, lifting her up and turning both of their bodies until they're facing the side of the bed. Then he lets her drop. She lands on her back with a squeal, tits bouncing and hair falling around her face as Anson dives back down, continuing to feast on her. It sets off something primal inside me.

Before I even know what I'm doing, I'm rounding the end of the bed, stalking to the edge, and yanking her down until her head falls back off the mattress. She gasps, her mouth dropping open, leaving a perfect spot for my dick. Without hesitation, I run the tip around her lips, spreading precum along the soft skin.

"Wren—" Her blue eyes are staring at me upside down, and she looks so fucking sexy I can't hold off anymore.

My dick slides into the warm wetness of her mouth, and my hands grip the back of her neck, tangling in her hair as I move in and out, barely managing to give her time to adjust when what I really want to do is slam my cock down her throat. It feels so fucking good, I know this first time is going to be embarrassingly fast.

Six goddamn years, man.

I glance up just as Anson pulls his shirt over his head, revealing the tattoos he's covered his entire upper body with. His long hair is loose, and his eyes are wild, and now I see what Fallon was talking about. We look exactly like the beasts she accused us of being, and I'll be damned if that doesn't make me want to pound my fucking chest a little. She's our mate. Ours. And after this, she'll have no doubts about that.

Fallon

Holy motherfucking feral alphas, Batman.

I know, I know. I said I didn't want to be fucked raw. I lied. So sue me. But I couldn't let them think that I was just going to take pity on their poor celibate little hearts. Six years? Try a fucking decade. I'm just as goddamn desperate as any of them, but am I losing my mind? No.

Of course, that was before Anson licked my pussy like it was his life's mission. And before Wren shoved his huge ass dick in my mouth.

Yeah, okay. I get it now. After years of touch deprivation, my body is so awash in sensations that I'm going a little wild too.

My hands reach back, gripping Wren's thighs, urging him to fuck my face. I want to feel it all. The pain, the pleasure, and everything fucking in between because I've been in a deep freeze for over ten years, and the warmth feels fan-fucking-tastic.

His groan echoes around the space as he thrusts in deeper, all the way to his knot. That's new. They hadn't quite acquired that particular part of their anatomy the last time we were together like this.

No, the second their designation came in, they were removed from the foster home we shared, and I was sent to live with another family that was younger and better equipped to handle a budding omega—or so they said. That started off the years I so desperately try to forget.

He hits the back of my throat and holds himself there while Anson roughly shoves two fingers into my sopping cunt. I gasp, the stretch just on the edge of too much, but Anson clearly doesn't have the patience for foreplay or little things like making sure he'll actually fucking fit. He pulls his fingers out, lifts my legs, and plunges in, all the way to his knot. He's big, the biggest of all the guys, and with the alpha haze pulling him under, I swear he's even bigger. The pain has me sucking in a breath, except no air is available because Wren is thrusting in and out of my throat.

I should probably panic, but if I'm going to go out, being fucked by two feral alphas is definitely the preferred way to go. Anson pulls out with another growl—the only speech he's capable of at the moment—and slams back in. This time, the pain is tipped with a hint of pleasure thanks to the intense tingling that shoots up from my toes and throughout my body. He does it again and again, each time a little harder, the pleasure more acute. I manage to sneak in some breaths when Wren pulls out, only to drop down over me, bracing himself on his hands to use the bed as leverage. He begins to throat fuck me in earnest, each thrust in unison with Anson destroying me at the opposite end.

"Mine," Anson rasps, his hips continuing to pummel me into the bed.

"Mine," Wren grunts, his movements becoming erratic. "Fuck, I'm gonna come."

He pulls out, his hand roughly stroking his dick. His head falls back, and the sound he makes sets off something inside me. As he comes, long spurts of his release covering my mouth, neck, and chest, I can feel my own release building.

Wren stumbles back and Felix replaces him, picking up right where his packmate left off. His cock slips into my mouth with ease, and I suck him down like I'm not covered in his brother's cum. Like I'm not being fucked by the other as his thrusts slide me up and down Felix's length. Unlike Wren, his hands grip my throat tightly, squeezing and applying just enough pressure to prove he owns me.

And I let him.

What's more?

I fucking *like it*.

But I don't have time to think on that too hard.

"Knot," is the only warning I get before Anson plunges in, his knot pushing against the tight ring of my pussy, and for a second, I don't think it's going to fit. He pulls out and thrusts back in until I feel my body stretching around the width of him. Then he's sliding home, nestling into a spot that feels as if it were custom designed just for him, and I swear I stop breathing. There's this incredible feeling of fullness coupled with the surprise of my first knot taking my breath away. He grinds into me, his knot getting fuller inside, almost to the point of pain. My body locks down, squeezing around him so tightly he roars. The throb and heat of his release sets off my own. I explode, my body going taut as Felix fucks me harder, using me like I'm his to do whatever he wants with.

I feel Anson collapse on top of me, his weight heavy, and his head rests against my breast. I don't have time to wonder if he's lying in Wren's cum because Felix hits the back of my throat, pulsing as the swell of his knot pushes against my lips. I have no idea what I'm doing, but I open just a little wider and let his knot fill my mouth, my lips closing around him.

"Fucking shit," he grunts out just before he shouts my name.

He comes, thick spurts filling my throat faster than I can keep up with. I have no choice but to try to swallow it all, and the excess slips out the corners of my mouth. His knot swells against my tongue, and he's still coming, even as I struggle to breathe. It isn't until I feel the bubbles slipping out of my nostrils that I start to panic, but Felix is right there, hands gently stroking my throat as he tries to pull as far back as the position will allow him.

"Easy, sunshine." His voice is deep and hoarse—raw, like he's the one that just got faced fucked, not me. "Fuck. I'm sorry. I didn't..."

He curses again, but just knowing he's with me settles something inside. Slowly, I feel his knot shrinking inside my mouth, and as reality starts to slink back in, I ask myself, *What in the hell did I just do?*

You fucked your foster brothers, that's what. You know, the ones you loved with all of your teenage omega heart. The same ones who discarded you like yesterday's trash.

Oh. Right. I'm going to have to have a long talk with myself where we discuss all the ways today went wrong and everything we have now discovered so we don't repeat the same mistakes. You know, like the fact that mouth knotting may produce cum bubbles. Lesson learned.

For now, though, I'm too blissed out on post-knotting sex to worry about any of it.

Chapter 6

Fallon

I'm so damn comfortable, except for the teensy weensy problem of needing to use the restroom. Unfortunately, the two alphas sandwiching me are passed out and pinning me down. At some point, when I finally untangled from all the knots, they carefully rearranged us and cuddled in close. No one said a word. In the darkened silence, surrounded by their scents, I fell into the most peaceful sleep I've had since they left. My nightmares were replaced with dreams—a highlight reel of moments from our past all woven together in an odd order, so vivid and real it was as if I was back there all over again.

Now, light floods across my face, and with it, all the feelings I was able to ignore the night before begin to bubble up inside. From their scents alone, I know who's with me. Wren is spooning me from behind, his arm wrapped around me, holding my boob in his hand. His morning wood is nestled in the crack of my ass, and when I roll my hips, earning a tit squeeze for my efforts, I tell myself I'm just stretching. In reality, I'm already feeling needy again.

Felix is cuddled up in front of me, his nose touching mine, with our legs intertwined and his hand on my hip. I grin despite the way my heart pounds in my chest. It's one thing to give in to your instincts in the heat of the moment. It's another to have to face the consequences in the light of day.

Felix stirs, his lips brushing mine and his hand slipping to my ass to pull my body into his. His hard length is ready, willing, and able against my abdomen.

"Mmmm... I want to wake up like this every morning, sunshine," he murmurs with a slow roll of his hips.

Wren nuzzles into my neck from behind, his nose brushing against my ear. Goosebumps break out along my body, but not because I'm cold. No, I'm burning up for them, my body primed and demanding attention. But without the frenzy of the night before, my mind is a mess of contradictions, and I have no idea what I want right now.

"Where's Anson?" I ask, looking for a distraction.

"He went running," Wren replies, kissing my shoulder.

"He's probably feeling guilty for how he behaved last night."

My eyes finally open, finding Felix staring back at me.

"Guilty?" I whisper, an unexpected shyness sneaking through. When was the last time I allowed anyone close enough for them to feel anything like concern or guilt for me?

"We were all a little rough last night. It's not exactly how we antic-ipated that moment would go."

"Nothing happened that I didn't *allow* to happen."

"It doesn't matter, sweetheart," Wren adds. "It's our second chance. The last thing we'd ever want to do is fuck this up."

That little ball of hurt manifests itself in my belly. All of the unre-solved feelings didn't go away just because they fucked me. They're all still very much there, lurking and ready to pounce.

I can feel the heaviness in my chest, the way my gut twists itself around in knots, and my breaths become shallow as confusion whirls itself into a frenzy inside. Felix's eyes spark with worry once I begin to wiggle free and untangle myself. I sit up, suddenly needing just a little bit of space.

"Where are you going, sunshine?" Felix asks, his voice rolling over my naked skin, making me shiver.

"I need to use the restroom." It's a lame excuse, and we all know it. I'm a total coward for running, but I can't have this talk right now. I need to clear my head first, and that requires just a little bit of distance to gain some perspective.

Quickly scooting off the bed, no doubt looking awkward as fuck, I grab the first shirt I see and throw it over my head. I slip out of the room and close the door behind me. Their low murmurs reach me as they no doubt discuss my hasty retreat. I just can't find it in me to care what they think right now.

The bathroom is only a couple steps away, a much needed bit of peace and quiet since everything else feels so loud right now. The second I'm safe inside, I lean against the door, my head dropping back and my eyes closing while I take a few calming breaths. I know what an oncoming panic attack feels like. I used to have them regularly. It's several long minutes before I feel like I can breathe again.

Straightening, I turn toward the mirror and get a good look at my face. The gasp that escapes is pure horror. My mascara is smeared down my cheeks, there's cum crusted on my jaw that got missed during the quick wipe down before we all passed out, and my hair is a tangled rat's nest around my head. Turning on the faucet, I wash away the mess that is my face, then attempt to finger brush my hair until I appear almost normal.

You've got this, Fallon. Just take a deep breath. You can do this. Remember, you're here on a job. Not for them. You can have this conversation then put everything back on lockdown. Easy peasy. I snort.

But maybe find some coffee first.

No one could ever say my stalling game isn't strong.

Quietly leaving the bathroom, I head for the small kitchenette and pray to all that is holy for something that can brew a cup of coffee, or, hell, even instant would do. Luckily, I find just what I'm looking for. I throw in the coffee pod and press start just as a door suddenly opens. Anson steps up into the bus. He's shirtless, showing off the jewel-toned tattoos, stark black lines, and scrawled words that cover his broad chest that's glistening with sweat. When he catches me watching, he freezes.

"Good morning," I chirp a little too brightly, startling him.

Honestly, I'm not entirely sure if it's morning or afternoon, but I roll with it.

"Morning," he responds softly, not moving an inch.

"Have a nice run?"

He nods, his eyes trailing over my body. I'm in nothing but Wren's white t-shirt that just barely covers my ass cheeks, leaving my long legs and feet bare. Swallowing harshly, he runs a hand over his hair that's pulled up into a bun.

"Fallon, I—"

"Anson, don't." I shake my head, leaning back and bracing my hands against the counter.

"Please, just let me apologize."

"There's nothing to apologize for."

He steps forward, his shoulders hunched and chin down. This giant alpha, one who was so perfectly rough with me last night, is now this big fluffy marshmallow. A wave of familiarity hits me. *This* is more like the boy I remember. Big and intimidating to most, but never to me. He hangs his head in defeat. I want to step into him, wrap him in my arms, and comfort him, but I don't. Maybe this makes me a bad person, but knowing he's feeling just a fraction of what I've felt for ages puts us that much closer to even ground in my eyes. Especially considering the special spot he once held that not even the others could touch.

"There is nothing, and I mean *nothing* in this world more important than you. And knowing that I might have fucked this up—that I took away your voice when I..." Both hands run down his face before he squares his shoulders. "When I knotted you without your permission. I'm not sure I can ever forgive myself, and I wouldn't blame you if you decided that I wasn't worthy of a second chance."

His voice catches in his throat, and my heart breaks. In that moment, all the years, all the hurt, all the times I swore I'd fuck them over just like they did me, it all evaporates as I stare at the pain written into every tense line of his body and the sorrow plastered on his face.

I can't do it. As much as I always thought I'd want to, I can't. There's still a lot that needs to be discussed, but I can't stand here and let him suffer—no matter what they did or didn't do in the past.

"I liked it."

His head whips up, shocked eyes meeting mine.

"You were my first, Ans. My first love, my first kiss, my first *knot*, my first...so many things. Before the other two came along, for those few short weeks, it was you and me. I'm surprised you tolerated me, honestly. I clung to you like a burr in your ass." I chuckle, the sound self-deprecating even to my own ears. "I was five and so goddamn sad. You were eight and trying to hold yourself together. I'm not sure I would've survived those early days without you."

"Baby girl—"

"And then you left, and my world shattered. It was..." My throat threatens to close up, so I turn away in order to finish what I need to say. "It was painful on more levels than I care to explain right now. And I never thought I would be whole again."

His fists are clenched at his sides, no doubt holding himself back, awaiting my final verdict. I could draw it out, but I don't want to. Right now, I just need him to hold me like he did all those years ago and tell me that everything is going to be okay.

"I'm not sure where we go from here. There are a lot of old scars..." My eyes meet his. "But if you needed me, I'd never turn you away, Anson. Ever. You're as much a part of me as the air I breathe or—"

He's on me before I can finish, hugging me so damn tightly that I might pass out from lack of oxygen. But I let him because my personal Squishmallow needs this as much as I do right now. He nuzzles into my hair, marking me with his scent and soothing me in that way only alphas do, and a little piece of my broken heart begins to mend itself.

"I'm sorry. For everything. I'll make it up to you. I promise." Lifting his head, I swear his eyes are glassy when they find mine. He brushes a stray piece of hair out of my eyes with such reverence that the omega inside preens under his attention.

"Kiss me, Anson."

His purr is loud in the complete silence of the bus, and when his lips touch mine, fuck, I could weep with the joy of it. I'd forgotten how damn cuddly he is. His lips softly play with mine in possibly the sweetest kiss of my entire life.

He lifts me up, setting me on the counter to ease the height difference just as his tongue slips into my mouth.

Fuck. The man can kiss. *I had forgotten.*

The tile is cold on my ass, but I couldn't care less. Standing between my legs, I can feel that fat cock of his nestled against the apex of my thighs, and even though I can't stop the whine that slips between my lips, he doesn't push for more.

"Fuck, baby girl." He kisses me again, then pulls back and drops his forehead to mine. "First knot, huh?"

His voice is a mere rasp, and his hands tighten on my ass.

"Mmhmm. Wanna be my second too?" I don't know why I say it. It just slips out.

He growls.

"Why does *he* get to go again? How's that fair?" Felix whines before a loud smack echoes through the room. "Ouch! What the hell was that for?"

"For being a jackass," Wren mutters.

My head drops to Anson's shoulder as I giggle. "God, some things never change."

When I lift my head, I find Anson's serious face staring back at me.

"Where have you been, baby girl?"

My smile slowly falls, and I glance at the other two alphas who now flank us. Before I can find the right words, there's a knock on the bus door before it swings open.

"Boys, how did it go with the hottie from last night? I've got a set of sexy blonde twins that..." Sebastian's eyes go wide when he takes us in. "Oh. Well, guess that answers that question. Except...you're not her."

My eyes narrow at the fact that he was about to try to get them laid. For as long as I'm here, this is a no-groupie zone. I'll cut a bitch.

"Sebastian, this is Fallon," Felix says proudly, a wide smile curving his lips.

"Well, I'll be damned! It really was her. *The* Fallon, huh? Looks like Mystery Girl isn't such a mystery anymore."

Anson is studying my face. I'm not sure what he sees, but his brow furrows before he tugs me into him a little more. My eyes threaten to roll back in my head when his bulge presses against my clit.

He whispers in my ear, "Don't worry. He always tries but never succeeds."

"Yes. She's staying for the show tonight." Felix turns to me, a challenging gleam in his eye. "Right, sunshine?"

My stomach flips, but I plaster on a sexy grin. "I wouldn't miss it for the world."

"What's our call time?" Wren asks.

"Backstage by six o'clock. That gives you an hour. The record label set up a meet and greet before the show."

"That will give me plenty of time to run and grab a change of clothes." And get a little break from the alpha pheromones I'm struggling to ignore.

All three of the guys growl, and I raise my hand.

"In case you've forgotten, Edward Scissorhands over here cut my dress off of me."

Anson grimaces. "I'm never going to live that down, am I?"

"Never, babe." I kiss his nose, ignoring the way the endearment slips off my tongue just a little too easily.

Sebastian looks at me, an easy smile on his face. "She sure is a pretty little thing. I can see why you've been looking for her."

His words seem innocent enough, but there's a tone to his voice that sets my instincts on edge. And that's when I remember the job I'm supposed to be doing while I'm here.

Shit! These guys are gonna blow my focus to hell.

Chapter 7

The walk of shame doesn't feel quite so *shameful* at five o'clock in the evening. I step out of the taxi wearing Wren's t-shirt and a pair of Felix's sweats that I've rolled up to keep them in place. After a brief argument over how I was going to get back, they finally agreed that I was a big girl and could make the trip on my own. For fuck's sake, I know more than six ways to immediately incapacitate someone if shit went down. I'm *good*. Of course, they don't know that, so I'll cut them some slack.

My mind starts plotting out my targets for the evening as I enter the hotel. My phone dings, and I pull it out.

Hello, Ms. Parker. Looks like you had an interesting evening. With no communication, we were beginning to worry that you'd forgotten your mission entirely. Remember, we're always watching.

I pause in the middle of the lobby, phone in hand, and check out the area around me. Fucking creepers. To be fair, I'm not used to having to provide updates to anyone. Being a solo hitwoman comes with very little oversight. They can take it easy.

Tamping down my irritation, I type out a brief update.

Apologies. I don't work well with others. If you've been watching me, then you would know that. Let's chalk it up to a beginner's mistake that I'll try very hard not to make again.

With a distinct lack of evidence after a search of their tour bus, along with the fact that the guys are unavailable during the bulk of each show, (also not discounting my so-called connection to them), I do not believe the band has any knowledge or involvement in the suspected trafficking ring at this time. They may be giant assholes, but they're not kidnappers. Fuck knows my teenage self sure as hell wished they were.

Manager, Sebastian Fuller, is still an unknown. My plan is to get closer tonight and hopefully investigate the backstage area for potential clues.

From what I've seen of the tour setup, I do believe it would be incredibly easy to operate such a system with little to no chance of getting caught. If I find any evidence of such, I will be sure to send an immediate update—pinky swear.

Items needed: 1) Full wardrobe that is appropriate for someone connected to the band—think young, hip, edgy, and sexy. 2) Some sort of small recording device that is discreet enough to carry in a small clutch or on my person.

Will check in after tonight's show.

Parker—out.

Maybe I didn't hide my irritation so well after all. Oops.

Thankfully, an elevator is waiting for me, and in seconds, I'm heading for my suite. I need a shower...desperately. And sleep, but that doesn't look like a possibility for a while. I need to get ready and prepare for tonight.

For the first time in my life, I'm conflicted. There are two distinct sides of myself that are at war. One wants to find the person or persons responsible for putting omegas in danger, no matter the cost. The other is worried about putting the guys in the line of fire and is torn about keeping them in the dark. But it's not like I have a choice. The Syndicate was clear. I'm not to mention them or what they've sent me to do, or I risk them taking extreme measures to silence me. Of course, there's also the fact that I don't want them anymore. I don't. Right?

Fuck my life.

The phone dings again.

Asshats? Appreciating the professionalism, Ms. Parker.
Expect a delivery within the hour.
Syndicate—out.

At least they have a sense of humor—or are just sarcastic as fuck like me. The depth of their connections is honestly a little mind boggling. Delivering everything I asked for within an hour? Who are these people? With unlimited funding and an organization willing to do what is necessary for the betterment of omegas across the globe, my brain sparks with excitement, imagining all of the good I could do with that kind of backing.

Entering my room, the door clicks shut, and for the first time in hours, there's blessed silence. I make my way over to the chaise in front of the window and decide that taking a few minutes to collect my thoughts wouldn't be such a bad thing. Sitting, I pull my legs up to my chest and rest my chin on top—my thinking position since I was a kid—and look out over the traffic and tall buildings.

My mind is a fucking disaster.

I love them.

I hate them.

I love my life.

But I hate it a little too.

More so who I had to become to do the things I get paid to do.

At sixteen, I walked out of the only home I had and went on the run, doing things no sixteen-year-old omega should ever have to do to survive. Do I regret it? No. It meant I lived when the only alternative was to die, so I accept my sins and all that came after.

Meeting Jimmy my first night in Chicago. Hearing how his daughter was forcibly bonded by an alpha and taken to the other side of the country, never to be seen again. The anger that rose up and the desire to do something about it. That was my first paying job—the day I became a contract killer. It was sloppy but extremely effective. No one would so much as look twice at a small teenage omega with wide eyes and curly blond hair as a potential suspect, and I quickly made a name for myself. Despite my age, designation, and even my inexperience, word spread through the darkest parts of the Chicago underworld, and offers began to come in. Over time, I honed my skills by taking martial arts and self-defense lessons. Made friends in low places. Became the woman I am today. Hardened, cold, *lethal*, and a slew of other things that I hide behind a pretty face. No one ever sees the lonely, hurt little girl residing within.

Yet somehow, *they* did. They so easily stripped off that rough outer layer, and it fell away, revealing someone I haven't seen in a long, long time. I had been so sure the girl they loved was dead, until suddenly, there she was—battered and bruised, her innocence long gone but a spark of love still alive in her chest. It feels almost wrong to be in her skin again. Like I might taint that last hint of goodness with the stain of my present.

What the fuck does this all mean? I can't be her and do the things I need to do, yet they don't see anyone else. What will they do when they find out I'm just a poorly made replica of the girl they so desperately want?

I don't know the answer, and that's terrifying. Because, at the end of the day, if forced to choose between my current life and the one I used to dream of when I was a young girl, I'm not sure which one would win. My brain and heart are very much conflicted on the matter. There's too much unfinished business, and until it's all resolved, I don't expect anything to get any easier.

There's a knock on the door, dragging me out of the loop my thoughts have entered, but I welcome the reprieve. Walking over, I go up on my tiptoes and, through the peephole, see the same middle-aged beta that delivered the disguise, makeup, and other essentials yesterday. Pulling the door open, he greets me with a smile.

"Delivery for Fallon Parker."

I motion for him to come in, pointing toward the open living room. "You can put it all right here."

The cart squeaks as he wheels it in—garment bags swinging on the metal rod and shoe boxes stacked along the bottom.

"They also asked that I deliver this." He holds out his hand. In his palm is a small white box. "It's a set of earrings that are voice activated. One touch turns them on. *Record* will begin a recording and *Stop* will end it. Recordings are automatically uploaded to the cloud and can be played back from any electronic device, including your phone. If you require a laptop, that can be requested as well."

"Interesting," I murmur, intrigued despite myself, as I take the inconspicuous box from his hand.

"Do you require anything else at this time, Ms. Parker?"

"No. Thank you... Sorry, I didn't get your name."

"You can call me Agent W, ma'am."

"Don't make me feel old, Agent W."

He grins. "We're only as old as we feel, Ms. Parker."

"Then damn, I feel ancient some days."

He chuckles. "Best of luck tonight, Ms. Parker. I know you'll do well. If you need anything else, don't hesitate to reach out."

"Will do, Agent W. Oh! One thing," I say.

He looks at me expectantly.

"Does the Syndicate ever bring people on board after they've completed their missions?"

"The Syndicate is a very harsh but ultimately fair organization, Ms. Parker. They only accept those who share a similar end goal and have a particular set of desired qualifications. I caution you to think carefully about your interest. Once you're in the organization, there is no getting out."

With a pointed look, he tips his imaginary hat and walks out.

Glancing at the clock, I realize I'm already running late. I rush through a shower and sift through the garment bags until I find a leather outfit that looks both sexy and a little badass. Just what I need for a confidence boost. Doing my makeup a little heavier, with a thick winged eyeliner and deep red lip, I add extra waves to my hair so it's full of volume and throw on the small studs. Looking in the mirror, I can almost believe that I'm a normal twenty-five-year-old dating a group of rock stars. *Almost.*

By six thirty, I'm back at the amphitheater, watching the huge crowds line up to get in. The guys told me to ask for Sebastian at the Will Call window, saying he'd escort me to the room where the meet-and-greet is happening. The girl at the window picks up the radio with a skeptical glance and asks if he's available, attitude dripping from her bright pink lips. In seconds, I'm directed to head to the security guard at the main entrance because he's "handling a situation."

After a quick thank you that goes unacknowledged, I walk past the long line of fans and up to the row of security guards blocking the doors. There are plenty of dirty looks and catcalls, but I ignore them. My only goal is to get inside, using my charm to sweet talk Sebastian into accidentally dropping some damaging information, before having to face the guys and my duplicity again.

Talk about an identity crisis.

"Excuse me," I say to the big burly security guard that's chatting with two of the others at the door. He eyes me up and down, immediately dismissing me, but before he can turn his back on me, I paste on my friendliest smile and continue. "Sebastian told me you'd all be expecting me. I'm with the band."

"Right, and so is everyone behind you. Get in line." He turns away from me, acting as if I no longer exist.

My temper rises, but I keep my cool. "I'm Fallon Parker. Sebastian Fuller—the band's manager—maybe you know him? He sent me here."

"I don't care who you are or who you claim to know. You don't have a pass, you don't appear to have a ticket, and the band *never* allows groupies into their shows. Try again, sweetheart."

I kind of want to punch his smug face, but his walkie-talkie chirps.

"Go ahead."

"It's Sebastian. Be on the lookout for Fallon Parker. Blonde. Sexy as fuck. She's *the* Mystery Girl and gets the V.I.P. treatment."

Burly glances back at me, shock written all over his face. "Roger that."

"Should we start over?" I ask sarcastically, holding out my hand. "Fallon Parker. Nice to meet you."

He cautiously shakes my hand. "I apologize, Ms. Parker. *Truly*. I'm Roland Hayes, Head of Security. If you need anything, just ask for me."

Well, isn't that convenient. A security guard in my back pocket.

"Tell me, Roland, who hired you?"

"Along with a few others, I was personally hired by the band. The facility provides added security of its own as well."

"Hired by the band or hired by their manager?"

"The band, Ms. Parker."

He swallows harshly, no doubt wondering if I'm going to get him fired for acting like an asshat, but I have a different agenda. I need to know who I can and can't trust around here, and if the guys hired him, then he's probably trustworthy. Good.

"Care to point me in their direction, Roland?"

"Is it true? Are you her?"

"I used to be."

He eyes me for a moment, then nods. "Come on. I'll take you to them."

He leads us through the door and down the hidden corridors the public doesn't get to see. Passing the tech crew who are busy setting up the stage for the night's opening act, the steady flow of people makes this an ideal backdrop for trafficking of any kind. Add in the multi-city stops and potential global exposure, and I'd be surprised if I *didn't* find any evidence of wrongdoing.

"Have you known the band long?" I ask, making conversation as we turn down another corridor.

"Been with them practically since the beginning. I consider them friends."

For some odd reason, that relieves a little bit of tension inside that I didn't realize I was harboring. The world is a scary place—I should know, after all—and the fact that they have someone watching their backs gives me peace of mind.

"Soooo...they really don't ever take groupies to their bus?" I ask, shooting him the side eye.

One corner of his lips quirk up. "Never."

I fight my smile and lose, a hint of girly giddiness coming to life inside me. Sebastian rounds the corner, his suit a little askew and hair slightly tousled.

"Oh good. You found her. I'll take her from here, Roland."

I try to unobtrusively look him over, and that's when I see it. A small scratch above his eye.

"Sebastian, you're bleeding." I point to his brow.

He freezes, then a deep sigh escapes. "I had to break up a fight. Got caught in the middle of it. That's why I couldn't escort you myself."

"You should've called me," Roland chastises.

"If I can't stop a catfight now and then, I'm in the wrong line of work." He chuckles. "C'mon, I'm sure you'll be a sight for sore eyes. They won't admit it, but they've been worried."

He takes my hand, placing it in his elbow before I can stop him.

"Check in with facility management and make sure we're all set with the extra precautions I mentioned to you earlier."

Roland glances at me, then turns back to Sebastian with a nod. "You got it. It was a pleasure meeting you, Fallon."

"Likewise."

He walks off as Sebastian steers us down the hall.

"So why were they worried?" I ask to fill the silence, my mind stuck on the *extra precautions* he mentioned. What's that all about?

"They thought you might not show up. They've waited years for this."

I can't admit that if the Syndicate wasn't forcing my hand, I might have considered just walking away no matter what my heart thought on the matter. The complications this adds to my life are too many to calculate.

"I always assumed it was a gimmick—a genius marketing ploy," I murmur, mostly to myself, but Sebastian abruptly stops.

Looking down at me, there is a multitude of emotions crossing his face. Surprise, frustration, and even a hint of anger I don't understand as his scent goes sharp.

"Every song, every tour, every interview, literally *everything* they do is with you in mind. You're incredibly important to them, and now that they're so close to having what they've always wanted, the fear of losing it again has them all on edge. You hold incredible power, Ms. Parker. More than I think you realize."

He starts to walk again, dragging me along with him while his words play on repeat in my head.

"I didn't ask for that power," I mutter like a petulant toddler.

"Neither did Spiderman," he shoots back.

Touché, Sebastian. Tou-fucking-ché.

Chapter 8

I hate meet-and-greets. The long lines. Awkward interactions. The *groping*. God, the groping. Don't get me wrong. We're grateful for our fans, but these forced interactions are just not my cup of tea.

"How much longer do we have?" I whine, earning an elbow from Anson as he signs yet another shirt.

We're all on edge—anxious for Fallon to get back. Until I physically see her, this ball of worry is going to continue to fester in my gut. Will she come back? Will we ever see her again? What will I do if she doesn't show up?

I'll hunt her ass down, that's what. I don't care what the label says. I'll cancel this whole motherfucking tour until she's back in my arms again. Thoughts of last night are on permanent replay in my head, thinking about her curves and her hair and those lips.

Good god. If I was hungry for her before, it has nothing on the primal need I have for her now. When her lips closed around my knot, I thought I'd died and gone to Heaven. Of course, I was practically suffocating her with my cum, but I'd be lying if I said that wasn't sexy as hell.

Shit, there's something wrong with me.

"Bro!" Wren barks.

I snap back to reality and see the woman in front of me. Her makeup is so thick, I'm not entirely sure what she even looks like under there, and her breasts are damn near spilling out of the deep v-neck shirt she's wearing. She's holding out a copy of our latest album and one of those metallic markers with a too-wide smile on her face.

"If you could make it out to Holly, that would be great," she says excitedly.

"Sure thing," I reply, taking them and slapping on my messy signature. There's no table, so it's the best she's going to get. "Here you go."

"Would it be possible to get a picture with you guys?"

I withhold my groan, barely, and give her a nod along with my camera-ready smile. In other words...the fake one.

She steps up, sliding her arm behind my back, and I lightly place my arm around her shoulder. It feels wrong—every time—to be touching someone other than Fallon, but I keep the disgust I feel climbing up my throat from showing on my face. Wren steps up to her other side and Anson on mine. One of the tour assistants counts down.

One. Two. Three.

The flash goes off just as I feel a squeeze on my right ass cheek.

Son of a bitch!

I quickly remove myself from her grabby hands and step back, fully prepared to call an end to this shit right now, but one look from Wren tells me that's not a possibility. We're contractually obligated to do this. With a sigh, I turn my back on Holly Grope's-A-Lot and face the next person in line, ready to go through the whole process all over again.

Fuck. I know what I really want to be doing...my girl. It's going to be a *long* night.

What feels like hours later but is really only thirty minutes or so, the line is down to only a handful of people. The others mill about the room, grabbing refreshments and snacks while they wait for another potential opportunity to talk to us. Yeah, that's not happening. I'm in no mood for small talk.

I glance up, seeing Sebastian walk in, and to my utter relief and surprise, Fallon is on his arm. Possessiveness rears up, and the pen in my hand cracks under the pressure when my fists clench in order to avoid knocking out our manager for touching what's ours. My hindbrain doesn't care that we told him to escort her here when she arrived. He's an alpha, and *my* alpha side doesn't like that shit one bit.

Then she turns to me, eyes bright and gorgeous lips spreading into a wide smile, looking fucking amazing in skintight black leather pants and a sleeveless black leather crop top. Her hair is in massive waves around her face, her lips a deep red, and for a moment, all I can do is wonder when the skinny little girl grew into all those womanly curves.

"You're drooling," Anson snarks beside me, and I glare at him while he chuckles.

"How are you not? She's the sexiest fucking thing I've ever seen."

"We are lucky bastards," Wren murmurs.

I swear, if we were cartoons, we'd both have hearts for eyes, and our tongues would be falling out of our mouths and rolling onto the floor.

She winks at me, and that's my undoing.

Handing the pen to Anson, I stalk over to the prettiest omega in the room and snatch her off Seb's arm. One hand slides behind her neck as the other wraps around her back, just above her ass, and I pull her into me.

"Well, hello to you too, Felix."

My lips smash into hers in response. Her arms twine around my neck, and just having her against me settles something inside. My hand grips her hair, tugging her head back the slightest bit as I ravish her, not giving a flying fuck who's watching or what they think. I'll never take a second with her for granted ever again.

She pulls back, eyes closed and lips parted, and a growl slips free. If it wasn't a total jackass move, I'd fucking claim her right here and now because she's perfection She's *mine*.

"I love you, Fallon."

The words leave my lips before I can think them through. I mean them with my entire heart, but I can sense her withdrawal and realize she wasn't ready to hear them yet. There's still so much left unsaid between us. Songs and interviews only tell half the story, and she deserves the full, unedited version of events. Maybe then we can start to earn back her trust and her forgiveness.

"Felix—" she begins, trying to escape my arms.

"Don't, sunshine. Don't run again. They're just words—words that come from the very center of my soul, but they don't require anything from you in return."

Her eyes search mine, body still tense under my hands.

"You don't know me, Felix."

"I know you smell like peaches and taste like sin. That you make this little sound in your throat just before you come. That you feel this thing between us, whether you like it or not. We can rediscover everything else as we go because I'm not letting you get away again."

Her eyes flicker with an emotion I can't quite place, but it doesn't matter. I'll be here, pushing for what I know we both need in order to convince her she wants it too.

I drop a kiss on her forehead and turn, seeing an entire room of strangers staring at us. Shit. The fucking tabloids are going to have a field day with this. The Mystery Girl has been unmasked. Maybe I should have Seb put a security detail on her just in case.

Grabbing her hand, I drag her over to where the other guys are signing the last of the fan merchandise.

"Thanks for leaving us hanging," Wren grumbles, but there's a smirk on his lips. He reaches for Fallon, and in one tug, she's in his arms, then he's kissing the shit out of her too.

I can hear the whispers around the room. Out of the corner of my eye, I see the cell phones being held up, no doubt recording the members of Feral Lyrics making out with the smokin' hot blonde. Anson and I share a look, and I know we're both thinking the same thing. We need to prepare Fallon for the media shitstorm that's headed our way.

"Hi, sweetheart," Wren whispers against her lips while his hands stroke up and down her back. "You came back."

"I told you I would, and I keep my promises," she replies, taking aim with that last line and hitting her target right in the bullseye.

I almost rub my chest, worried I'll be bleeding out from the strike.

"Come on, baby girl." Anson wrestles her away from Wren, tucking her into his side and kissing the top of her head. "Let's give you the backstage tour before the show starts. Do you want to watch from back here, or would you prefer to be in our reserved box?"

"I'll probably hang back here. See how everything works." She glances between the three of us. "If that's okay?"

Like we'd deny her anything. "Of course. Whatever you want."

"Thank you all for coming," Sebastian calls out. "Feral Lyrics needs to get ready for the show now, so if you could please exit through that door right there, ushers will direct you to your seats."

Sebastian slowly herds the stragglers out of the room, but my eyes stay locked on Fallon. My fists clench at my side because, with every breath I take, it's becoming harder and harder to ignore the need to have her in my arms. They say omegas will beg for a bite during their heat, and if denied without proper care, they can suffer severe anguish until the alpha makes it right, but I'm pretty sure alphas experience the same thing. Even though the man doesn't need her to say those three little words back to him, the alpha inside demands a response. He wants to know that she's just as invested as he is. That she feels what he does every time he looks at her. Without that, he's anxious and frustrated and a whole slew of other shit I can't even name. Those emotions translate into this urgent need to claim her in the only way he can in order to prove he's worthy of her love.

"Mind if I take her on the tour?" I ask, noticing the way my brothers share a look.

"I have to run and replace a couple of parts on my drumset before the show, so I can't join you guys anyways," Wren says, his brow furrowed and lips turned upside down as he no doubt fights his own internal battle where she's concerned.

"I should probably talk to Sebastian about a preliminary media intervention," Anson murmurs, studying Fallon.

She looks up at him. "Media intervention?"

"After Felix kissed the shit out of you in front of the entire room, there's no doubt going to be photos and videos popping up on the Internet, if they aren't there already. The secret of Feral Lyrics' Mystery Girl has been revealed, and the media is going to go nuts. We need to work out a plan."

She blinks. I'm sure she never even considered the ramifications of shagging the members of a popular band whose fans have theorized on her existence for years.

"Don't worry. We'll make sure everything is under control," he adds, kissing her forehead. "We'll be waiting for you before we have to go on."

Wren cups her face, dropping a soft kiss on her lips before they both walk out, leaving us alone. I'm not sure if they really had stuff to do, or if they could tell that I needed this time with her. Either way, I owe them one.

I hold out my hand, and the second her skin touches mine, it becomes a struggle not to spin her around, bend her over, and fuck her hard and long until she's screaming my name. Taking a deep breath, I pull her closer, needing her scent to calm me down.

"What is it, Felix?" Her fingers trace the furrow between my brows, just like she always used to do when I started overthinking everything. It's simple, sweet, and so totally Fallon. I'm not even sure she realizes she's doing it while she stares into my eyes, trying to understand this vibe I'm no doubt giving off.

"I don't want to scare you off, sunshine," I whisper softly, "but I need you to know how I'm feeling because there's never been anyone else who could get me this twisted up inside."

"I'm not sure if that's a compliment or a criticism."

"Neither. Just a fact."

She steps into me, burying her face in my chest. My arms instinctively wrap around her just like they used to. Drawing her in and nuzzling into her hair, her peach scent is just a little bitter when it washes over me, but she still smells too fucking good. My dick strains against my tight jeans.

"What are we doing, Felix? We're not kids anymore." Her voice is muffled as she talks into my dress shirt, but I hear every word. My heart pounds in my chest.

"Whatever we want to, sunshine. We make the rules here. No one else does."

She pulls back, her eyes so damn big and blue with this sense of wonder that's sparking to life right in front of me.

"Show me something that tells me about who Felix is *now*. Give me some insight into the man behind the sexy dress shirts and bow ties."

She playfully tugs on the green and black striped bow tie as her fingers run down the buttons on my green shirt. She's attempting to lighten the mood even though I can still read the uncertainty in her eyes, and I decide I can let her have this.

"Ever seen a concert from high in the sky?"

"I've never been to a concert at all. Wow me, Felix."

"How have you *never* been to a concert? That's blasphemous."

She shrugs, a hint of darkness crossing her otherwise bright features.

With an idea forming in my head, I let a smirk curve my lips. "Prepare to be wowed then, sunshine."

I tug her along behind me, determined to give her as much of me as she's willing to take. Hopefully, it's the whole damn package.

Chapter 9

The opening act, Knotty Boys, is just beginning their set as Felix drags me up to what he calls the catwalk. I can feel the music's heavy beat in every bone of my body, every strum of the guitar giving life to this feeling that's bursting inside me. It's dark, and so damn high, that my adrenaline is already amping up. Maybe I'm a little bit acrophobic.

"Are you sure it's safe up here?" I ask, letting him guide me to a spot that's just in front of the stage, looking down at the band.

"Would I have brought you up here if it wasn't?" he asks, pulling me over to the railing and boxing me in from behind. "This is always the best seat in any house. I come up here sometimes when I just need to get away from everyone else. No one will bother us up here."

"Can they see us?"

"No way. Too many lights and other distractions."

Taking a deep breath, I glance down. It looks like a kaleidoscope as the music plays in sync with the light show that bathes everyone in a sea of color. It's beautiful.

"This is amazing, Felix."

His nose skims along my ear, giving me goosebumps.

"It is now that you're here with me."

My heart skips a beat, and my fingers curl around the metal bar in front of me to keep myself from doing something really stupid up here. He's always been the risk taker—the intense one of the group with a level of passion that sometimes becomes too much, even for him. These stolen moments with just the two of us have always been his way of making sure I was the sole focus of all that intensity he keeps bottled up inside.

"Are you happy?" I ask softly, wondering if he can hear me over the rhythm of the music.

"I haven't been happy since the day I walked away from you, sunshine. Every moment since has been about surviving until I could find you. Hold you." One hand slips around my hip. "Now that you're here, I can smile again because I feel whole. I don't have to fake it for the press or the fans because I feel it in my soul."

I glance over my shoulder, just barely able to make out the emotions playing across his face. Does it ease something inside to know that he was hurting just as much as I was all these years? I'd be lying if I said no. But do I also wish I could take that hurt away because I understand how awful it feels? Hell yes, I do.

I kiss his lips, slowly pulling away until our eyes meet again. In the darkness, it's always so much easier to say your truths—all this bottled-up emotion eager to spill out into the night.

"I've had nothing to be happy about since the boys I loved broke my heart and left me alone to face hell by myself."

His jaw is clenched tight, but despite the tension written in the lines between his brows, his palm gently cups my cheek, his thumb stroking along my jaw.

"And now?"

I consider that question and how best to answer it. With the truth, I realize. There's so many lies between us already. This is one thing I can offer him that has no hint of deceit.

"Honestly?"

"Of course. I've never wanted anything else from you."

"I'm confused. Overwhelmed. There's so much *feeling* inside me after being numb for so long that I can't untangle the individual emotions well enough to know which one is predominant."

"After the show tonight, we'll have that long overdue talk. We owe it to you, and maybe it will help clear up some of that confusion and hurt I still see written all over your beautiful face whenever you look at us."

"I'm sorry. I—"

His fingers touch my lips. "Never, Fallon. Never apologize. We understand. I promise. Just be with me and forget the past for a little while. Can you do that? For me?"

I nod, telling myself it's just a means to an end. I can get closure, have some epic sex, and tally up some orgasms to get me through the following years when I'm alone again. I'll finish what I came here to do, tell them goodbye and thanks for the fun, then walk away.

The lies don't come as easily as they usually do.

His purr rumbles his chest as his fingers stroke through my hair, and I realize that no one has ever looked at me the way they do. It makes a girl feel powerful. Now I understand Sebastian's warning.

My hips begin to sway as the lead singer croons out the words to a slow song that talks about love and loss and the despair of letting go. If he only knew how much this song was speaking to me right now.

Felix's body molds to mine, his erection evident against my ass, and his hands trail over the bare skin of my belly while we move together. His scent deepens, the chocolate tang turning richer, and his fingertips brush against my pussy through my pants.

"Sunshine," Felix murmurs in my ear, "I need you."

There's a hesitant plea in his words, a barely hidden desperation that I can't ignore because I need him too. More than I'm willing to admit to myself.

My face turns so that my lips can brush his. "Fuck me, Felix."

He growls, his lips crashing into mine as his fingers work the small button on my pants, somehow managing to shimmy the tight leather down until it puddles against the metal mesh at my feet.

I hear the rasp of his zipper, feel the brush of his thighs against the back of mine, then his hand pushes one leg out as far as it will go with my feet tangled up in the taut material.

His fingers trail through my pussy, discovering a ridiculous amount of wetness.

"Fuck, sunshine, you're so goddamn soaked for me." His palm presses against my lower belly, and I arch my back, opening myself up for him. "Just like that. Be a good little omega and stick that ass out for your alpha."

His words, in that deep ass voice of his, are like gasoline to a flame. My body is on fire for him, my heart pounding in my chest.

"Felix..."

He leans forward, his body draping itself against the back of mine as his dick slips between my thighs. He slides through my slick, the wide head of his cock nudging my clit.

"You want my dick, sunshine? Want it to fill that pretty little pussy of yours?"

"Yes. *Fuck...please.*"

He pulls his hips back, his hand helping to guide him in. He's thick, even the tip stretching me open.

"Fuck, you're so goddamn tight. This is going to be fast. Hold on."

He slams into me and immediately pulls out only to thrust back in. It's hard and it's fast and it's dirty.

When I glance down, trying to catch a breath, I white knuckle the metal railing. People are rocking out to the lyrics of an upbeat song that I can't hear over the pumping of my blood through my veins and the groans of the man behind me. There's something incredibly fucking erotic about standing above a crowd of thousands, my pussy out in the open as slick drips down my thighs, my alpha's dick relentlessly plunging in and out of me.

With every thrust, I inch closer to the edge.

"Fuck, you're squeezing me so damn good, sunshine. This tight little pussy was made for my dick."

His hand slides up my belly and over my breasts to my throat, squeezing lightly as he lifts my upper body until I'm flush against him. The position has him hitting deeper, harder, and his grunts turn into growls. His knot presses against me, sending a pulsing ache thrumming through my core. No one ever told me that an omega's demand for a knot was so fucking intense or that it was damn near impossible to deny.

"Tell me you want my knot. Beg me for it," he demands, just shy of his alpha bark.

"I...*shit.*" His hips clap against mine, fucking me without mercy. I've never said the words out loud, never begged someone to fuck me, let alone knot me, but instinctually, I can feel the whine building in my throat because I want it. I want to have him fill me up so fucking full I don't know where he ends and I begin. "I want your knot, Felix. Please fucking give me your goddamn knot."

He chuckles darkly, rolling his hips back. "You're such a naughty fucking girl, sunshine. I love it. But we're *both* going to love this."

He hasn't finished saying the words when his hand tightens around my throat, his other arm wrapping around my waist so he can use my body for leverage. He slams me down on his dick, the swell of his knot stretching my sopping cunt until my body relents, letting him slip into a spot that molds around him, locking him tightly inside me. His growl turns feral, and a scream slips through my lips when the pleasure becomes so intense my entire body feels like a livewire sparking with too much electricity.

"That's it. Be a good girl and come on my goddamn cock."

This time, his bark holds a hint of his alpha power, and my body heeds its command. My orgasm tears through me while his hips continue to grind against my ass, my body milking his cock for every last ounce of pleasure he has to offer.

His forehead drops to my shoulder, his hands sliding to wrap round me in an embrace that rocks my entire being.

"Fuck." His voice is hoarse, emotion catching in his throat. "You feel so fucking good. I can't... I don't... Shit. I'm screwing this up."

My hand raises, soothing down the back of his neck.

"You're not screwing anything up, Felix. This was perfect, and I'm so fucking glad you shared it with me."

"I'd share it all with you, sunshine," he whispers.

Immediately, I know that I can't share everything with him. I have too many secrets. Too many skeletons in my closet, ones that could be dangerous to both their careers and their lives. How could I ever truly be theirs when the chasm between us is miles wide? No, I won't do that to them. I refuse to put them in the line of fire for my own selfish reasons, but that doesn't mean I don't want to.

"I don't need it all, Felix. All I ever needed was you. But now there are years that stand between us, and we're not the same people we were back then. We've each got our own lives. Our own responsibilities."

"Our lives have been on pause for the last ten years, Fallon. Now that you're here, we're ready to live again. We want what we always talked about—to be a pack, to be family. We want a future with you."

"Felix—"

"I know. I'm moving too fast. I'm just scared that if I don't put it all on the table, I'll miss my opportunity. That's all." His arms squeeze me just a little bit tighter. "Like I said, we'll talk after the concert and answer all of your questions. Just don't make any decisions until then, okay?"

I nod, and he nuzzles into my neck and along my jaw while I close my eyes, wishing things weren't so complicated. With each minute I spend here, every time I let them touch me, I'm sinking myself deeper into a pit I may not be able to climb my way out of.

"Shit. We need to meet the guys, but..."

I glance over my shoulder. "But what?"

"Well...uh... This is going to be messy, and we're standing above a crowd of people who very likely could end up getting jizzled on."

My nose scrunches up. "What the hell is jizzled?"

"Like drizzle, but with cum—jizz. Jizzled."

I blink. It's already been a really weird twenty-four hours, and it's not over yet.

"Then you better be good at catching."

"Catching? What? No!"

"Yup. You're going to have to put those big hands of yours under me and not let a drop slip through the grate under our feet."

"I didn't think this through."

"You didn't, and now there are consequences."

"Fuck. Okay. Their set is almost over. We need to go. Ready?"

"Ready."

He drops his hand under where we're joined, and I feel his knot stretch a little against me when he pulls out. He curses as I moan, then does a quick swipe between my legs, lifting his hand with a disgusted grunt.

"What am I supposed to do with it now?" he asks.

I shrug. "Hang on to it until we get down from here?"

"Gross."

"Welcome to the plight of sexually active women everywhere."

"Y'all deserve a medal."

"Come on, let's go tell the boys you got jizzled on." A large smile tilts my lips.

"You're enjoying this, aren't you?"

"Tremendously."

"Fuck, I'm never going to live this down."

"Never."

He grumbles the entire time we get redressed—with me having to help him pull up his jeans—all the way to the ground level, and the entire walk to the restrooms where we do a quick clean up. The guys are standing around talking when we walk up with minutes to spare. Their heads come up, nostrils flare, and for a split second, I get a little worried that they might not make it on stage after all because Anson and Wren are getting that feral look in their eyes I'm starting to recognize all too well.

"No." I hold out my hand and shake my head. "You all keep your knots in your pants. You have a show to do, and I won't have you fucking up my first concert."

Each one steps forward with a wide grin, dropping a quick kiss on my lips, and my belly flips. Felix was right, earlier. This is all moving so fast. I went from loving them, to hating them, to fucking them, to loving... No, I can't go there. Not yet. Maybe not ever again.

"You're on in two minutes." Sebastian stalks up, no doubt catching a heavy dose of satisfied omega since his eyes flick between Felix and me. I notice he's sporting a band-aid over his eye and make a mental note to check out that story he told earlier. "Fallon, here's your pass. Make sure you wear it at all times while you're on the property."

I slip the lanyard over my head, noticing the guys all sharing a look.

"Thanks, Sebastian. Am I okay to hang out here?"

"Of course. If you need anything, I'm usually around, or you can flag down one of the stage assistants."

"Got it!"

"One minute," Sebastian notes before walking over to talk to one of the security guards who has two blushing girls standing with him.

My eyes narrow, watching them walk away, but then the lights go down, and the crowd goes wild. I'll wait until the guys are on stage, then I'll go look for them.

"As soon as the show's over, we all need to head for the bus. It's time for a talk."

Anson and Wren look at me, then nod to Felix.

As I stand in front of the three of them, I see all the small ways time has changed them, but I also see so many more ways that prove they're the same men my heart still beats a little differently for. I'm pretty sure I'm fighting a futile battle here, but with few other options, I straighten my shoulders and smile.

"Break a leg, boys."

Anson kisses my forehead.

Wren tugs me over, wrapping me up in his arms, and drags my mouth in for a passionate kiss.

When I'm passed off to Felix, his hand twists in my hair, and he tugs my head back so he can feast on my mouth.

And I... I stand there and let them, wondering where everything went so damn wrong.

Chapter 10

Looking out from the curtain beside the stage, I see the crowds of women calling out their names, holding up signs asking the guys to claim them, and even catch the moment one brazen girl lifts her shirt, flashing her tits. My stabby side rises up, and this inner possessiveness that I have no business feeling threatens to take over until I hear Felix begin to sing.

"The taste of your skin, so sweet," he belts out soulfully.

The slow, heavy beats of Wren's drums and the deep tones of Anson's guitar create this entrancing combination that calls to me.

"The way you looked, staring up at me."

He's gripping the microphone with one hand, the other gripping the air as if there was someone kneeling at his feet. There's no doubt what he's referring to, and my pussy throbs to the rhythm.

Fuck. I'm not sure what it is about these guys, but they pull me under their spell with little effort. There's no fighting it, no escaping it, and that makes everything about this situation a million times harder.

"No way I could ever forget her," he sings, then Wren softly joins him in the background. "No one's ever loved me better."

I turn away, my heart pounding wildly in my chest. Fuck. When they said *every* song, *every* lyric, I assumed it was an exaggeration. But with every word they sing, I realize the depth of their suffering, and it's as gut wrenching as it is alluring.

The hair on the back of my neck begins to stand on end, that feeling of someone watching me creeping across my skin. My gaze scans over the groups milling around backstage. They're *all* staring at me. Word travels fast.

Two female members of the crew give me a nasty look when they brush past, not bothering to lower their voices despite talking about how I'm nothing special and they can't believe the guys waited all these years for *me*. When I hear them talking about all of the women that would kill to be in my shoes, I finally tune them out.

Standing tall, I straighten my shoulders. I've never been worried about what other people thought of me. I've simply brushed it off and moved on, but this strikes at the heart of my relationship with these alphas.

I've always wondered why I wasn't enough. Hell, my parents didn't even want me, so why should they? What could a girl like me have to offer men like them? Now that I'm older, and I've learned a thing or two about the designations, I can see the flaws in my reasoning. Maybe I was *too* much. Too loud, too aggressive, too independent. Alphas want a meek omega, right? Fuck. I don't even know. The guys never seemed to mind my intense nature, never seemed to want me to be anything other than what I was. Which brings me right back to the age-old question. Then why did they leave me?

Frustrated with myself, I walk away from the stage, suddenly needing a little fresh air. I was sent here on a mission—not to rekindle old flames—and I'm going to do my damndest to see it through. Taking one of the rear exit doors that lead back to the bus, I step outside. The night is cool, with clouds forming to the south as another storm rolls in. It's the perfect complement to my mood.

Gripping the metal railing, I close my eyes and try to recenter my thoughts. Stay focused. Get the job done. That's what I'm here for. That's when I hear soft whimpering. Slinking into the darkness, I head for the area where the crew and trailers are parked. There's very little light over here, but the moon is bright in the sky, providing just enough visibility. I peek around the front of the bus, seeing two security guards dragging a young woman under her arms. Her head flops from side to side, and a moan slips into the night. Her heeled boots are dragging across the blacktop as the trio heads for a black SUV. No way in hell am I letting them get her in that car. I touch my earring.

"Record," I whisper, praying it's actually doing what it was designed for, and step out of the shadows before I fully think it through.

"Hey, have either of you seen Roland?" I ask, glancing down at the petite blonde between them. "Oh gosh. Is she okay?"

They share a brief glance, then the taller of the two looks back at me. Their scents are heavy in the air, deepening as they take me in. Alphas.

"She's fine. Can't handle her liquor and got a little combative when we asked her to vacate the premises. We're giving her a lift home since the closest ride share is almost thirty minutes out."

"I wouldn't mind waiting with her. I'm sure you all have better things to be doing than dealing with some drunken fan."

"It's fine. We've got her," the stockier guard says, his eyes narrowing. "Hey, aren't you the band's Mystery Girl? What are you doing out here alone?"

"Is it a crime for a woman to be outside by herself?"

"It is when she looks like you. Those boys better be careful, or you may get snatched up by some alpha who isn't going to worry about your connections or your consent."

"Is that a threat?" I ask. Inside, I'm a bundle of fury, but I keep my voice even.

"Just saying it like it is, sweetheart. Now, run along. We've got this handled."

"And if I decide to stay? I'm starting to worry about this woman's *consent*."

"Your choice, but don't get upset when we're forced to make our own," he says menacingly, dismissing me as he and his friend hoist the girl into the back seat of the black SUV.

I have a decision to make. My gut tells me they aren't being knights in shining armor. This is potentially the evidence I've been waiting for, and fuck knows I'm not going to let an innocent girl get hurt just to get one hundred percent confirmation for the Syndicate.

Fuck. Why is nothing ever easy? Looks like I get to play bait.

Slamming the door shut, they turn to me.

"You really should've heeded our warning." The smile on his face is sinister as his eyes trail over my body. "But damn, I'm glad you didn't."

They split off, thinking to sandwich me in between them. Silly, silly boys.

"Boss is going to be fucking thrilled when he sees the extra we snagged for him," the taller one says.

"Two for one is always a good deal." The stockier one licks his lips. "But I may take first dibs at her before we hand her over. She's a sexy little thing. Now, be a good girl and make this easy, and I promise not to hurt you...*too* much."

They chuckle.

Until my leg flies up, jamming a heel right into the stocky one's family jewels. He immediately collapses, clutching his limp dick and howling in pain. The other one roars, diving for me, but I'm faster. I spin out of the way just in time to see him barrel forward at full speed with nothing to stop his fall but his buddy writhing on the ground. He trips, stumbling to his back.

I walk over, placing my heel in the center of his chest as I lean down. His eyes widen dramatically, breath stuttering in his throat.

"I'm going to ask you a question. If you're honest with me, I promise not to hurt you...*too* much." The wicked smile that tilts my lips has his skin paling. "Who's your boss?"

"Fuck off," he grunts out. "I'm not telling you shit."

I dig my heel in just a little harder, forcing a cry out of his mouth.

"Wrong answer." The knife in my ankle holster is in my hands faster than he can blink, and I hold it to his throat. "Who. Is. Your. Boss? You'll tell me if you cherish your tongue."

"He'll kill me. I can't tell you," he sputters out.

"*I* will kill you if you don't tell me, so it looks like you're fucked either way. At least with me, I'll make it quick."

He glances at his friend, and I see it too late. The stocky guard is aiming a gun at his partner's face. The shot goes off, and blood sprays through the air. My ears ring, but I don't have time to worry about it. He aims the gun at me, but I'm already in motion. My arm swings, knocking the gun to the side just as he pulls the trigger. The gun goes flying across the pavement as my knife slices into his meaty thigh. He screams in pain, clutching his leg.

Quickly assessing my surroundings, it doesn't appear that we've drawn any attention. I grab my phone out of my back pocket and type out a message to the Syndicate.

Backup requested ASAP.

You wanted proof. I got it.

Behind the amphitheater. Recordings should also be uploaded to the Cloud.

One potentially drugged and terrified omega in the back of the black SUV.

One security guard with a knife in his leg. Can't remove it because he'll bleed out. Bring a paramedic.

One security guard dead. Shot in the head by his pal with the knife in his thigh. Clean-up crew requested.

Please return the knife—sans blood—to me at your earliest convenience.

Parker—out.

A response comes within seconds.

Nice to see you being discreet.

Backup will be arriving in less than three minutes.

Do try to keep a low profile, Ms. Parker.

Syndicate—out.

"You fucking bitch. They'll get you for this. You're a dead omega walking."

I wipe blood spatter off my lips.

Gross. Low-life alpha is not in my diet, thank you very much.

I lean over Stocky, my hand gripping the knife. "It takes a lot to kill a girl like me. Hope they're up for the task." Then I twist it, causing him to howl in pain.

Lights flash across the parking lot, then two blacked-out Escalades come to a stop feet from where I'm standing. Guys in head-to-toe black combat gear swarm out of the vehicles, with two heading for the omega, two heading for the dead guy, and three heading toward me and Stocky.

"We'll take it from here, Ms. Parker," he says from behind his mask.

"Y'all are quick."

"It's our job, ma'am."

"All this fucking ma'am shit."

"You might want to go clean up. You're covered in blood."

"Thank you, Captain Obvious."

One of the guys behind me snorts.

"Thank *you* for leaving us one hell of a mess to clean up." He sighs. "But good job. You saved a life tonight."

"You're welcome," I say, throwing up the middle finger as I head for the tour bus, praying no one is around to see my Carrie impersonation.

Twisting the handle, I say a silent thank you that it's unlocked and make my way inside. I head straight for the bathroom, risking a glance in the mirror. Blood is splattered across my face and chest, and looking down, I see it dotted along my belly and arms. As much as this is going to suck, I step into the shower and turn it on. The cold water rains down on me, rinsing the blood down the drain. Once I'm fairly certain it's off my clothes, I struggle out of the leather and wash my hair twice to make sure all the blood and brain spatter are gone.

With very little time to spare, I quickly finish, wrapping a towel around myself so I can clean up any evidence I might've trailed in. It's been a long, exhausting forty-eight hours, and when I'm finally done, I sit on the sofa with every intention of relaxing for a few minutes before the guys get back, except my eyes start to feel heavy. Within minutes, I'm falling asleep with Felix's words playing through my head.

No way I could ever forget her. No one's ever loved me better.

Chapter 11

I walk off the stage and hand my guitar to one of the roadies, eagerly searching the mass of people for Fallon. Since the second I walked out there tonight, I've been waiting for the moment I could walk back off and get her in my arms. Felix got some alone time with her earlier, and I don't begrudge him that, but my instincts are going a little crazy. The need to hold her close is driving me to the brink of insanity.

"Where the fuck is she?" I growl, startling a few stagehands that are walking past.

"She's not here?" Wren asks, his tone laced with disappointment.

"Maybe she's with Sebastian in the box?" Felix offers.

Just then, our manager rounds the corner.

"Great show tonight, guys. That's a wrap on Chicago. On to the next!"

"Have you seen Fallon?" Wren asks, his eyes scanning backstage for any sign of her.

"One of the crew mentioned that a couple of the female road-ies were openly talking shit about Fallon earlier. They said she left through one of the back doors and never returned."

My heart sinks to my toes.

"What did they say?" Felix growls.

"People are figuring out who she is, and not all of them are happy about it."

"Well, they can fuck off. They don't get a say in our personal lives. If I find out anyone is harassing her or talking shit behind our backs, they'll be looking for another job." I'm not quiet about it. I say it loud enough that the people eavesdropping can pass it along.

"Don't worry. I'll take care of it." Our manager looks around at the people moving about. "Look, the buses are scheduled to head out first thing tomorrow morning. Have you talked to her about where you all go from here?"

We all share a look.

"We were planning on asking her to join us for the remainder of the tour when we talked to her after the show." Wren looks at Seb. "Are there any logistics that need to be worked out to make that happen?"

"I'll just need to add her name to the roster so the label can account for the added head count. Other than that, no. Not until the second leg of the tour when we head overseas."

Fuck. I hadn't even thought about the international portion of the tour. What if she doesn't want to come with us...or can't? We don't know if she has a job or other responsibilities. We haven't taken the time to ask her about her life now. How selfish are we?

"We'll get it all worked out tonight." Felix nudges me. "C'mon, let's go check the bus."

We all follow him out the door and into the quiet of the night. Roland is walking toward us as we descend the stairs.

"Hey, Roland. Have you seen Fallon?" Felix asks.

"I haven't," our head of security replies, pausing to look out over the parking lot. "You haven't happened to see Scott or Marcus, have you? I've been looking all over for them. They were supposed to be watching the east entrance but went radio silent sometime after you all went on stage."

I shake my head. "We just got done with our set and haven't seen them. Talk to Seb. Maybe he can check with the rest of the crew."

"Will do. If I see Fallon, I'll send her your way."

"Thanks, Roland." We nod at each other before my brothers and I head for the bus.

"Do you think she'll come on the tour with us?" Wren asks nervously.

"I think once she has answers, she'll consider it. Worst case, we have all night to convince her." Felix twists the handle to the door and stalks inside.

He comes to a grinding halt at the top of the stairs. Wren and I step up beside him and see Fallon asleep on the sofa.

"She's exhausted," I whisper.

"We have to wake her up, Ans."

"Felix, let's give her a couple hours. Then we can—"

"I see you all haven't forgotten how to be creepers when I'm asleep."

Her voice is raspy from sleep, and it settles over me, calming my nerves.

She's not wrong. Even when we were young and stupid, there were many times one or more of us would just stay awake, watching her sleep. It's as if our instincts knew she was precious and to be protected even then.

"Sorry, baby girl."

Her eyes open, and she stretches, the towel slipping just the tiniest bit down her cleavage. Instantly, I'm hard. Not that it takes much around her. When she sits up, her damp hair falls down her back, and she stares up at us with a face free of makeup and a mark from the pillow marring her cheek. Fuck, she's still the prettiest thing I've ever seen in my life.

"Are you hungry?" I ask, knowing damn well she hasn't eaten shit in the time she's been with us.

"A little. But I think we should get this talk over with first."

I share a look with Felix, then Wren.

"I'm a big girl, guys. I can handle the tough discussions even if they hurt like hell."

"But can we?" Wren murmurs, running a hand down the back of his neck as he looks at Felix.

"I don't know where to start," he whispers.

"We never wanted to leave you," I begin, taking the leap for my brothers.

Watching her face fall and wishing the story was different, I so vividly remember the shock and gut-wrenching terror I felt when we realized she was gone and there was no way to find her. Even now, my gut churns with the all-consuming dread of that moment.

"But you did. You left and never came back."

"We wanted to, sunshine. Fuck, did we want to."

"But you *didn't,* Felix. For years, I've wondered what I could've done wrong. Was it something I said? Did you find someone else? Was I too damaged? The mess of self-deprecating thoughts playing through my head were probably enough to have me committed if I had so much as whispered them out loud."

"If there's one thing you should know, it's that you did *nothing* wrong," Wren asserts. With both hands on the top of his head, I know he's fighting every instinct pushing him to go to her and comfort her. We all know we need to get this out first. "Getting in that car and driving away was the single hardest thing any of us have ever had to do. They told us that if we resisted the relocation, it would just make things harder on you, and we were too naive to realize it was a ploy to get us to go quietly."

Staring at the carpet, I remember those early days with stark clarity because I've never felt as miserable and desperate as I did then. "When they moved us out of the foster home, we were placed in temp housing until we could manage to get jobs and find another place to live. We were eighteen hours away, and none of us had a car. It took us months—working odd jobs and saving up every little bit of money we had—just to buy a piece-of-shit vehicle. By the time we were able to make the drive back to the old house, you were gone. We asked around, tried to figure out where they'd placed you, but no one would tell us anything."

"We didn't know what to do," Wren adds. "We got so desperate we started calling the local radio station and dedicating songs to you on the off chance you might hear them. We had no way of knowing if you were even still in the area, but what else could we do? We were young and broke and stupid."

I watch her face, take in the way she's sitting so primly while her eyes meet ours head on. She's so fucking strong—she always has been—and incredibly smart. I have no doubt, if she had been in our position, she would've figured out a way to get back to us. As it was, she was young and at the mercy of a broken system. For the first time, I wonder if we were ever truly worthy of her in the first place, but I'll be damned if I can give her up.

Felix's foot is tapping on the floor, a rhythmic sound that gives away his frustration at our situation—back then and now. "We checked in with the foster agency once a month, begging them for answers. They always refused, giving us a new reason every time. You were a minor, so your file was sealed. We weren't your legal guardians. Privacy laws restricted the information they could give out, and there was all sorts of other shit we didn't understand. We didn't have anywhere else to turn. We'd exhausted all of our options."

"Where were you, Fallon?" I repeat the question I asked her earlier.

She swallows harshly, the color draining from her face.

"When you all left, the family decided they were getting too old to continue to foster—especially with a potential omega on their hands. I was moved to a new home. New family. New city. New…"

"New what, baby girl?" My gut twists. Something tells me I'm not going to want to hear this next part.

"New problems." Her blue eyes sparkle with unshed tears.

She fights against them valiantly, but I know it's a losing battle. Fuck, this woman guts me, and not being able to hold her as she faces her past is damn near killing me.

"Problems?" Felix repeats, clenching his fists at his sides.

"An asshole of a man who liked to use his alpha designation as a way to intimidate and abuse a young omega whose designation had barely come in. Then add in a young son who was destined to be an alpha asshole like his dad—he learned from the best after all—and it was a living hell. Beatings to get me to understand my place. Inappropriate touches that escalated to non-consensual acts that no young girl should ever be subjected to—all under the guise of *training*."

The silence in the room is absolute as realization hits us like a freight train. Without us there to protect her, she was on her own, facing an enemy she didn't stand a chance against.

"Baby girl—" My voice breaks.

She shakes her head, and the first tear rolls down her cheek. "I survived. Barely. And when he pushed for the one thing I refused to give him, I got the hell out of there."

"How?" Wren asks, his voice wavering.

"I don't think you want to know the answer to that particular question," she whispers.

"Give us the address. We're going to fucking murder him and his fuck nugget of a son for what they did to you." Felix's growl has her wincing.

"He's already dead," she says, her voice void of any emotion despite the tears falling like rain.

There's a collective intake of breath, and for a long moment, none of us move. It's not hard to piece together the details and come up with the obvious outcome. She killed him. Good fucking riddance. I, for one, am so goddamn proud she had the strength and courage to protect herself when we couldn't, and I'm sure my brothers feel the same way.

When I see the look in her eyes, resignation staring back at me like she expects me to walk away from her again, I stalk forward without thought. I kneel in front of her, taking her face in my hands. Her eyes are focused on something I can't see, so lost to her nightmare that she barely notices I'm sitting right in front of her. I drop a soft kiss on her lips and linger there for a long moment, trying to draw her out of the past. I might've been too late to rescue her then, but I'll do my damndest to be her hero now.

"I'll never be able to apologize enough for what you've been through, but I'm here now, Fallon. We all are. Let us share the burden. You don't have to carry it alone anymore."

Her eyes slowly focus on mine, her bottom lip beginning to quiver, and I can't take it anymore. I wrap her up in my arms like I've longed to do all night. She buries her face in my neck, her scent taking on a tart edge.

"We're here, sweetheart. We won't ever leave you again." Wren sits beside her, stroking her hair.

"You're about to leave on a world tour, Wren. It could be months before I see you again."

"About that," Felix murmurs, sitting on her other side. "We want you to come with us."

She pulls back enough to meet his eyes. Her face is flushed and her eyes are red from crying.

"Come with you?" she whispers.

"You can travel with us, go to all of our shows. We can spend time getting to know each other again," I explain.

She turns to me. "I don't know—"

"Do you have people here who count on you? That would miss you if you were gone? A job? Friends? Family?" Wren asks.

She blinks as if the thought is so foreign she's not even sure what he's talking about, and the noose around my heart squeezes just a little tighter. At least we all had each other. Didn't she have *anyone*?

"There's no one. I just..." She looks away, worrying her bottom lip between her teeth.

"Please, baby girl. If at any point you don't feel like this is working out, we'll get you a flight back home. Just give this a chance. Give *us* another chance," I beg.

The thought of leaving her here, alone, is like swallowing nails. We've waited so long to have her with us, we never considered she might not want to be here.

"There's a lot about me you don't know, and—"

"There's nothing you could say or do that would change how we feel about you, Fallon," Felix states, the use of her real name telling me just how serious he is. "We've loved you our entire lives. Let us start proving it to you."

She glances between all of us. "I don't have anything with me. No clothes, no makeup."

"We can run and grab whatever you need. Stop stalling," I chastise, earning an eye roll for my efforts to lighten the heaviness in the air.

"I'm not sure I like the idea of you all getting to boss me around."

Wren's lips tilt up in a grin. "As if we've ever been able to do that."

"I can't make any promises. This would only be a test run, going in with no expectations. Do you all understand?"

Turning to Felix, then to Wren, I know none of us are happy that she's still so damn unsure, but we also understand it. Regardless, we'll make sure she has no doubts about where this is going, and if I have any say in it, she'll officially be ours before the last show of the U.S. tour because I want her at my side for the rest of my life.

"We understand."

"Then I'll need to run and grab my things. I can be back here in—"

Felix shakes his head. "Not gonna happen, sunshine. We'll go with you."

"That's really not necessary."

"He's right. You might need an extra set of hands. We'll borrow one of the crew's SUVs and drive you to your place."

She purses her lips, her nose scrunching up adorably.

"Why don't you want us to come with you, sweetheart?" Wren asks.

"My place was too far away. I…" She bites her bottom lip again, and I growl before I tug it safe from her teeth. "I'm staying at a hotel for the weekend."

"Then what's the problem?" Felix demands, patience growing thin.

"Nothing. *Nothing.* No problem. Let me get changed, and we can go," she grumbles, extracting herself from my arms and heading for the bathroom.

Once I hear the soft click of the bathroom door, I look at my brothers.

"What do you think she's so scared of?"

"She doesn't trust us," Wren adds.

"Well, she better get over it because we aren't going anywhere and neither is she. I'll fucking bite her if it comes down to it and deal with the repercussions after."

I run my hands down my face. "We can't fucking claim her without her consent, shithead."

"Watch me." Felix crosses his arms over his chest.

I wouldn't put it past him. Where Fallon is concerned, we've never been able to maintain a clear head. We've always acted on impulse and instinct—every cell in our bodies dictating our actions. It's hard to stay rational when she smells like peaches and looks like ours.

Now we just have to convince her that's exactly what she is before Felix gets impatient and ruins everything.

Chapter 12

The damp leather is chafing my skin, but I refused to borrow the guys' clothes again. The SUV pulls out of the parking lot and barrels down the freeway, heading for the hotel. The guys recognize the signs, even after all these years, that I'm struggling with my thoughts, so they let me think in silence as I stare out the window, watching the city skyline whizz by.

Knowing they didn't purposely abandon me, that they never stopped wanting me, really has begun to mend the cracks in my heart after it was shattered all those years ago. But with that, comes a new problem. The lies I'm keeping from them. The Syndicate's involvement in my return isn't my secret to tell, but they may not see it that way. And my *job*? Well, I'm not sure there's ever a good time to tell the men you love that you kill people for a living.

Major mood killer, am I right?

But that's who I am. What I do. I could no sooner change that part of me than they could stop making music. The rock stars and the killer—has a nice ring to it if you ask me.

But going on this tour with them under false pretenses feels wrong. If it had been solely up to me, I would've said no. It's easy to get caught up in the excitement of the moment, the adventure of hopping from city to city, but that's not real life. Real life is arguing over which way the toilet paper roll goes and who left their dirty socks lying on the bathroom floor. Real life is being stressed out over work and coming home to a messy house. I would've forced us to work toward a new relationship as the people we are today. Forced us to find time to spend together and see if this connection can withstand the test of separation. Sex and pretty lyrics don't mean anything if the foundation under them is as fragile as glass.

At the end of the day, though, I said yes. Because it's not my decision to make, and that just pisses me off. Pulling out my phone, I send a quick text to the Syndicate.

I've been asked to join the band on tour. I bet you're jumping for joy over that, not giving a damn what I think about it. You say you're all about equality, but there's nothing equal about using an omega as a pawn in a game she has no control over.

Regardless, I'll be grabbing my things from the hotel.

Will send another update when I have more information.

Disgruntled omega—out.

God. One of these days, my mouth is going to get me in trouble with the wrong people.

My phone dings. Discreetly, I lift it up and glance at the screen.

You're wrong, Fallon. We do care, but this mission is important enough that we're willing to make the risky plays in order to save lives. Please try to understand.

We'll still be with you every step of the way—watching from the shadows, ready to lend a helping hand.

Sympathetic Syndicate—out.

PS—We are truly sorry we weren't able to save you all those years ago, but since you took care of the problem yourself, kudos to you for surviving.

Fucking creepers. Until this moment, I'd just assumed they meant it in a general sort of way. Now, I'm starting to realize they mean it quite literally—they're *always* watching. Maybe I need to request a signal jammer next time to make sure private conversations stay private.

Shaking my head and sighing deeply, I have to admit they *are* right, though. I'm but a small fish in a big sea. So many others aren't as strong as I was back then and can't save themselves. That leaves their lives in my hands.

Shit. I don't want to commiserate with them, but I fucking do.

Anson pulls into the parking lot a short while later and whistles. "This place is swanky. "

"Yeah, a little rich for my tastes, but it does its job."

"What *is* your job, sweetheart?" Wren asks. "You know so much about us, but we know very little about you."

I honestly expected this question, and I've practiced my response multiple times, but the lie feels like acid on my tongue after the discussion we just had.

"I was an independent contractor, working toward safer environments for omegas, but I recently partnered with an organization that's striving for much of the same thing. It's proving to be an eye-opening experience."

"That's amazing," Wren says, reaching for my hand as I exit the vehicle.

The guys throw on hats and sunglasses, doing their best to disguise their faces since they didn't want to bring security. I'm still not sure that was a good idea, but before I can voice my concern one last time, the sliding doors of the hotel open, and we stroll through the lobby with its marble floors and elegant chandeliers. We get quite a few surprised looks, but no one seems to care too much about who we are or what we're doing.

"Fallon?"

I whirl around, hearing my name called from one of the seating areas tucked off to the side. Stalking toward us in a custom tailored suit is Chance—the bartender from the Thirsty Alpha...otherwise known as the beta who drugged me and a member of the Syndicate.

My eyes narrow in warning, though I'd be lying if I said he didn't look just as handsome as he did behind the bar wearing a shirt and jeans. His blue eyes are bracketed by smile lines, his hair a messy sort of perfect, and he's staring at me with a look on his face that I can't quite decipher.

"I thought that was you," he says, stepping into my personal bubble and wrapping his arms around me in a hug.

I'm frozen in place, not sure what his fucking deal is right now, but his fresh laundry scent floods my nose, and I'll be damned if the urge to lean into him doesn't rush through me.

"Chance. What are you doing here?" I ask as I pull away, *accidentally* stomping on his foot...hard.

Fucker.

He grunts, gritting his teeth at the pain, but recovers quickly with a knowing smile.

"I just got done with a business meeting, and I was about to head out. I have to catch a late flight to Nashville."

"We're heading there tomorrow morning," Anson offers, and I curse the entire situation right now.

"I'm so sorry. Guys, this is Chance Donovan, my…"

"Her new business partner." His smirk gets under my skin as he uses my explanation from the car.

I withhold the growl stuck in my throat. "Chance, this is Anson, Felix, and Wren."

His eyes go wide. "You're the members of Feral Lyrics."

He holds out his hand to each of the guys, shaking theirs in return. My gut twists at this game he's playing right now. I glance around us, but it doesn't seem as if anyone is paying us any attention.

"Let's keep that down. They're trying to keep a low profile."

"Right. *Right.* Sorry." He turns back to me. "How funny that we'll both be in Nashville tomorrow. Maybe we could meet for dinner before the show?"

My jaw is clenched so tightly, I'm surprised they can't hear my teeth grinding.

"I'm not sure if there will be time—"

"We could get you a ticket if you're interested," Wren offers, glancing at me. "I bet Fallon might like some familiar company while we're on stage."

Felix shoots Wren a dirty look, but Chance doesn't see it because he's still staring at me. To be the focus of this man's attention is to feel like an ant under a magnifying glass. If you're not careful, you could get burned.

"That sounds like fun. I'd love to take you up on that."

"I'll have our manager set it up at the Will Call window for you."

"Sounds like a plan." His eyes glint mischievously. "I thought you said they were asshats—"

"Would you excuse us for just a moment?" I ask, my hand already latching onto Chance's arm and tugging him a few feet away.

When we're out of earshot, his eyes trail over my body. "Leather looks good on you, Fallon."

"What the hell do you think you're doing?" I whisper yell.

"After tonight's close call and your brash admonishment, the Syndicate decided I need to take a more active role in the investigation, which is unprecedented, I'll have you know. But they decided me staying behind a phone screen wasn't going to keep you safe."

"Wait a goddamn minute, *you're* the one I've been talking to this whole time?"

"Yes, pussycat. The Syndicate assigns each of our *projects* a handler. You're the lucky one that got me."

"First off, I am *not* your pussycat, do you hear me? Second, I am more than capable of taking care of myself, as evidenced by the mess you all had to clean up tonight—you're welcome by the way. Third, you need to get back behind the scenes where you're meant to be. I don't work with a partner. Ever."

"My pussycat has claws. I kinda dig it." He grins when I growl. "But remember, what the Syndicate wants, the Syndicate gets. We'll just need to learn how to work together."

Wishing I could scream my frustration, I grit my teeth instead. "I sort of hate you right now."

"I've seen firsthand what you do to the men you supposedly hate..." He glances over at the guys who are watching us with rapt attention then turns back to me. "I've gotta say, I'm here for it."

A blush rushes over my cheeks, and my heart rate spikes when my perfume fills the space between us. I silently curse my traitorous body.

"Keep your hands to yourself, and maybe I won't have to cut them off, got it, beta boy?"

He leans in, his smell growing impossibly stronger as his lips brush my ear. "I can do some interesting things completely hands free, just sayin'."

I narrowly avoid shoving my fist in his face, choosing to walk back over to the guys instead. I know the minute they smell my arousal. Their nostrils flare, and three sets of eyes home in on Chance with a much more possessive look.

His smug grin has a dimple appearing, and for some stupid reason, it makes him even hotter.

Son of a bitch!

"We should probably get going before people start noticing you," I say, grabbing Felix's hand.

"It was a pleasure meeting you all," Chance murmurs as he puts his hands in his pockets.

"Likewise," Anson replies.

"I guess I'll be seeing you tomorrow. Have a good evening, fellas. Night, pussycat." With a wink, he mouths, *Always watching,* and walks off.

I'm going to murder him in his sleep at the first opportunity.

I can feel their eyes on me, but I just straighten my shoulders and plaster a fake smile on my face.

"Are we ready to do this?"

Tugging Felix along, we make it all the way to the elevator. The doors close us in before he boxes me against the wall.

"What is your relationship with your *partner*, sunshine?" His voice is deeper than normal, his tone low and menacing, but I'm not afraid. No. It actually turns me on, seeing this possessive, jealous side of him. It didn't go unnoticed that they said they'd been celibate for six years. That leaves the four before that unaccounted for, so they're not entirely innocent.

"I'm not fucking him if that's what you're asking."

He growls. "You're. Mine."

"Ours," Anson interrupts, leaning his shoulder against the wall beside us. "You're *ours,* is what he meant to say."

My eyes narrow at the alphas who are suddenly looking a helluva lot more like alphas and a lot less like lovesick puppy dogs.

"Do you really think I would've fucked any of you if I was with someone else?"

"No. You wouldn't," Wren interjects, "but I'm not so sure he got the just-friends memo, sweetheart."

"And let's not forget I can smell your goddamn arousal," Felix barks.

"We... *We* can smell your arousal," Anson corrects, his eyes glinting with barely banked heat.

I shrug, pretending to be unaffected by this whole alphahole thing they have going on right now, when really, they're just amping up my arousal even more.

"He's an attractive guy. I can't help my body's reaction to that."

Three snarls echo through the elevator just as the door dings, and before I can protest, Felix picks me up, throwing me over his shoulder.

"Your body's about to react to something," he grumbles. "Room number?"

I'm bouncing on his shoulder, lifting my head to find Anson's hungry eyes on mine. There will be no help there.

"Thirteen ten."

In seconds, we're standing in front of my door.

"What's the code for the keypad?" Wren asks, his voice huskier than usual.

"Five six nine six."

The pad chirps, then the lock clicks. Anson opens the door, letting Felix and me in first. He doesn't stop in the living room, instead carrying me to the bedroom where he sets me on my feet and takes a step back.

"Strip," he barks, alpha command in his tone.

My eyes widen, and without hesitation, I unbutton the leather pants and shimmy them down my hips, letting them pool at my feet. Reaching for the zipper on the side of the leather crop top, I slide it up and wiggle out of it.

I'm standing before them, completely naked. In the back of my mind, a voice whispers, *always watching,* and I know that Chance is seeing me naked right now too. I get impossibly wetter, imagining him watching the guys fuck me. My perfume floods the room, and their nostrils flare.

"I can see the slick dripping down your inner thighs, sunshine. Is that for us, or is that for *him*?"

Felix's voice has gotten impossibly deeper, settling into a place inside that's begging for him to touch me, needing it with an urgency I don't understand.

"For you," I rasp, the urge to ease the ache growing more powerful with every second their hands aren't on me. "Fuck, Felix, please."

"I don't believe you," he murmurs. "So prove it to us."

I blink. "What?"

"Get yourself off. I wanna see you come."

"How in the hell does that prove—"

"You're going to tell us what you're thinking about while you touch yourself. Give us the play by play. We'll know if you're lying."

Fuck. My. Life.

Chapter 13

Fallon

They're lined up at the foot of the bed, looking large and imposing and so damn hot as their eyes rake over me lasciviously. I've never been more turned on in my life.

"Get up on the bed, Fallon," Felix commands.

I do as instructed, my heart pounding in my chest and my ass sinking into the plush mattress, and force my body to relax.

"Spread your legs. We want to see that pretty little cunt of yours." Anson's hand drops to the bulge in his jeans, stroking himself through the rough material.

The whimper is stuck in my throat, but my hands fall behind me and my feet slide apart, the cool air in the room hitting the wetness between my thighs. My clit is already throbbing and swollen, desperately needing attention that I'm going to be forced to provide myself. It's one thing to get yourself off in the darkness of your room with no one watching. Another knowing three possessive alphas have a front row seat to your pleasure while a beta watches from who the hell knows where. To be the center of attention is not something I thought I would ever be comfortable with, but being the center of *their* attention has need shooting straight to my core.

"What are you thinking about right now, sunshine?" Felix murmurs.

"That I like your eyes on me."

His purr is loud in the silence of the room. "Show us just how much you like it."

I swallow down my nerves, lifting one hand and sliding it down my belly until my fingertips brush against the smooth skin between my thighs. I'm so fucking wet it's dripping down the crack of my ass to the bed beneath me.

My eyes close as a flush works its way up my chest, over my throat, and into my cheeks. I've pleasured myself before—I'm not a fucking saint—but I use toys, not my own fucking hand. The couple times I was desperate enough to try, it took forever to get out of my own head enough to find release.

"I'm not sure I can—"

"You can. Touch yourself, baby girl. Let us see you come undone."

My fingers slip between my folds, brushing over my clit, and I can't contain the gasp that slips out. It's so fucking sensitive and swollen that even a small hint of friction feels amazing. My knees fall apart even more, my hand growing more confident as I tease my hole.

Wren's fists clench at his side. "Tell us, sweetheart. If I can't touch you, I want to know what you feel like. What you're thinking."

My chest is rising and falling, the lightest touch of my fingers making me ache for more.

"Fuck. I'm wet and so damn needy. I wish it was your hands touching me."

A finger slips inside my pussy, pumping in and out, but it's not enough. My breath catches in a whine, not wanting them to know just how fucking much I need them.

"Two," Felix rasps. "Fuck yourself with two fingers."

My middle finger pulls out, only to be joined with another as I thrust them in as deep as they can go. My head drops back with a groan, but I need more.

"How does it feel?" Anson's voice is low, a growl edging his tone.

"It feels warm and wet and...and...not enough." The whine finally escapes thanks to this building ache that's pushing at the edges of my control.

"Imagine it's our cocks slamming inside you," Felix purrs. "That we're fucking you so damn good."

My eyes slowly open, my lids heavy as I take in the men watching me. Their dicks are all out, their hands stroking their erections. What a fucking waste.

I'm surprised when frustration begins to well inside, followed by a blooming anger that they're making me do this instead of fucking me like they rightfully should. They said I'm their goddamn omega after all.

This time, after I withdraw, I plunge three fingers in a little harder and roll my hips against my hand, reveling in the obscene noise. I drop back onto the bed in a huff, willing to do just about anything to find the release I'm so fucking ready for.

"Fuck, I need to come." They're as deep as I can get them, my fingertips teasing along my inner walls as the heel of my palm grinds against my clit. "I need your fucking dicks, but you won't give them to me. Knowing you're all watching while I fuck my own hand, needy and aching and so damn wet, just has me wanting you even more."

My free hand tangles in the comforter to ground myself, and my hips begin to buck up into my hand. My breaths are coming in deep pants, a perpetual whine slipping from my lips.

"All because you think I want him. I bet if he were here, *he'd* fuck me. He'd fill me up so damn fast, and I'd be coming all over his cock instead of my goddamn fingers."

The thought of him sinking into me while the other three look on is like a spark to kerosene. I can feel sweat forming on my skin as I fuck my hand harder, hearing low growls coming from the end of the bed.

"Don't you dare think of him right now, Fallon." Felix's voice is so low that I know I'm edging toward dangerous territory, but I don't care.

Pulling my hand back, I roll over and thrust my ass into the air, giving them the perfect view of everything they're missing out on. My hand slips underneath me to find my clit while the other grips my own hair. My fingers have no finesse now, desperately rubbing circles around the sensitive little nub in the hope that I can ease the pressure building.

"Fuck. Here I am, presenting like a good goddamn omega, but I feel so fucking empty."

My hips roll against my hand, the grip on my hair getting tighter as I imagine Chance's face beneath me. I would grind my pussy along his tongue, all while the guys watch us together and wait their turn.

"Shit. My pussy is clenching around nothing, but it feels so fucking good. I..." I've lost all sense of rhythm now. I just fuck roughly against my hand. I'm damn near incoherent, rambling and whimpering their stupid fucking play by play. "My slick is dripping down my arm. Dammit. I want a fucking knot. I need to come so goddamn bad."

"Fuck, sweetheart," Wren groans, but I don't stop.

"I want someone to pull my hair and shove their fat cock inside me, want one of you to lick my clit while the other fucks me hard until I'm so damn sensitive I can't take it anymore. I want... I want him to watch..."

Snarls sound out through the room, but I don't stop. I can't at this point. Guess I've proven something after all, just not what they wanted.

"I want him to see you fucking me, see your cock in my mouth as you come down my throat. Want him to see you knotting me until I'm a writhing mess and coming so hard I can't even speak." My pussy is clenching down so hard, begging for a knot as I feel my release skimming down my back. "I want his dick in my ass as you sink knot deep into my aching fucking cunt."

I choke on my next breath, and my body goes taut. I can hear them in the background, but I can't make out what they're saying. I'm lost to the most empty pleasure I've ever experienced, and I know the ache afterward is going to be even worse.

"Fuck, I'm gonna...."

It rolls over me slowly until it pulls me under with the force of a tidal wave. My fingers continue to rub my clit, praying for more even though my body's already soaring. My hand finally drops to the mattress, knowing it's useless. I hadn't realized I'm tugging on a fistful of hair, or that I'm crying into the mattress, until the first hiccup slips out. I bury my face into the soft comforter, praying they didn't hear it.

I've only just realized that I'm attracted to an asshole who drugged and kidnapped me, and I just announced that fact to the men I've always loved who watched me unravel for their own pleasure because it sure as hell wasn't for mine. What sort of twisted web am I weaving right now?

"Sweetheart?" Wren whispers.

"I just…" I can't face them yet. My vulnerability is written all over my face. "Give me just a second."

"What do you need?"

"I don't know," I murmur.

My head shakes back and forth. There are so many things I need right now, and I wouldn't even know where to begin. Then I feel the brush of thighs against my ass and strong hands gripping my hips. I hiccup, turning my head to look down the length of my back.

Wren is there, naked, his abs streaked with sweat, staring down at me with his mouth in a tight line and his eyes wild.

"This what you need? Need an alpha to take control?" Felix appears beside the bed, looking down at me with slitted eyes. He brushes hair back from my face, and the gentle touch, so comforting yet still so far from what I want, is both mesmerizing and torturous in equal measure. "Need Wren to fuck you for being such a naughty girl?"

And just like that, my body coils up tighter.

"Please," I whimper, the sound pathetic and needy at the same time.

Without hesitation, Wren slams in. He's long and so fucking thick that the stretch is phenomenal. My groan is swallowed up by the mattress as he begins to thrust in and out of me. I'm still wound up so tight, my pussy clenches down on him as if to hold him in place.

"Holy shit, she's…" His fingers dig into my hips. "She's squeezing me so fucking hard I can't…" But despite his words, he continues to fuck me through it, and the sound of skin slapping skin echoes through the room.

"Fuck. Yes. Harder, Wren. Please."

"This is ours, Fallon. Say it."

The words stall in my throat. I am theirs, but now that the idea has sparked to life, a small part of me wants to be *his* a little too.

"Fucking say it, Fallon." Felix is suddenly kneeling before me, lifting my head until our eyes meet. "You're ours."

"I *was* yours," I manage to rasp out, watching Anson kneel beside us.

"You still are."

Felix's hand grips my jaw, forcing my lips to part, and without hesitation, he thrusts in. He hits the back of my throat, making me gag. Eyes watering, I look up at him from beneath my lashes, letting him throat fuck me as if he thinks that will somehow change things.

Anson pulls one of my hands up, wrapping it around his dick.

"Stroke it, baby girl. Make me come."

With my hand moving up and down Anson's dick, Felix's in my mouth, and Wren's slamming in and out of my pussy, I'm overwhelmed in the filthiest way.

"God, she's fucking perfect," Wren mutters. "I'm not gonna last."

"Want Wren's knot in that greedy little cunt, sunshine? Want him to show you just who fucking owns it?"

I nod, our eyes locking.

"You've got two alphas who need to come first, sunshine. Get to it."

I whimper around his dick, taking him deep over and over again while Wren pounds into me, forcing me forward. Both of Felix's hands move up into my hair, grabbing fistfuls, and he forces me down, holding me there until I can feel him throb against my tongue.

"Fuck yes. Just like that, sunshine. Holy shit."

My hand has a stranglehold on Anson's dick as he thrusts between my fingers, getting himself off while his packmates use me for their own pleasure.

"I'm gonna fucking come," Felix groans. Pulling out of my mouth and squeezing his dick hard, he pumps it over and over while holding my face up with his free hand.

He roars, thick spurts of cum covering my face—eyes, cheeks, chin—and dripping down my neck.

"Move. I need to mark her too."

Felix stumbles off the bed, with Anson taking his place. My big alpha shares a look with Wren, then I'm pulled up against my alpha's chest as he grinds into me from behind, just shy of his knot slipping inside.

"I'm going to come on those pretty little tits, baby girl. Spread it all over you so there's no doubt about whose omega you are."

He strokes himself hard and fast as Wren's free hand grabs one of my breasts, pinching the nipple. I groan, and it sends Anson over the edge. With a roar, he comes all over my chest, even on his brother's hand, but Wren doesn't flinch. He continues to thrust up into me harder.

Anson reaches forward, his fingers swirling around in his cum as he does exactly what he said, spreading it all over my body, his scent combining with Felix's.

"Fuck. My turn," Wren groans, his fingers slipping up to grab my shoulder. The other wraps around my waist as he pulls out the slightest bit. He slams me down onto his knot, the fully swollen width of him stretching my pussy to its limits as he slides home.

"Take my knot, Fallon. Fucking take it," he growls just before I feel him bite down on my shoulder.

My pussy locks around his knot, milking him for everything he's got, and I detonate. All of the pieces that make up who I am explode out around me until they slowly start to come back together again, but they fit together differently than they did before, and I have no idea what that looks like yet. Who I am now.

When I finally return to reality, I'm surprised to find no bond, no connection, nothing lighting up between us. Disappointment wells up even though relief slowly follows.

Anson is still staring into my eyes when I can finally focus again, and whatever he sees there has his brow furrowing and concern sparking in his eyes. My body slumps against Wren, and his arms pull me into his chest, holding on tightly as he nuzzles into my hair, marking me with his scent.

Anson's fingers brush a hair out of my face, gently tucking it behind my ear.

"You look fucking stunning covered in our cum and smelling like pack, baby girl."

Pack.

That single word makes my heart pound in my chest. It was all I ever wanted. A pack to call my own. People to love and care for me. But will they still want me when my secrets are revealed, or will they leave me to pick up the pieces again? Do I want to wait around until I have the answer?

"Let him try to take you from us now, sunshine," Felix murmurs from beside the bed. "He doesn't have shit on our history together."

Maybe he doesn't, but I bet he understands the woman I am now a helluva lot better than any of them ever could, and that's an alluring draw. Never once did I expect my past and my present to collide, but now that they have, I'm almost eager to see where this all goes. Will the boys I loved love me in return, or will the new guy swoop in and steal the girl?

Of course, maybe I can have the best of both worlds. We'll just have to wait and see.

Chapter 14

What the fuck am I doing?

What I'm *not* doing is my job. The one the Syndicate pays me to do.

Never in all my years with the organization have I ever developed...fuck, I don't know...*feelings* for one of my assignments.

Until her.

The second she came into the bar, looking gorgeous and tired and lonely, everything inside me went still. Staring at her picture was one thing. Seeing her walking toward me was something totally different. It was as if my soul recognized its counterpart, and for the first time in my life, all the voices that usually struggled for dominance in my head were silenced. Blessed. Quiet. It took everything in me to stand my ground and do what I was there to do.

Drug and kidnap her.

When she looked up at me, those bright blue eyes full of confusion as she slipped into my arms, I felt immediate regret. Regret that it had to be me she looked so betrayed by. Regret that I couldn't have just met her somewhere else—anywhere else—where things could have developed naturally. And now regret that I have to hide behind a screen, watching her fuck three other men. Regret that she isn't fucking *me*.

Running my hands down my face, I pick my phone up, watching Felix hand Anson a wet towel. He cleans her face and chest with a gentle sort of reverence that I wish I could emulate, but I'm too rough around the edges for that. Too many years of diving into the depths of depravity will do that to a man.

When Anson's done, Wren carefully maneuvers him and Fallon onto their sides, spooning her from behind while whispering sweet words into her ears.

She's the perfect omega for them.

Their lives would be pointless without her.

Please give them this second chance.

They're good men. She deserves the love, support, and care they can offer her, but they can't feed her dark side like I can...and she wants it. I heard it all. Whether it was for their benefit or mine, I can't be sure, but it was reassurance enough. The next time I get her alone, I'll take the next step and see just how far she's willing to let me push.

My phone rings, and I startle out of my daydreams of the sexy omega. Glancing at the number, I immediately answer.

"Donovan."

"Did you secure the package?"

My hackles rise, and for the first time in years, I'm half tempted to tell the Syndicate to fuck off. Of course, that would probably mean my untimely demise, ruining all my newly laid-out plans, so I hold back. But Fallon is not just *a* package. She's the *full* package.

Fuck. I have issues.

"I'm meeting her in Nashville, the band's next tour stop. They've offered me a ticket to the show, and I should be able to cement my position by her side. She told them I was her new business partner."

"Smart girl."

Also strong and beautiful, not to mention so fucking vulnerable underneath it all that I can't stand it.

"I'll check back in tomorrow with an update."

There's silence on the other end of the line, and I know I'm not going to like whatever it is they're about to say.

"I know I don't have to tell you the ramifications of getting emotionally attached to an assignment."

My teeth grind, and I force down a surge of anger.

"I'm fully aware of the protocol."

"She's a beautiful, dangerous woman, Donovan. I can see why you'd be intrigued by her, but at the end of the day, she's just a job who will go on her way as soon as her mission with us is done. They don't ever stay."

A small voice in my mind tells me I could convince her to.

"Like I said, I know protocol. I'll follow up tomorrow night."

"Good job tonight, Donovan."

The line goes dead as I drop back against the hotel room bed. She doesn't know I'm just across the hall. That I'm so close I can damn near smell her arousal from here. When I pull up the video feed again, they're all in bed, talking softly, sharing stories about the band's time on the road and the crazy things they've seen.

At one point, when Wren's knot finally eases, Fallon excuses herself to use the restroom. I switch cameras, watching her walk up to the sink and grip the cold marble, staring at the mirror. It's like she's looking right at me. My finger slowly traces her features on the screen. Fuck, she's pretty. Big eyes, plump lips, long blonde hair, and curves that make me want to do nasty things to her body.

But it's the war I see hidden in the depths of those icy blues that draws me in the most. She's torn between the woman they think she is and the woman she's become. They're both spectacular, but the darkness in the present version of Fallon is what calls to me on levels I can't explain.

"What the fuck are you doing?" she whispers to herself, brow furrowing. "They love you, you know they do."

"But not like I can," I whisper back, knowing she can't hear me.

She's naked, her perky breasts and pink nipples in my direct line of sight. She really is motherfucking perfection. Quickly taking care of business, she comes back to wash her hands and glances in the mirror one last time. Her eyes narrow.

"If you're watching, Chance, this doesn't change anything."

She heads out of the room, shutting off the light, so I switch over to the other camera with a big ass grin on my face. She climbs back onto the bed, settling into her place between Wren and Anson, who immediately pull her in and wrap their bodies around her. Felix is passed out on the other side of the big guy, and in minutes, the others' voices trail off, and the room goes silent.

I don't really have a flight to Nashville. I'll be following discreetly behind the bus, in case something were to happen along the way. Always watching, just like I told her. Carrying my phone into the bathroom, I open the video feed and set it up high on the ledge above the shower, so I can keep an eye on things. As soon as the water is steaming, I step under the spray, letting its warmth wash over me.

Like hell tonight didn't change anything. I heard every single dirty thought she had, and I let her words play on repeat as my body responds. I'm hard and aching for her as I have been every night since

I met her. My hand wraps around my dick, and I hiss at the sharp pleasure that simple touch elicits. Closing my eyes, I imagine it's her smooth, wet pussy gripping me so fucking tightly as I stroke myself. Imagine her mouth on mine while she rides me, her tits bouncing and hair falling down her naked back.

One hand falls forward to rest on the tile as the water continues to pour over me. My hips roll, sliding my dick through my grip, working myself over to an image of fucking her while the guys watch. My fingers tighten, and my groan echoes off the shower walls. I'll fuck her tight ass while she rides one of her alphas. She'll be warm and wet and gripping me so fucking good that I know I'm not going to last long. I'll fill her up, coming in that pretty little puckered hole of hers until it's pouring out around me.

"Fuck, just like that, Fallon." My hand tightens, strangling my cock, as my hips buck wildly.

Heat spreads up my spine, and my balls draw up as my release edges closer. With the warmth of the water running down me, I can almost imagine it's her warm, wet mouth sucking me down, taking my length to the back of her throat and swallowing around the head of my dick.

"Shit, I'm gonna come, pussycat," I growl in the silence. "Swallow it all."

With a few last pumps between my fingers, I come with a shout, spurt after spurt hitting the shower floor as I squeeze tighter, aching for every last drop of pleasure my imagination can conjure.

My head falls forward, and my breaths come in quick pants as I recover. I already need her again, but I tell myself that the real thing is almost within my grasp. By this time tomorrow, I'll be that much closer to having her in my bed. Whether the others are there too remains to be seen. I honestly don't care as long as there's room for me somewhere in the mix because my soul has already claimed hers, and it's not going to give her up that easily.

Chapter 15

The restaurant is busy, with people lined up outside the door as I slip inside. I thought Chance was kidding when he mentioned dinner last night, but then his text came through earlier, giving me the time and location. I hesitate. This thing between us was bound to get complicated. Fast. And I'm not in the mood for more complications. Even sexy ones.

There's this divide inside me—this feeling of living two separate lives that was making my head hurt. I don't know how to reconcile the two into one whole person, but I have to. For all of our sakes.

"Fallon."

Turning, I catch sight of Chance standing up from a table not far from the door. He's wearing a suit coat unbuttoned over a loose shirt, the neckline dipping low to show off the leather band of a necklace hanging down against his chest. His hair is pulled back, revealing the shaved sides of his head, and stubble graces a jawline that is strong and masculine. He looks amazing, and I have to fight the arousal that sneaks up on me.

He lifts his hand, palm up, and motions me forward with a come-here gesture. The smirk on his face has my eyes narrowing. I don't like being told what to do. At least, not outside the bedroom.

Making my way toward him, I can't help but add a little extra sway to my steps, watching the way his eyes skim over my body. There's a barely banked heat in his gaze, a look that says he likes what he sees.

"You look stunning," he murmurs when I stop in front of him.

I may have picked the sexiest outfit that was delivered, solely to torment him. My sheer black geometric, long-sleeved top shows off the black bra underneath. The red suede skirt hugs my hips, and the thigh-high black boots add a couple extra inches to my short frame.

"Thank you. Considering you probably picked out the outfit, I figured you might appreciate it."

His grin is immediate. "I'm surprised they let you come alone."

I shrug. "They had a meeting with the label exec who's in town, so they didn't really have a choice."

He motions toward the table, and I take my seat. Stepping up to my back, his warmth washes over me when he helps push in my chair. Glancing up at him over my shoulder, I'm sure my surprise is evident on my face.

He leans in, his lips brushing the back of my ear. "I can be a gentleman, Fallon."

My brow arches as he rounds the table and takes his seat.

"A gentleman wouldn't drug an innocent omega and rip her away from her life."

The smug expression on his face drops, jaw muscles clenching, and he considers me thoughtfully.

"I'd apologize, but we both know I wouldn't really mean it. My job is what brought you into my sphere, and I find that I wouldn't change anything, even if I could. I recognized the loneliness in your eyes that night, Fallon. Even if you try to deny it."

I ignore the feelings he's so effortlessly stirring and try to reason with him. "Chance, this can't go anywhere."

"Why not? You and I are a lot alike, Fallon."

I glance around the room, trying to get my thoughts in order. He's right, but I'm not sure how I feel about that. The waitress arrives, buying me a few extra minutes while we place our orders. He takes a sip of his water then sets it back onto the table, his eyes on me the whole time.

"Admit it, Fallon. You feel it too."

"Feel...*what*?" I ask, tilting my head and tapping my bottom lip with my index finger while I pretend to think on it. "Anger at being fucking drugged in a place I've always felt safe? Confusion over being thrust into a situation I've carefully avoided my entire adult life? Or maybe the insanity I now feel as I question who in the hell I am and what I want?"

Leaning forward, he places his forearms on the table. "You're too smart to pretend to be so goddamn stupid. You know what the hell I'm talking about, or you wouldn't be here."

"I'm here because the Syndicate said I needed to be."

"This isn't the Syndicate's doing any more than that outfit you're wearing. This is solely about me and my pleasure."

"Wow," I growl, scooting the chair out a little harder than necessary. "Your gentleman persona needs a little bit of work, Chance. Better practice before you lure your next unsuspecting victim to her doom."

I've always thought alphas were the only ones that used and abused omegas as their own personal pleasure holes. Turns out betas aren't much better. But for some reason, this particular beta's asshole-ish-ness hits a little harder than any other.

"Fallon, that's not what I—"

"It's been positively lovely chatting with you tonight, but how about we stick to the anonymity of a phone screen from here on out until I'm able to get the hell away from you?"

Standing, I stalk out the front doors, hearing him call my name. I ignore him and all the curious stares of the onlookers around us. The cool evening air feels phenomenal on my heated cheeks, and I let my eyes close as I take in a deep breath. Now that I can breathe again, I step up to the curb, trying to flag down a cab.

"Fallon, wait," Chance calls out from behind me.

His hand lands on my arm, and my entire body goes into defense mode, but there are too many witnesses. Slowly glancing down at the contact, then up into his pretty blue eyes that hide a wealth of sins, I keep my voice level and calm even though inside I'm a riot of fury.

"You've got two seconds to remove your hand, or I'll remove it for you regardless of who's watching."

"Just, please..." he begs, withdrawing and stuffing both hands into his pockets—probably to avoid grabbing at me again. "I'm sorry. I've never..."

He looks toward the street, eyeing the rush of traffic heading both directions as people get to wherever the night is about to take them. He clears his throat, looking back at me with an open expression I'm not sure I trust.

"I've never done this before," he murmurs softly.

"You've never talked to a woman? Never had dinner with an acquaintance? Never had some fucking *manners*? Like you said, I'm too smart to be stupid enough to believe that you don't know how to behave in normal society."

"I don't know how to behave around *you*." He runs a hand over his head. "I'm so used to just taking what I want—"

I snort, crossing my arms over my chest. He shoots me a glare, and even that bit of irritation is damn sexy on the man. "You don't say?"

"You know what I mean. I don't do *feelings*. I don't do *relationships*. But I'm a fucking man with needs. I usually prefer straightforward interactions—no games, just a mutual understanding that any interaction is strictly a business arrangement and means nothing beyond sexual gratification. Women who are with me know the score."

"That…" My mouth drops open, then closes again because there are no words for just how appalled I really am. "Sounds really sad, even to someone like me."

"Says the woman who went ten years without physical sex." He raises a brow when I start to argue. "Your battery-operated boyfriends don't count."

I growl.

He holds up his hands. "All I'm saying is you're *different*. You're beautiful and mysterious, a whole helluva lot dangerous, and I can't fucking stop thinking about you. For the first time in my life, I'm overwhelmed in the best way possible, willing to dive straight into the deep end, knowing damn well I can't swim. But trying to decipher your signals is like trying to decode an encrypted message. I'm fucking it up. I don't know what I'm doing here, so I'm just asking you to cut me a little bit of slack, okay?"

I study him. In our line of work, we wear masks to hide our true selves away from our targets. We present the person we think they want to see, the person most likely to get a positive response. For the life of me, I can't tell if this is the real Chance or some act he's putting on to get what he wants out of me. I should leave, head back to the guys and stick with what I know is safe, but on some level, he's right.

When you do the types of things we do, getting close to anyone is a liability. You close yourself off from any connections because they create a vulnerability. I chose to be alone. He chose differently. There's no right or wrong way to protect yourself when your life is always one misstep away from coming to an end.

"I don't trust you," I murmur, meeting his eyes.

"I know, and I don't blame you. Just tell me if you feel the same insane draw to me that I do to you. If you do, I'll work to earn your trust. If you don't, then I'll step back and let you complete your mission without any further distractions."

It would be so much easier if I said I didn't feel a thing. That I could walk away and have no regrets. I try to put on my mask of indifference, prepared to tell him exactly that, but it keeps slipping, the words struggling to form on my lips. When I feel the warmth of his hand sliding around my back, my head lifts and our eyes connect. I want to believe it's honesty staring back at me, but there's no way to be sure. It's a risk. One I'm not sure I can avoid taking.

"Please, Fallon. Tell me what you want."

The plea in his voice is real, and I can't avoid it any longer.

"I want you..." I whisper.

He pulls me into his chest, eyes narrowing. "But...?"

"But I want them too."

His features soften. "I know that, pussycat, and I'd never force you to choose."

The nickname doesn't seem quite so absurd when he's holding me close like this.

"But they might."

The hand on my back flexes, the only sign he's not as calm as he appears.

"And if you choose them, I'll leave graciously. Might hurt like hell, but I give you my word. No hard feelings."

Fuck, I believe him. His soft scent washes over me, along with this internal sense of calm that I've never experienced before.

"You do feel it, right?" he whispers. "This...connection between us?"

I nod because it's impossible to deny. Even while I was passing out in his arms, I felt it—safety in the middle of the storm.

"I want to kiss you." His nose brushes mine, and my eyes drift closed.

The blaring of a car horn draws me out of this almost hypnotic state he's lulled me into, and I jolt, taking a step back and drawing in a much needed breath of fresh air. Whatever the fuck this is between us is potent, and I'll need to be careful not to get pulled too far under his spell before I decide what the hell to do about it.

His grin is tight as he grabs my hand. "C'mon. My car is parked in the lot behind the restaurant. We can grab some food on the way back to the venue."

I let him pull me down the sidewalk, his stride long and sure, demanding, just like the man. Where the other guys fill the gaping hole they left inside me years ago, there's something about Chance that settles into the deepest depths of my soul, filling that empty space that I was sure no one would ever be able to touch. His darkness is the perfect complement to mine, and for the first time in over a decade, I feel full. Complete. Like balance has been established within me. The war between the two opposing sides has come to some sort of tentative truce.

I don't know if this will last, but I'll enjoy the peace it provides while I can.

Chapter 16

It's only been a couple hours since Fallon left for dinner with her business partner, but all of us are on edge, waiting for her to return.

Fuck, who am I kidding? Where our lovely little omega is concerned, we're always on edge, waiting for the moment she decides we're not what she wants and walks away.

We're standing around backstage with Seb, Roland, and Raphael Montoya, the head of Theta Records. The guys are discussing how the opening nights of the tour went and any issues we saw that might cause problems down the road.

I tune them out, my eyes continually darting around the space, looking for my girl.

"You cool, man?" Roland asks.

"Yeah. Of course. Just keeping an eye out for Fallon, that's all."

He nods. "Girl is stronger than you all give her credit for, I think."

He's right. She managed without us for a decade. Who's to say she couldn't manage for a decade more? The thought sours my stomach.

Just then, the backstage door opens, spilling moonlight into the darkened space. Fallon walks in, Chance beside her with his hand on her back. It's a gentleman's gesture, but it sets off something inside, especially when I watch her look up and laugh at something he says. My gut pitches.

She catches my eyes, straightens her shoulders, and walks toward us. I can feel Anson and Felix go still beside me, catching their scents that linger heavily in the air. She's wearing a sheer black shirt, her black bra clearly visible beneath it. Her red suede skirt shows off the curve of her hips, and those thigh-high boots that do miraculous things to her legs have me reaching down to adjust my dick in my pants.

Felix beats me to it, stepping forward and reaching for her hand so he can tug her into his arms. His mouth smashes into hers at the same time his hand grabs her ass.

His possessive claim doesn't go unnoticed, and a grin spreads across her face. Her arms wrap around his neck, clinging tighter to him as her perfume takes on a sweet edge.

"I fucking missed you," he murmurs against her lips, dropping his forehead to hers.

"I missed you too."

"Have a good dinner with your *partner*?"

I don't miss the slight growl or the way his scent turns just a little bitter. Apparently neither does she.

"It was okay. Couldn't wait to get back here to you guys," she soothes.

I can practically feel his purr through the pack bond rather than hear it over the upbeat Knotty Boys' song blaring through the space. When he pulls back, he drags Fallon over to the rest of us.

"Raphael, this is Fallon Parker. Fallon, this is Raphael Montoya, head of Theta Records. He's here to make sure everything with the tour is going smoothly so far."

Raphael holds out his hand, and she reluctantly reaches forward to shake it.

"So this is the girl who's had our boys in knots. Literally." He laughs at his own joke, not releasing her hand, instead bringing it up to his lips and kissing the back of it. My body tenses, the urge to rip her away growing stronger the longer the other alpha holds on. Which is strange, I realize, because Chance's touch didn't elicit this same angry reaction. "It's truly a pleasure to meet you, Ms. Parker. I can see why the boys would be so enamored with you."

His eyes trail over her cleavage before he takes a step back, his eyes widening slightly when he finds that Anson has stepped up on her other side. I'm flanking her back without even realizing I'd moved.

"Protective, aren't they?" Raphael murmurs, smirking at Sebastian. "I'm surprised you haven't bonded her yet. An unclaimed omega like her doesn't usually last long."

"I don't know. I've managed to remain unclaimed for twenty-five years." She shrugs, playing off the sharp bite to her tone, but I can sense her unease.

His charming grin kicks up just a fraction more. "Hmmm. All it takes is one overzealous alpha, and you could find yourself in a situation you're not prepared for."

Is it just me, or did that sound like a threat? The other guys must think so because their bodies are as rigid as mine. Raphael has been with the label since our original contract was signed, and while he's a manwhore, I've never known him to be this outwardly aggressive toward a woman—especially considering she's *our* woman.

"Hi, I don't think we've been introduced. I'm Chance Donovan, Fallon's business partner."

Risking a glance at the beta, I inwardly thank him for taking the attention off Fallon before one of us did something really stupid—like tear out the throat of the man who signs our paychecks. They begin to have a conversation about Chance's business, but my focus is on Fallon. We've circled around her, shielding her, and her bitter peach scent tickles my nose.

"You okay, baby girl?" Anson asks softly, running a hand up and down her back.

"I'm fine."

It's a lie—one we can all sense from her scent alone, but none of us call her out on it.

"He's got a reputation with the ladies, but I never thought he'd be that way with you. I'm sorry," I murmur against the top of her head, then I kiss her hair and slide an arm behind her back.

I'm still on edge, but when I can feel her body slowly start to relax against mine, it settles something within me.

"Don't worry. He usually doesn't stick around long. He drops in, shows his face, and is gone before we go on stage." Felix is staring over her head toward the group of men still chatting away.

"Really, guys, I'm fine. It's almost time for you to go on, right?"

Anson nods, his eyes raking over her. "You going to hang backstage tonight, or will you and Chance go up to the box?"

"We'll probably go to the box. Stay out of the way until you all are done."

We share a meaningful look.

The thought of her spending a couple hours in a secluded box with the beta doesn't sit well with any of us, though I'll be the first to admit that I wouldn't blame her if she was interested. He's non-threatening.

There's no chance of a forced bond. No knot—not that she's taken any issue with that particular aspect of alpha physiology. In simplest terms, the beta is *safe*, whereas I'm sure we represent a certain level of threat even if it's only subconscious. We left her before, and she spent years avoiding us because of that. Is she worried we'll do it again?

All this talk about bonding strikes a nerve. We've begged her for a second chance, and we've tried to show her how we feel about her, but we haven't come right out and told her what we all truly want in the end. Instead, we've been skirting around the issue so we don't frighten her off. Maybe it's time to change that.

"You know that we want to claim you, right, sweetheart?" I ask quietly, drawing Anson's and Felix's stares.

Her breath catches, and my heart begins to pound in my chest.

"All you have to do is say the word, and we'll make it official," Anson adds, studying her face.

"We're just giving you time to figure out what you want." Then I hear Felix grumble under his breath, "Though if it were up to me, you'd already be wearing my bite."

Before she can respond, Chance walks up.

"Nice guy," he mutters, interrupting the moment. When no one says anything, his gaze bounces between all of us. "Sorry, did I interrupt something?"

"It's fine," Fallon says, looking decidedly relieved, and I'm not sure how I feel about that. "I was just telling the guys we'd watch the show from the box, if that's okay with you?"

The Knotty Boys walk off stage, which gives us maybe fifteen minutes before we have to take our places.

Chance slides his hands into his pockets. "Oh, sure. I'm just along for the ride."

"As long as that's the only thing you're riding," Felix murmurs, and Anson elbows him in the ribs. "Ouch! What'd I say?"

Chance's eyes shine with laughter. "Don't worry. I'll take good care of her, and I'll have her back to you at the end of the show."

Twisting her around to face me, my hands cup her jaw, and I wish for the millionth time the bond was already in place so I would know what she's feeling. I stare into her eyes, willing her to see how much I love her. How much I need her.

"We'll see you after the show, sweetheart. Okay?" I whisper, gently brushing my lips against hers.

She tries to follow when I pull back, and a purr rattles my chest.

Her smile is breathtaking. "I'll be waiting."

Anson draws her over for a deep kiss, murmuring something in her ear before handing her off to Felix. I'm not surprised when his hands grip behind her thighs, lifting her off the ground. The man has no shame. One hand tangles in her hair while he mouth fucks her in front of everyone backstage, making it clear who she belongs to. When he finally pulls back, she's breathless, flushed, and a little unsteady on her feet once he sets her down. But Chance is there with a hand on her back, earning himself a growl from the possessive alpha.

The beta is unfazed, his smirk impossible to miss. He knows what he's doing, and he's enjoying every minute of it. They turn to walk off, and Fallon glances over her shoulder, shooting us a wink.

"I fucking hate him," Felix growls.

Anson and I share a look before the big guy turns back to our packmate. "He's harmless."

"He most certainly is not. Have you seen the way he looks at her?"

I shrug. "Pretty sure we all have."

"And you don't care?" he asks, stupefied.

"At the end of the day, I care about Fallon and her happiness. In whatever form that takes."

"Hold up." His hand shoots up into the air. "You're telling me that if she wants him, you're okay with that?"

I consider the idea, rolling it over in my head and thinking back on her words from last night when she rode her fingers and imagined us all together.

"I think it's pretty obvious she does, but she wants us too. As long as it's not a him or us sort of deal, I'm good with it."

Felix's mouth opens and closes like a fish out of water, and Anson chuckles.

"I've got to agree. After everything she's been through, I'm not sure I could deny her even the smallest bit of happiness."

"Dude isn't that small," Felix grumbles.

"But he's gentle with her, attentive, and the way he looks at her says he's just as into her as we are."

"Like hell," Felix snarls.

"Felix..." Anson's sigh is long. "She keeps saying we don't really know her, and to some extent, she's right. We've barely scratched the surface of who that woman has become. The fact of the matter is that he knows her *now*. We knew her *then*. He might actually help bridge that gap. Would you really issue an ultimatum if it opened up even the slightest possibility of losing her again?"

"I hate you all." He turns, stalking toward the stage.

"He'll come around," I say.

Anson watches Felix leave. "I hope so. For all our sakes."

Chapter 17

T he box is really just a section of the upper balcony blocked off with walls on three sides, leaving the whole front of the space open to the venue below. It offers a little bit of privacy but no lack of views.

Anson is strumming the first chords to their opening song as Felix yells out to the crowd. It's my first time watching them front and center, seeing the way Felix works the stage and the speed of Wren's movements as he twists around his drum set. Anson looks fully concentrated on the notes he's playing, whipping his hair back and forth while he moves his large body to the rhythm of the music on the two large screens on either side of the stage. They start flipping between close-ups of the guys as they move through their setlist.

One song ends, then Felix steps to the edge of center stage.

"Have you ever loved someone so much it hurts? Yearned for them until you thought you'd lose your mind? But what if that person doesn't feel the same? How would you cope with the realization that they may love another?" Felix talks to the crowd like they're old friends, drawing them in with his story. He's drawing *me* in, and I already have a pretty good idea what brought this on. "This song is one of my personal favorites, but we don't play it often because we're firm believers in manifesting our own energy."

His chuckle echoes around the venue, and the crowd cheers wildly.

"So here it is. 'Unconditionally.'"

The beat of Wren's drum starts off slow and soft, building the anticipation of what's to come with every strike.

"From a distance, she looks happy with him," Felix sings softly, his face closed off and almost angry. "Smiling and touching, soft looks when he holds her close."

The beat of the song has turned wickedly sensual, dark in a way most of their music rarely is.

"But does she think of me when the lights go dim?" Felix croons, his voice deep. He practically snarls the next line as he looks up at the box. "Wishing it was my hand wrapped around her throat."

I swear he's staring straight into my eyes. I'm standing at the railing, fingers wrapped around the thick metal bar, letting the music hum through me. There's a quick rush of his fresh laundry scent just before the warmth of Chance's body wraps around me from behind, caging me in. The position is intimate and possessive. I expect to feel uncomfortable with a strange man at my back, but instead, it feels natural and almost wickedly attractive to have one man reaching out to me through my body while another reaches out through song.

"Are you picturing him behind you right now, Fallon?" Chance whispers in my ear. "Wishing it was his dick pressing against your round ass?"

He steps in closer, leaving no doubt about his desire for me.

I shake my head, completely incapable of words. It's almost as if I'm stuck between them—sandwiched between the alpha and beta—and I'm struggling to find some sort of steady footing. I feel like no matter which step I take, one of us is going to stumble to the edge and fall.

The music drops off, leaving Felix to sing acapella.

"Maybe one day she'll leave him and come back to me," Felix sings softly into the microphone. "Though, I suppose it doesn't matter. I'll love her unconditionally."

As the notes to the song drift off, morphing into an uptempo beat, Chance nuzzles into my hair.

"They love you," he whispers.

"I know," I whisper back.

"Do you love them?"

There's only a second of hesitation before I confidently respond, "I do."

He hums, dropping a gentle kiss on the back of my ear.

How fucked up is it that I just revealed that to a man I barely know before I told them? Panic itches up my throat at the realization that I'm still in love with them. Despite all my previous denials, despite all that stands in our way, I *love* them—so much more than before. I'm a grown woman now with grown feelings. This isn't young love that's blind to the trials and tribulations of a relationship. This is true love that is stronger because of them. But what about the lies? What about the beta who came into my life like a hurricane, ready to break down all my carefully constructed walls? I'm suddenly finding it hard to breathe.

"I'll be right back."

Before I can walk off, he grabs my arm, searching my eyes in the dim light.

"Don't run, Fallon."

"I'm not. Promise. Just need to use the restroom."

His fingers release their grip, and I slip out of the room. My heart is pounding wildly in my chest, and I can't seem to get myself to calm down. With every step I take away from Chance, I wonder what the hell I'm doing. How did I go from being entirely alone to dealing with more dick than I rightfully know how to handle?

I don't owe him anything—I don't owe *anyone* anything. I should go back to my quiet little life where I could keep all these messy feelings wrapped up tight.

Numb. That's the word for it. Feeling nothing but what you allow yourself to feel. On the rare occasions I accept a job, I give myself those few brief moments where I open those little boxes inside and let the feelings rush over me. Then I package it all back up and tuck it away, keeping it nice and tidy.

Voices up ahead have me slowing to a stop, and I silently stalk to the end of the hall. When I peek around the corner, I expect to find Sebastian. Instead, it's Raphael Montoya and three security guards I don't recognize. With music in the background, I can't quite make out what they're saying, but I'm pretty sure I hear my name. My shoulders straighten, and I surreptitiously feel for the blade strapped high on my thigh just as a hand lands roughly on the back of my neck.

Risking a glance behind me, I see yet another burly beta security guard whose glare tells me that he's not quite as harmless as the two from the other night. He pushes me around the corner, my feet stumbling in the heels.

"Found someone snooping," he mutters.

Raphael's eyes light up with wicked delight. "Ms. Parker! Enjoying the show?"

"I am. You?"

"I am now," he states, walking straight up to me with a cocksure grin on his face.

His scent is oppressive, heavy gunmetal and smoke, and I try to keep the disgust off my face.

"Chance is expecting me back any second."

"Funny. My team saw him heading down the stairs moments ago, talking on his phone."

I hide the surprise from my face, wondering if Chance would really walk away from this—from *me*—so easily, and try to keep my voice calm. "Must've been important."

"Mmm. Which means my job just got a helluva lot easier."

He eyes the security guard at my back and nods.

The big man is fast, but I'm faster. He releases my neck to grab for my arm, but I use that split second of freedom to spin away from him, grabbing his wrist and twisting until I hear the snap I was looking for. He howls, then curses as I maintain pressure on his shoulder, holding him facing away from me.

Raphael claps slowly. "Well, well, well, isn't this a pleasant surprise?"

"What do you want?"

"Thought that was obvious." His eyes trail up and down my body like he's undressing me right here in the hall.

"It's not. Spell it out for me."

"You. I want *you*." When his eyes finally meet mine again, a twisted smile quirks his lips. "And now that I know what you're capable of, I'll stop at nothing to have you."

He snaps his fingers, and the three security guards he was with rush me. Shoving their injured friend out in front of me to buy myself some time, I spin and make a run for it. I'm not stupid enough to think I can take on three men by myself with no planning and few weapons. I try to work through my options while I open the door to the stairwell, briefly glancing up and down, trying to decide which would be the smarter choice.

In a horror film, the clumsy heroine always goes up, leaving her standing on the edge of the roof with no other option but to jump. Since that doesn't sound at all appealing to me, I head to the right, taking the stairs down as fast as I can in these heeled boots. Loud shouts make it through the door before it closes, and I glance up, seeing two of the security guards raising their arms and taking aim.

I duck just as the first one fires, the silent bullet whizzing by my face with only inches to spare. I'm in trouble, and I damn well know it. The door in front of me opens, almost smacking me in the face, and another unknown security guard blocks my path with a gun aimed right at my head. I come to a grinding halt, hands held in the air. My phone is in the pocket of my skirt, my knife too risky to grab for. I am completely and totally *fucked*.

"Grab her and bring her to the town car. He's waiting for her there," one of the guards behind me says.

"Time to go, Princess." The one with the gun at my face motions toward the door. "Your choice whether we do this the easy way or the hard way."

"Or we could do this *my* way," Chance growls from behind him. "Fallon!"

I spin to the right, plastering myself against the wall just as he pulls the trigger. Blood sprays through the air before the big man drops like a sack of potatoes.

"You okay?" Chance shouts.

"Never better."

It takes Dumb Guard One and Dumb Guard Two a second to catch up, and I slide the knife out of its sheath, wishing I had my Beretta instead. Can't bring a knife to a gunfight, but I'll sure as hell try. I'm up the few stairs in record time just as One finally starts to pull the trigger. My knife plunges into his wrist, pushing his arm up and sending the shot wide. From this angle, I play the girl card and punch him right in the dick. He grunts, clutching his family jewels as his body crumbles. That means I'm about two seconds away from getting steamrolled by a large beta body. Fortunately for me, Two decides to grab a fistful of my hair and yanks me out of the way just in time.

Not that it was his intention to be noble, but it sure as hell helped me out.

"Thank you," I mutter, hanging from his fist by my hair.

He ignores me, yanking me up and wrapping his arm around my throat while the other raises the gun to my temple. Chance walks up with a cocky grin on his face and his own gun pointed at Two over my left shoulder.

"Pussycat, I haven't had this much fun in ages."

"You need to find a new hobby, beta boy."

"I did. *You*."

"Romantic."

"I know, right?"

I don't think he's kidding.

"I'm going to leave with the girl, and you're going to let us go, or I'll just put a bullet in her head."

Chance slowly walks us down the stairs and past a groaning One, his eyes locked on Two. Without even flinching, Chance shifts the gun and shoots One in the head. The shot makes Two jump, but thankfully, he doesn't have a twitchy trigger finger.

"See what I just did to your buddy right there?" Chance asks, his tone low and menacing. Admittedly, it's also hot as fuck. "That isn't half as bad as what I'll do to you if you harm one more hair on her head."

"Look, man, I bring her to Raph, or I'm a dead man anyways. I've got nothing to lose."

The cold metal is digging into my temple, and I can smell the tang of his sweat as he continues to push us toward the door, never turning his back on Chance.

"Pussycat, how would you like to play this?"

"You're giving me a choice?"

"Of course. I'm a gentleman, remember?"

I snort. "This is all solely about me and my pleasure," I mutter in my best Chance impersonation.

"I do *not* sound like that."

I shrug. "To me you do."

He growls.

"You two shut the fuck up!" Two shouts, throwing his hand in the air in frustration. The hand with the *gun*. "You're like my fucking parents, always fucking bickering."

"You got the fucking bit right," Chance says seconds before he pulls the trigger. Two goes slack...with his heavy ass arm still around my throat.

I fall back on top of the dead man, trying to catch my breath, and Chance's head suddenly appears above me.

"Comfortable?"

"Not particularly. Something is jabbing into me."

"Dude better not have a dead boner pressed into my girl's ass, or I'll kill him again."

He offers his hand, tangling our fingers together as he lifts me up and into his arms.

"I'm not your girl," I grumble.

"Yet." He rubs his nose back and forth on mine.

"There's definitely something wrong with you," I murmur breathlessly, lust beginning to tingle up my spine.

"Obviously. I haven't actually kissed you yet. Let's fix that."

Before I can respond, his lips smash into mine, sparking an inferno in my blood. My legs wrap around his waist, bunching my skirt at my hips, and his hands find my ass as I grind up against the not-so-small dick trapped inside his jeans. Adrenaline is still racing through my veins, and with the immediate threat gone, I need an outlet for the excess energy. Chance seems more than happy to oblige.

"We need to call in a clean-up crew." He ignores me, nipping along my jaw, then slamming my back against the concrete wall.

"I already did."

I pull back, confusion furrowing my brow. "When?"

His lips are skimming over the sweaty skin of my throat, teasing me with light kisses. "The Syndicate called right after you left. They had eyes on Raphael and noticed you were heading right for him. They told me to be ready, and *I* told *them* to get ready for a mess."

"Convenient."

He pulls back an inch, his fingers dipping between our bodies to trace the slick up my thighs until he's sliding over my clit. I don't even try to fight back the groan.

"Yup, just like the fact that you're not wearing any underwear beneath this skirt," he damn near purrs. "God, you smell like fucking peach pie."

My hands drop to his belt, undoing the buckle and carefully sliding the zipper down.

"Pull me out, pussycat. Put me right where you want me."

My hand reaches into his jeans, slipping around his fat cock and running it through my wetness.

His groan rumbles against my mouth.

Fuck, what are we doing? "We shouldn't—"

"We most definitely should."

"The Syndicate's watching." And yet I'm still teasing my pussy with a fistful of his cock.

"Let them."

I no sooner have the head of his dick poised at my entrance than he thrusts in. My back hits the wall, his hands sliding up my arms until he's gripping my fingers and pulling them above my head. He's not the hard, demanding draw of an alpha, but the steady seductive pull of a beta. As he thrusts into me over and over again, I find myself centering. Find myself coming down from the rush of the night despite being fucked senseless against the wall with three dead bodies at our feet. It's fucking perfect.

"Shit, pussycat, you feel so damn good. Better than I imagined. And trust me, I imagined you'd be pretty fucking spectacular."

"You're going to give me a complex. Shut up and fuck me."

"Yes, ma'am."

His kiss is rough, his tongue battling mine as he does what I asked. It's fast and dirty, and it doesn't take long for the warmth to rush up my spine from my impending release.

"Don't stop, please."

"Wouldn't dream of it," he grunts out. "I need you to come for me, Fallon. Come all over my cock while I fill you up so fucking good."

He slams in, grinding against my clit, and I explode. My pussy tightens around him, and my orgasm goes on and on. With every harsh plunge into my cunt, he draws out my pleasure until his rhythm falters, and he makes this sound in the back of his throat. Burying his face in my neck, he comes with a groan, the pulse of his dick inside me setting off one last wave of my own release.

Releasing my hands, they fall to his shoulders as he pulls me into his chest, holding onto me tightly. We're both gasping for breath, our bodies slick with sweat.

"When I saw his gun pointed at your face, I lost it." He pulls back, his hands leaving me long enough to cup my cheeks. I can't be sure, but I think he's shaking.

"But you saved me," I whisper, softly brushing my lips over his.

"Hell yes, I did. I'm your white fucking knight."

"You got the fucking bit right." His dick twitches inside me when I repeat his words.

"Ready to go again?" he rasps.

"Sorry, Donovan. Cavalry is here," a deep voice calls out.

Men in black tactical gear and masks swarm the stairwell. One walks over, motioning to Chance with his tactical rifle.

"Pull up your pants and get Ms. Parker somewhere safe. We've wiped the cameras, but you all need to clean up before anyone sees you." His covered face turns to mine. "Seems to be a recurring theme with you, Ms. Parker."

I shrug, a ridiculous grin playing on my lips. "What can I say? Red suits me."

His head slowly shifts, and even though I can't see his eyes, I know he's eye fucking me.

"Yes. Yes, it does."

"Go find your own fucking badass omega, Nixon. This one's mine."

"From what I hear, she's got three alphas that might say otherwise."

Chance grunts, pulling out and carefully setting me on my feet and quickly pulling my skirt down before he tucks himself back into his jeans and zips up.

"Fucking buzzkill."

"Come on, beta boy. He's right. We need to clean up and catch the rest of the show before the guys realize we're missing."

"Take the rest of the night off, yeah?" Nixon grumbles, but I can hear the amusement in his voice.

"No promises," I chirp, walking out the door, hand in hand with my beta.

Yeah, I said it. He's mine. After this, I'm not sure I could let him go.

Chapter 18

We're waiting backstage when the band plays their last notes to the crowd's wild applause. Chance is leaning up against the wall next to me, his nose trailing up my neck. He's been awfully damn cuddly since he saved me then fucked me, and I'm not sure the guys are going to appreciate that. My nerves are on edge, waiting for them to walk out.

We have our first real lead, and now I have backup I know I can count on in a pinch. What else does a deadly omega need? Oh, right. Three possessive alphas with their knots that are definitely going to be in a twist when they find out what happened tonight—both the sex and the whole trafficking ring thing.

Chance and I have gone back and forth on whether we tell them or keep it to ourselves. He finally convinced me that keeping it from them could put them in danger considering their label is involved. That was all it took.

And he's right. The Syndicate called Chance and explained that Raphael Montoya has gone underground. He's taken a personal leave from the label, and they've assigned another exec. We don't know how deep the treachery goes, so there's no way we can trust anyone they assign.

The guys will find out from Sebastian either tonight or tomorrow morning when the label fills him in, and I need to be there to see his expression because it's not just Raphael we have to worry about. Raphael has someone close on the payroll—running things behind the scenes—which means everyone is a suspect.

Chance straightens beside me, and I hear the growl before I see the alpha responsible.

"Aren't you two cozy." Felix glares at my beta.

Redirecting his attention, I ask, "You all heading back to the bus?"

His eyes go wide. "Are you not?"

Anson lightly punches Felix's arm before turning to me. "Of course she is. Aren't you, baby girl?"

I nod, feeling the tension between Felix and me rise.

"We were hoping to talk with all of you actually," Chance finally speaks up, and I can feel his stare.

"Talk? About what?" Wren asks, glancing between the two of us with a nervous look in his eye.

"Let's wait until we're alone—"

"Why, sunshine? So we don't make a scene when you tell us you're leaving us for *him*?"

"Felix, that's not—"

"Fuck it. Might as well get it over with so we can start mending the broken fucking hearts you're about to rip out of our chests."

He spins on his heel, stalking toward the door. I roll my eyes.

"You've always been a fucking drama king, Felix!" I call out to his back.

He growls but doesn't turn around.

"He's just blowing off steam, baby girl," Anson whispers, combing his fingers through my hair. His eyes narrow when I grimace, my scalp stinging from Two's rough tug. "I think we need to have that talk. Now."

There's an urgency in his voice now that he's started to realize something is wrong. He's always seen more than the other two.

"Fallon," Wren begins, shoulders bunching under the weight of his worry.

"Not here," Anson says, grabbing my hand and looking up at Chance. "I assume you're coming too?"

Chance—for once in his life—doesn't make a sarcastic quip or snarky innuendo.

"Yeah. I can't..." He runs his hands over his hair. "I can't leave her right now."

I touch his chest, offering what little comfort I can.

Anson nods, sharing a look with Wren.

We head for the bus, and Wren drops back to talk to Sebastian when he catches all of us filing out of the venue. He's got a crowd of girls around him, all with some sort of drink in their hands. We make eye contact, but his expression is inscrutable. Should we do something? Make sure that these girls are safe. But how? Then I see Roland walking up to Sebastian and feel like I can let him handle it. I've done enough for tonight.

The moment is over when Anson tugs me out the door and into the quiet Nashville night. There are a ton of people bustling about, with roadies wheeling carts down a long ramp leading from a huge bay door. The bus will leave once everything is torn down and packed up, heading for the next stop of the tour. Atlanta.

The bus is quiet when we enter. Anson guides me up the narrow stairs where I find Felix splayed out in one of the two leather rocking chairs. He's already got a glass of whiskey in his hand, swirling it around. He sits forward, resting his forearms on his knees so his hands and drink hang between them.

"I love you, Fallon. I know I said it before, but you weren't ready to hear it. You probably don't want to hear it now, either, but I just..." He stares down at the drink. "I needed to say it one last time before—"

"I love you too," I whisper, walking over and dropping to my knees in front of him. "I'm sorry it took me this long to tell you."

Carefully setting his drink down on the side table, his hands bracket my face and his eyes study mine.

"You're not leaving?" he whispers.

I shake my head, while his thumb traces my lower lip. Then his eyes raise to Chance, standing anxiously beside Anson.

"You want him to stay too," Felix says flatly.

The others are quiet behind me, so I hear the door open and shut when Wren joins us.

"Yes, but—"

"Okay. I mean, I'm not sure I'm *okay* with it, but if it's between losing you or him staying, then I choose you."

"Felix, it's more than just that." I glance over my shoulder, making my hair tumble over my shoulder and down my back.

"What the fuck is this?" he growls suddenly, his fingertips tracing the faint mark on my neck from Two.

He's on his feet, slamming Chance into the wall before I can even blink.

"You fucking left marks on her and expect us to let you stay here?"

"Felix!" I shout, jumping to my feet. "They're not from him. Chance *saved* me!"

Slowly, Felix's hold on Chance goes slack, but he doesn't take his eyes off the beta.

"That true?" he asks, voice so deep I can barely hear him.

Anson and Wren are both at Felix's back, fists clenching and unclenching at their sides. Chance looks right into Felix's eyes and shifts his neck slightly, offering his throat. I'm not sure if it's a conscious gesture, but it has the tension in the room easing.

"Yes. I killed the man who did it."

Silence.

This is the part where I might lose them despite only recently discovering I want to keep them.

"Explain," Anson barks, and I see Chance swallow at the alpha command he's unable to avoid.

Chance details the encounter with the guards and Raphael's involvement in it all.

"You're not really her business partner," Anson states, his voice devoid of all emotion.

Chance shakes his head, his eyes darting to mine before three sets of growls have him turning back to the alphas. I know he could probably get away with ease—alpha barks or not. The fact that he doesn't means he's doing this for me.

I promise myself a good swoon later. Right now, there's too much shit going down to drop my guard.

"I'm a member of an organization that...acquired her services. We needed help with a mission that required her particular set of skills along with her connections."

Three sets of eyes turn to me.

"Sweetheart?" Wren asks, the plea in his voice breaking my heart.

"I told you in the beginning I'm not who you thought I was. I meant it. I'm not that young, innocent girl anymore." I swallow down my nerves. "I go by ABO007 on the dark web."

"Dark web?" Felix crosses his arms over his chest.

"People hire me to... Um... I... Well, I get paid to—"

"She's a badass who takes care of alphas who hurt omegas. For a small fee, of course." Chance's heated stare meets mine. "Did I mention she's a badass?"

"Wait a fucking second. You kill people—kill *alphas* for a living?" Felix shouts.

"Should probably keep that down, mate," Chance mutters.

The alphas ignore him.

Straightening my shoulders, I look him dead in the eye. He either stays or he goes. Nothing I can do at this point will stop him.

"I kill *bad people* for a living. Just like I killed the alpha who hurt me."

Anson blinks.

Wren's eyes are wide.

Felix adjusts his dick in his pants.

"And your *connections*?" Anson asks. The hint of hurt in his tone strikes right through my heart.

It figures he'd be the one to catch onto that little detail Chance blurted out. I get it, though. I'd be hurt too if I thought they were using their connection to me simply because someone told them to.

"The organization thought my connection to you all would make it easier to gain access to the mission I was assigned, but I had no intention of using my history with you or even coming face to face with you at all. I didn't want any of you involved in this."

"The disguise..." Wren straightens, eyes going wide.

I nod. "I stupidly thought I could get in and out without you noticing."

Felix snorts. "Fat chance, sunshine. You underestimated just how badly we wanted you."

Wanted. Past tense. My stomach drops.

"Want. *Want* you," Anson corrects, punching Felix's shoulder.

Everything inside me stills as I try not to get my hopes up. There's still a lot to discuss.

"Since when are you the goddamn grammar police?" Felix grumbles.

"Since our girl just went pale as a ghost."

Felix's eyes fly to mine. "Shit. Sorry, sunshine. Of course we still want you."

"But what could you possibly be investigating here with us?" Wren asks.

I glance at Chance, and he nods.

"A possible omega trafficking ring set up under the cover of your tours."

The guys all talk over each other, denials slipping from their lips.

"You can deny it all you want!" Chance shouts, getting their attention. "But the simple fact of the matter is that Fallon was almost taken tonight at the direct order of Raphael Montoya. If I hadn't been here..."

His hand shakes as he runs both down his face.

Walking over to him, I lift his arm and slip under it, wrapping mine around his waist and hugging him tightly while the alphas watch.

"Thank you." Felix steps forward, his hand outstretched. "We owe you a debt."

Chance shakes his hand. "You don't have to thank me. She's kinda gotten under my skin."

Felix snorts.

"We know a thing or two about that." Anson eyes land on mine, a smirk quirking up the corner of his mouth.

"Did you get him?" Wren's normally even voice is laced with fury.

"Raphael?" Chance asks.

The guys nod.

I shake my head. "He had already left the building when his guys caught up to me."

"So how can we help?" Felix asks, cracking his knuckles. "No fucking way is someone going to use our shows to traffic innocent omegas."

Chance looks down at me, then back to the guys. "Keep your eyes and ears open. Raphael had to have someone here on the payroll. We need to figure out who and stop them. The guards with him tonight were part of the tour, not the extras hired by the facility. Someone is organizing them."

"Who oversees the security staff?" I ask. "Not just the day-to-day operations, because I'm assuming that would be Roland as Head of Security."

"Sebastian has final say in hiring and firing, with the label being responsible for setting the overall budget for the security detail."

"Well, we've already confirmed the label's involvement, and Sebastian was one of our other primary suspects."

"No. No way!" Felix shakes his head. "He might be a horny jackass, but he's not a trafficker."

Chance and I share a look.

"What do you know?" Anson asks.

We quickly detail the encounters I've had with him and the situation with the omega outside the venue the other night. The guys start to look less sure.

"No one leaves Fallon alone." Anson crosses his arms over his chest. "She's always with one of us. When we're on stage, Chance will be there."

The beta kisses the top of my head, and I notice the alphas are significantly less antagonistic about the contact. A spark of hope blooms wide in my chest.

"So where do we go from here?" Wren asks.

"A foursome sounds pretty good to me. Who's down?" Chance suggests, slipping a hand down my back to take a handful of my ass before he pulls me into his chest.

My thighs clench tight, and my perfume floods the space despite exhaustion tugging at me. I risk a glance over my shoulder, seeing the alphas having some unspoken conversation.

Felix steps up to my back, sandwiching me between him and my beta. He leans in, voice deep as his breath whispers against my ear.

"That what you want, sunshine?"

"Fuck. I..." He drops a kiss on my neck, making lust rush through me. "Yes. I need all of you. I mean, if you still want me after—"

His hands grip my hips and spin me around, then he wraps a hand behind my neck. Chance's erection presses into my ass.

"Unconditionally, Fallon. I love you. Period. And I'm just so fucking grateful you're okay."

Felix's eyes are stormy and his body tense as his eyes drop back to my neck. They need this as much as I do, I realize—maybe more.

Chance kisses the top of my head as Anson steps up beside us, staring down at me with a look that I can't decipher.

"You survived. Then and now." His voice cracks, and he clears his throat. "I can't believe we almost lost you again."

"But you didn't. I'm here, Ans."

With a finger under my chin, he tilts my head up, placing a gentle kiss on my lips. After he pulls back, he glances over my head.

When I turn, I find Wren sitting on the sofa. His face is carefully blank, but that stare of his penetrates through to my soul. I expected Felix to be the one to turn away from what was happening. Not Wren. He's always been the steady one of the group, and I could count on him to have my back. *Always.*

"Wren?" I whisper anxiously, biting back the whine that wants to slip out.

Without a word, his hand grips the neck of his Feral Lyrics t-shirt and pulls it up and over his head.

"Come here, sweetheart," he beckons, a tease of his alpha bark in the command. "I need you in my arms...and on my cock. Let's get this thing started, shall we?"

Well, how the fuck am I supposed to say no to that?

Chapter 19

If anyone ever asked me if I thought I'd be okay sharing Fallon with anyone other than my brothers, I would've told them to fuck off and eat a dick.

Not even remotely kidding.

Now here I am, watching her saunter over to Wren, this seductive sway to her hips that hypnotizes me, and I'm willing to give her just about anything she damn well wants if it means I get a piece of her too. Even if it's a foursome suggested by a beta I'm still not sure I trust.

We watch her tug the sheer shirt out of her skirt, pulling it over her head and tossing it aside. She's in her bra and the red suede skirt, those thigh-high boots making my dick rock hard. She leans over to unbutton Wren's jeans, and that small bend has her skirt riding up just the barest fraction. I have to adjust my cock in my pants. Her smell, which had been too damn tart earlier, has gone sweet—like peaches and ice cream.

She removes his pants, and his hands slide her skirt down her toned thighs until she kicks it away. Her ass is on display, along with the light red scratch marks trailing up her back.

"Yeah, *that* was totally me. Not gonna lie."

I glance over at Chance with a raised brow. He's rubbing a hand over the bulge behind his zipper, and when he senses me looking, he turns to me.

"Adrenaline fuck. Against the wall. Should I apologize?"

"No. You get a pass on that cuz any of us would've done the same," Anson murmurs, lost in the image of Fallon climbing onto Wren's lap, grabbing hold of his dick, and sinking down onto him.

They both moan, then his hands make quick work of her bra, sliding it down her arms and off the side of the sofa before he grabs her ass and her hips start to roll. Her head falls back, long blonde hair trailing down almost to her waist. Wren's mouth latches onto her nipple, suckling her like her body could provide sustenance.

The image that hits me is swift and potent, damn near making me stumble back. I imagine her round with our baby—breasts full and ripe and ready to feed. The need to fill her up, fucking her so good until she's carrying our kid, is as unexpected as it is enticing. She's not even in heat, so it's not possible yet, but it will be, and suddenly that's all I can think about.

"Damn, sweetheart. You feel so fucking good," Wren groans.

"Who's next?" I ask, eager and horny and a slew of other shit that I can't identify.

"She's got more than one hole, my friend." Chance smirks. "Pick one."

He starts stripping right beside us.

Anson and I share a look, automatically following suit so we don't get left out.

"So how do we do this? Rock, paper, scissors?"

"I want her ass," Chance declares. "What about you guys?"

"Mouth," Anson declares, stroking his cock.

"I might sit back and watch for a bit," I say, surprising myself.

"A voyeur. I like it." Chance holds out his hand as if to fist bump me.

Ah, what the hell. We bump knuckles and turn to the pair on the sofa. Wren has already turned them so he's lying flat along the cushions, his hands gripping her breasts. Fallon's back is beautifully bowed as she bounces on his dick, just shy of slipping onto his knot. With zero shame, Chance settles in behind her, dropping a tender kiss on her shoulder.

"Ready for another dick, pussycat?"

Her lust-filled eyes glance over her shoulder. "I've never had anyone back there before."

For a second, they just stare at each other even though her hips continue to grind into Wren. I'm shocked when Chance turns to face us, an unspoken question in his stare.

"You saved her life. You've earned it."

I feel more than see Anson's nod beside me. Without further hesitation, Chance's hand grips her face, smashing his lips to hers in a kiss that's passionate and consuming. I wouldn't doubt that he's already head-over-heels in love with her and just hasn't realized it yet because there is nothing casual about their kiss.

He pulls away, his lips brushing hers as he says, "Fuck your alpha, pussycat, while I prepare this tight little ass for my cock."

I've got a stranglehold on my balls because it would be really fucking embarrassing if I come before I even get near her. I walk over and situate myself on one of the spinning leather chairs in front of the sofa, giving myself a front row seat to the fucking action. No pun intended.

Chance places a hand between her shoulder blades, pushing her down until her breasts are pressed against Wren's chest. The second she's in reach, Wren's lips take hers, kissing her and sucking on her bottom lip.

Chance glances over at us. "Lube?"

"Side table drawer," Anson murmurs, his voice barely a rasp. He walks over to the far end of the sofa, placing his knee on the arm and using his hand to guide Fallon back up just enough for her to be eye level with his dick.

"Open wide, baby girl."

Her whine slips over me, making my dick throb in my palm. But she does as he asked, her mouth opening in a pretty little "O" so he can push his length between her lips. Her eyes go wide when Chance teases her ass with a thick finger, pushing it in to the knuckle.

"You're doing so fucking good, pussycat, taking my fucking finger in your ass. Let's try two."

He doesn't give her time to protest, just gently pushes two fingers in, slowly thrusting in and out, and she hums her pleasure around Anson's cock. The alpha's hands grip her face, lightly moving in sync with Wren's thrusting from below.

"Fuck, I don't know if I can last much longer," Wren rasps.

"Don't go yet, alpha. Your beta is almost ready."

Wren doesn't even disagree with the possessiveness of that statement, and I find myself considering the logistics of accepting a beta into our pack. Bearing witness to his protectiveness when it comes to our omega, I'm finding I'm not as opposed as I once was. These small gestures of respect earn him a little credit in my book. It's also a relief to know someone has her back when we're not able to. Fallon's moan draws me out of my thoughts, and I look back in time to see Chance guiding his cock in, inch by excruciating inch.

"Fuck," Wren gasps. "I can... I can feel you inside her. It's like being stroked on the inside."

"Just wait until you shove that fat knot in her. She's going to suck us both dry." Chance's hands land on her hips, his knuckles white. "Fuck, pussycat. You're strangling my dick. I need to move."

Her hand comes up, gripping his thigh, and he takes the invite for what it is. After withdrawing, he instantly plunges back in. The motion sends her forward, forcing Anson's dick deep into her throat. Eyes watering as she gags, the big alpha curses and tries to pull out, but she shakes her head. Her glassy eyes stare up at him, begging him to do it again.

"Gonna be the fucking death of me, baby girl. Swallowing me down between those swollen lips. Fuck."

My legs are splayed wide in the chair, my hand slowly working up and down my shaft with hardly any pressure because I'm not fucking stupid. I want my chance to get inside her and have no plans to shoot my load anywhere else.

She looks fucking stunning between the alpha and beta, the sound of their fucking like no music I've ever heard. One of her petite hands reaches up, wrapping around Anson's knot and squeezing. The alpha's knees damn near buckle, his growl so fucking thick that it stutters when he comes, thrusting in and holding her mouth down on him while his head falls back. I can see her throat muscles flexing as she swallows again and again.

When he pulls back, he falls into the chair beside me, breathing rapidly, and Fallon licks one last drop of his cum off her lips.

"Holy hell," I mutter, earning a searching look from the pretty little omega still being used as the meat to an alpha-beta sandwich.

"Felix," she purrs, lips swollen and pink, "I want your cock, baby."

"And you'll get it. As soon as Chance is done with your ass."

The beta looks over at me with a smirk. "Oh. Two fucking knots filling her up. This I've gotta see. Hang on, love."

His next thrust is hard, making her shout end with a ragged gasp.

"Fuck. She's so goddamn tight, man. You're going to lose it the second this ass swallows your dick." His voice is hoarse, the strain from holding back clear in the bulging muscles in his arms as he repeatedly slams into her. "Gods, yes. I'm gonna come so fucking hard."

"Fuck, wait for me." Wren's sweat is trickling down the sides of his flushed face, the poor alpha damn near desperate to get his knot squeezed.

"What do you think, pussycat? Ready for knot number one?"

"Yes! Knot me, Wren. Knot me so fucking good."

Wren's purr battles his growl as he places his hands over Chance's on her hips.

"On three." Chance pulls back. "One, two, three."

They both thrust at the same time, and Wren's knot pushes past the slight resistance in Fallon's pussy. She screams, her body going taut as she collapses on Wren's chest. The alpha growls into her hair when he comes.

"Oh holy fucking fuck," Chance groans. "Your knot just made everything so fucking tight. Her ass is acting like a cock ring. I can't... Shit, I need to..."

He pulls out, and the second he's free of that tight ring of muscle, he explodes all over her ass cheeks, his hand pumping his cock as he comes.

"Fuck, man. She might be too tight—"

Fallon turns her wide-eyed, pleading gaze on me. "Felix, please. Knot me, alpha. I've been such a good omega."

The growl sneaks up my throat as I stand, watching Chance stumble back. Anson hands him a wet washcloth, and I surprise myself again when I hold my hand out to stop him. I don't want his scent off of her. If he's going to be pack—which is a conversation we'll need to have—then the bond starts now. What's a little cum between brothers?

Taking the beta's place, my fingers swipe through the sticky mess of his release, using it for lube before I place the head of my cock at Fallon's ass. Wren's hands are skimming up and down her thighs, but her face is turned so that she can look back at me. Suddenly, I realize this is a first for me too, and my dick throbs in anticipation.

"C'mon, alpha, show me what you got," she challenges, a wicked grin on her lips.

"You might regret that, sunshine." I thrust in, and her ass immediately clenches around me.

Wren's knot skims along the underside of my dick, the sensation unlike anything I've ever felt before. Her back bows, and his grip tightens on her thighs.

"Son of a bitch," he growls.

She really is fucking tight, Chance was right about that, but she feels so fucking good. I pull out and drive in again, my knot hitting between her cheeks, and I know there's no way I'm going to last. But I'm also not sure it's a good idea to shove my knot in her ass.

"Felix," she gasps, my name a plea on her lips.

"Do it, alpha," Chance whispers. "Give it to her good."

"Sunshine?"

"Knot fuck my ass, Felix. Fill me up."

I glance down, catching Wren's eye. He nods, sliding his hand up to Fallon's neck and tangling his fingers in her hair. He pulls her mouth to his, distracting her while I slowly slide out. Fuck. This is going to shatter me in the best fucking way.

I lean forward, my chest hitting her back as I whisper, "I love you, Fallon."

The urge to bite her is so fucking strong, but I hold myself back. That will come—sooner rather than later if it's up to me. No way is she getting away from us again, but for now, I'll claim her the only way I can.

My hips slam forward, and my knot meets the resistance of her asshole until it finally gives way, letting me slip into her heat. My knot presses into Wren's as her body locks down tight on both of us. The pleasure is almost painful, sending fire skirting up my spine as I roar my release. It continues in long waves while her body milks us both. I'm not sure, but I think Wren is coming again too. How could he not? It's like nothing I've ever felt before.

When it finally starts to ebb, and I can breathe again, I kiss the back of her neck, her shoulders, anywhere my lips will reach. This woman is fucking spectacular, and she's *ours*.

Chapter 20

O mega locks are no joke. It takes almost twenty minutes for Felix's knot to go down enough that he can unsteadily climb off the sofa. Wren's fingers are playing through my hair, the poor guy having taken the brunt of my weight for a while now.

Lifting my cheek from his chest, I glance down to find his eyes closed and the sweetest smile on his lips. I drop a kiss on his nose, then gasp when a warm washcloth is run over my ass and between my cheeks. A twinge of pain follows, but I hide that from the beta who is studying me intently.

"God, the way you squeeze me," Wren murmurs, opening his eyes to glance down at Chance. "Whoa! My balls are good, dude."

"No, they're really not. You should see what's dripping out of her back here."

I bury my face into Wren's chest and giggle. "He's cleaning your balls?"

"Apparently so. Dude has no shame."

"I don't. A huge lack of boundaries too, or so I've been told."

The beta straightens, trailing his fingers over my back. "You're all good now, pussycat. Fresh as a daisy. At least until the alpha beneath you pulls out the plug."

I chuckle. "Definitely something wrong with you."

"There's plenty to choose from. Take your pick."

Slowly sitting up, I glance down at Wren, who nods sweetly at me. Gently, I start to stand, letting his knot slide out of me, then I immediately realize Chance was right.

"Towel," I demand.

He laughs, holding out the hand with the towel. "Told you so."

Stepping over to the side on weak legs as I clean myself up, Wren swings his body so he's sitting on the soft leather. Anson is laid out in one of the chairs across from us, with Felix in the other. Chance is standing close by, probably to catch me if I collapse into a satisfied heap in the middle of the floor.

I'm surrounded by naked dick, and my greedy omega pussy definitely takes notice.

"I recognize that look, pussycat. You want our dicks again so soon?" Chance purrs.

"This hungry cunt might, but I'm not sure my exhausted body is up for the challenge."

Felix laughs until his eyes land on the marks around my neck. "Come here, sunshine."

He pats his knee, and I close the short distance between us, climbing into his lap and wrapping my arms around his neck.

"I'm good, Felix. I promise."

His fingers brush against the marks. "You've been hurt so much already. I can't stand the thought of you being harmed right under our noses by people we were supposed to trust."

"There are so many people that make these shows happen. Finding the mole is going to be like finding a needle in a haystack." Wren runs his hands over his head, leaning back into the sofa.

Do not look at his dick, Fallon. Do. Not. Look.

Shit. I looked. I promptly squeeze my thighs together. *Down, girl.*

"Unless we can somehow draw them out. We'll have to come up with a plan," Anson says, looking toward me. "You have more experience with this than we do, baby girl. Any ideas?"

He's looking at me with trust in his amber eyes, and something inside my soul soars. He knows who and what I am, and he's asking for *my* advice. Mind. Blown.

"What?" he asks.

"I just..."

"Don't get shy now," Chance chastises. "You've had our dicks in all your holes, honey. Ain't nothing more personal than that."

I snort. "I just never thought we'd be here. Like this. Or that you guys would accept the woman I am now once you learned what I've become."

Felix nuzzles into my throat, his chocolate scent sweet and syrupy, and a purr rumbles his chest.

"We never gave up hope, sweetheart." Wren's smile is warm and open, making me wish he was closer so I could kiss him. "Who you are now is a byproduct of the shit hand you were dealt. We'd never hold that against you. I only wish we could've saved you from it all."

"He's right," Anson murmurs. "As shitty as it is, maybe this is the way it had to be. We had to fall apart so we could come back together stronger."

Stronger. I like the sound of that. It settles into my heart, patching up the few remaining cracks from our past.

"I'm just so fucking glad you're back. Period." Felix's hands are trailing over my thighs, fingertips teasing along my skin, making my perfume thick and pungent.

"You guys keep that up, and we'll be fucking again in no time." Chance's grin is wicked. "Not that I would complain about that, but we do need a plan."

My fingers are combing through Felix's hair, my eyes focused on the way his jaw clenches the longer I'm quiet.

"I have an idea, but you won't like it."

Felix is already shaking his head. "Not a snowball's chance in hell, Fallon. Find another way."

"What?" Wren asks, brows knitted in confusion.

"She wants to use herself as bait," Felix grinds out.

The entire room is in an uproar before the sentence is finished.

"How did you know that?" I grumble.

"I know *you*, sunshine."

"You're out of your ever-loving mind if you think any one of us will allow that to happen, pussycat."

I huff. "Do you have a better idea?"

Chance starts to pace the floor, arms crossed over his chest. His semi-erect dick bounces as he moves, and I'm fascinated. When he turns to face me, he catches me checking him out, and a smirk lifts the corner of his lips.

"Eyes up here, love. Unless you *want* an eyeful, that is."

That's the third time he's changed the endearment, and I don't even know if he realizes he's doing it, but the butterflies in my belly take flight regardless. The longer I spend with him, the more names I want to collect. Pussycat, love, honey... I want to be all of those because it means I'm his.

"There's no fucking way we can think straight with her naked." Felix glances at Chance. "Throw me Wren's shirt."

Chance walks over, picks up the shirt, and tosses it to the alpha, who immediately slides it over my head. The scent of gooey caramel apples rushes over me, and I bite my bottom lip.

"Not much better," Wren mutters, his eyes sparking at seeing me in his shirt. "Fuck."

He runs both hands down his face.

Anson chuckles. "Kinda just makes you want to undress her all over again, huh?"

"Mmhmm," Wren agrees.

"Plan first. Fuck later?" I suggest, earning groans from all the men in the room.

There's warmth pooling in my belly, this itch crawling across my skin. Whether it's from their constant looks or their pheromones, I can't be sure. Either way, it's making rational thought increasingly difficult.

"I don't think we're going to get anywhere tonight. Let's try to figure something out tomorrow after we get some rest," Anson suggests.

Felix hasn't taken his eyes off me.

"What?" I whisper.

"You're mine," he whispers back, eyes narrowed at me.

"Why do you look so pissed off by that?"

"I want to make it official."

My heart pounds in my chest, my fingers pausing in his hair.

"Felix..."

It's not that I don't want what he's offering. More so that there's a small part of me that keeps expecting them to change their minds once they realize the full scope of what I'm capable of. By holding off, I feel like I'm giving them an out—giving them the ability to walk away when shit hits the fan. And it will. There's no doubt about that.

"I want you to wear my mark. Let everyone know who you belong to. Be able to feel you in the bond and know you're safe."

My hand strokes down his neck, resting over his heart. My hesitation disappears in the face of his worry. He needs this as much as I do.

"Oh, Felix."

"He's right, baby girl." I turn to Anson. He's leaning forward in his chair, a possessive expression on his face. "Knowing what we do now, I want to sink my teeth into you more than ever."

"If they don't, I might," Wren adds, and I feel like I can't catch my breath.

There's a knock at the bus door, and we all look at each other.

"Who is it?" Anson calls out.

"Sebastian."

"Give us just a minute." Felix lifts me off his lap, setting me on my feet.

The guys sift through clothes, slipping into whatever they find, while I stand there, wondering if I need to give Wren his shirt back.

"It smells like fucking sex and satisfied omega in here," Chance grumbles. "I don't like the idea of him getting a boner off her scent."

"Someone's getting possessive," I tease, earning a glare.

"Damn right I am. I might not be able to bite you, but you're mine regardless."

He's looking at me with that same intensity I've come to expect, and something shifts inside. Four guys—all wanting *me*. The thought of keeping this forever, being *pack*, is starting to settle a little easier in my heart.

He clears his throat, jolting me out of my inner musings.

"I'm yours, just like I'm theirs," I admit, and he smirks sexily. "But we know why he's here. We need to let him in and see what he's got to say."

"Still don't like it." The beta stands in his jeans and loose tee, looking sexier than sin.

"Me either, but not much we can do about it," Felix mutters.

"Shit, baby girl." Anson rakes his eyes over my outfit...or lack thereof. "Here."

He grabs a blanket off the back of one of the chairs and wraps it around me, effectively making me look like a burrito. I don't even complain because their concern is fucking adorable.

A shirtless Wren walks toward the door, and I'm biting my bottom lip again.

"Knock that shit off, pussycat." Chance saves my battered lip, his eyes searching mine before turning to our guest.

"Holy shit," Sebastian whispers, his pupils blown wide once he gets a hit of our combined scents. He tugs on his tie, loosening it slightly. "Maybe we should have this conversation outside?"

"What is it, Seb?" Anson asks. "Just make it quick."

Their manager's eyes scan the bus, coming to a halt on the beta wrapped around me.

"I thought he was Fallon's business partner?" he asks.

"He is." Felix walks into the kitchen, grabbing a couple bottles of water. As he heads back to me, I can't help but notice the way his jeans ride low on his hips, putting that lovely Adonis belt on full display.

Chance's hand reaches down and lightly pats my ass.

"Stop it, or that pat is going to be a helluva lot harder once he's gone," Chance whispers in my ear.

Dammit. My thighs are going to get a helluva workout around here with all the clenching I'm doing.

Felix hands me a water before removing the cap and taking a long swallow of his own. A tiny drop of water dribbles down his throat, and I can't help but imagine licking it off.

What the hell is wrong with me? I know my decade of celibacy has ended, and I'm suddenly a thirsty bitch, but for fuck's sake, this is getting ridiculous!

"He'll be staying with us too."

Felix's words draw me out of the lust haze I'm being swept under, and I try to focus on the topic at hand.

Sebastian's eyes go wide. "He'll need to sign an NDA. Hell, they both should, honestly."

Wren shakes his head. "An NDA isn't necessary."

"Wren—"

Felix growls in frustration. "Sebastian, they're going to be pack. It's just not official yet. No fucking NDA."

Chance and I stare at each other, mutual surprise lighting up our faces. I keep forgetting I've known this man for less than a week. He fucked me for the first time less than twelve hours ago. Now, we're going to be *pack*? Is that what he wants? Is this all moving too fast?

His hand grips mine, the other softening the lines between my brows. Then he drops a sweet kiss on my forehead.

Right. Calm down, Fallon. We'll talk about this after the potential trafficker leaves.

Sebastian runs his hands down his face. "You guys are killing me here. It's been a shit fucking night, and now you drop *this* on me?"

Anson crosses his arms over his chest. "What happened? Why are you knocking at our door after midnight?"

"I just got word from the label. Raphael has taken a leave of absence. They're working on a replacement, but until then, if anything is needed, I'm to contact the head of the label directly." His shoulders sag, and I realize the man just looks exhausted. "I'm not sure what the hell is going on, to be honest, but maybe I'll find out more tomorrow. For now, I'm going to need a drink. And definitely some fucking pussy after this. Jesus."

One of the guys growls.

"Oh, piss off. You know I'm not suggesting anything. The scent in here is enough to send ten alphas into rut. Give me a break, yeah?" He glances at Chance and me. "Welcome to the club, guys. If you need anything, just call. Program my number into your phones just in case. Mr. Donovan, I'll get you a permanent pass. The rest of you, we'll talk when we get to Atlanta. Maybe I'll have more information by then."

"Sounds good. Goodnight, Seb," Wren offers, walking their manager to the door.

When it closes, we all stand around, looking at each other.

"Do you believe him?" Chance asks me.

My brow furrows as I try to piece together the puzzle that is Sebastian Fuller.

"I mean, it's hard to tell. His scent didn't change. Maybe just a little bit thicker because he's stressed. He's either an excellent actor, or maybe the guy really is innocent."

The guys all look at each other, varying degrees of discomfort written on their faces.

"It's late. We should get some sleep." Anson walks up, unwrapping the blanket and lifting me into his arms.

"How's that going to work, by the way? This bus isn't a luxury hotel."

"We can all Tetris it up on the bed tonight. If anyone needs space, they can use one of the bunks."

"You guys have bunks?"

He grins, "Yeah, in the hall outside the bedroom. They're fancy and look more like cabinets when the curtains are closed."

Carrying me down the hall, he pauses just past the bathroom and points to the wall.

"These offer privacy." He pulls back one of the panels, showing off a fairly decent-sized bunk with built-in shelves for storage. "This one's mine."

There's one more on this side and two on the opposite. Four private spaces when the crowd on the bus gets a little too much. Good to know, since it appears this will be our home for the foreseeable future.

Home. Pack. Mine. Theirs. All these *forever* words when nothing in my life has ever been permanent. Instead of feeling rattled, I feel steadier than ever. That sense of stability—security—is forging something strong and solid at my foundation that I'm not sure I've ever experienced.

Anson crawls up onto the bed, laying me down and situating himself beside me. With one hand, he pulls me back against his chest, wrapping his arm around me and nuzzling into my hair.

"You smell so fucking good, baby girl."

I hear the others padding down the hall toward the darkened bedroom. Their low murmurs whisper through the open door, followed by the sound of skin softly slapping skin.

"What the hell is going on?" I grumble, my eyes falling closed as exhaustion and contentment fight to pull me under.

Anson snorts. "They're doing rock, paper, scissors to see who's sleeping where."

My lips curve up into a smile no one can see, but my heart is warmed by the overwhelming sense of peace I feel in this moment. I'm sure it won't last—reality has a way of crashing the party—but for now, I'll soak it up and let my guys cuddle me into oblivion. Everything else can wait until tomorrow.

Chapter 21

Fallon

The Atlanta air is muggy, making my black slip dress cling to my skin the second I open the bus door. I'm greeted by loud shouts and the clicks and flashes of cameras snapping photos. Anson is waiting for me, hand held out, and the second my palm touches his, the irritation inside me settles somewhat.

I'm antsy, my skin feeling too tight thanks to the impatience clawing at my throat. Exhaustion and stress are a nasty combination, and I don't see an end to either anytime soon.

"Fuck, baby girl," he says in that low voice of his. "You look amazing."

I smile when he tugs me into his chest, the sound of reporters calling his name forgotten. One hand slides up to the middle of my bare back, and the other cups my jaw. There's this reverent sort of look in his eyes that tells me this isn't just for the cameras. It's real, and it's all for me.

His hair is loose, acting almost as a curtain when he leans forward, lips brushing against mine. Tonight he's wearing a black button-down, the sleeves rolled up to reveal his sexy forearms littered with tattoos. His jeans are worn, hugging his muscular thighs in all the right places.

"You keep looking at me like that, and I might just pick you up and carry you right back into the bus."

"Promise?" I purr.

His low growl sends shivers up my spine. Keeping an arm around the back of my waist, he pulls back.

"Come on, the guys are waiting inside. Chance wanted to do a quick check of the exits and some other super secret spy shit, so I offered to come out and walk you in. The fucking paparazzi finally caught wind of the story, and they're going a little nuts."

"You don't say?" Looking out at the crowd of people lined up behind the metal barricade, the flashes are damn near blinding.

I'm not sure how I feel about being outed as Feral Lyrics' Mystery Girl. Not only will my face be plastered all over newspapers and tabloids, but this is going to make our lives that much harder. Dodging the press while trying to find the traitor amongst the crew is going to take some added discretion. Let's hope someone gave Chance that particular memo.

Striding toward the back entrance, Anson's fingers twine through mine, and this girlish sense of excitement rushes through me, momentarily blocking out the frustration I was experiencing earlier. The darkness consumes us when we enter the backstage area, and I faithfully follow his lead until my eyes finally adjust.

The Knotty Boys are rocking out on stage, the crowd's eager anticipation practically a living thing, even back here.

"Sunshine." Felix's low growl comes from behind, then a warm hand slides around my belly and tugs me backward into his chest and out of Anson's hold. "What the fuck are you wearing?"

"A new dress. Do you like it?"

"I fucking hate it," he murmurs against my ear, and an enticing thickness begins to push against my ass. "Because all I want to do is take it off you."

"You're welcome," Chance sing-songs as he walks over to Anson with a wink in my direction.

My grin is wicked. "Chance pretty much handpicked my wardrobe, so you can blame him."

His hand skims over my ass cheek. "And do I have him to blame for your lack of any type of undergarments as well?"

"Nope. That one's all me."

He pushes his face into my throat, lips skimming along my skin, teasing the warmth unfurling in my belly.

"Felix...baby," I plead, though I'm not entirely sure what I'm asking for.

"Goddamn. Do you smell that?"

I look up, finding Wren poised in front of me looking like sex personified. His dark hair is messily styled, a tight black tee stretches across his well-defined chest, and a pair of silver charms hangs from suede straps around his neck. His gray jeans are tight, and black combat boots hug his calves. When his hazel eyes finally make it up to my face, his grin is sinful.

"You keep perfuming like that, and the entire stadium is going to turn into one huge fucking orgy, sweetheart."

I shrug, pretending like the thought of a big fuckfest isn't at all a turn on.

Side note: it totally fucking is. I'm so damn horny.

"I can't help it if you all are too tempting for your own good. Your pheromones are killing me."

His hands land on my hips, right above Felix's, and he tugs me forward. His lips find mine with ease before he kisses me senseless. I can feel the slick literally dripping down my thighs and know a trip to the restroom is going to be in order. *Maybe I can convince them to come along with me?*

"I'm not sure if you all are aware, but we are in a *very* public place with people all around. Fucking in the middle of the backstage area would probably be frowned upon."

Chance's voice plays over me, making my need grow by insane degrees when he steps closer. My vision starts to blur, sweat beading at my temples. The noise becomes almost intolerable as realization slowly begins to dawn.

Pulling back, my forehead drops to Wren's chest.

"Oh, shit."

"What is it, Fallon?" Wren asks.

"My heat is starting," I whisper into his shirt. "I should've known."

"I'm sorry. Did you just say your *heat* is starting?" Felix rasps behind me.

When I nod, Wren's hands rub up and down my back, attempting to soothe me, but the soft contact is just making me even more desperate for their touch.

"We've got two days off after tonight, then another day of travel until our next show in Miami. Maybe we should see if there are any heat suites available?" Anson suggests.

"I'll call a couple of the local hotels." Wren pulls back, dropping a kiss on my forehead. "It's going to be okay, sweetheart. Don't worry."

Felix's chin rests on my head as the other alpha walks away with his phone up to his ear. "Sunshine, I have a question for you."

Glancing over my shoulder, I study him. Rich brown eyes, hair styled to perfection, tight black dress shirt accented with a deep red bow-tie. God, he's so fucking handsome.

"Are you on birth control?"

Tension is thick in the air, with Anson and Chance now standing directly in front of me, eyes searching mine. My belly flutters at his tone, noting this almost hopeful quality to his voice that I'm not sure how to interpret.

"Yes. I have an appointment to renew it in a few months. My heat's at least a week early." I turn in his arms, tilting my face up to his. "Why? Omegas can only get pregnant during heat, and we typically only have them twice a year. What we've already done shouldn't—"

"I'm not worried. Maybe just a little bit...excited about the possibility is all."

I blink. The thought of children was always such an impossibility in my mind that it never even occurred to me to consider it. But now, seeing the look on my alpha's face, I'm reconsidering all *kinds* of things.

"The Regent Hotel and Suites has a heat suite available, so I booked it for the next few days." Wren walks back up, phone in his hand. "What did I miss?"

Chance slides his hands into his back pockets. He's wearing dark gray jeans with a gray plaid vest. Under it is a tight white dress shirt and black tie. His hair is tied back into a mini-bun, the scruff on his face grown out, and I'm licking my lips before I even realize it.

"Alpha over here wants to fill her up with a baby already."

Wren's purr can be heard over the sound of the crowd's cheers.

"I can see the appeal," he murmurs, half-lidded gaze sweeping over me.

A whimper escapes. The idea of them filling me up with their cum has become this vivid image in my brain.

"Agreed." Anson is suddenly beside us, brushing a lock of hair behind my ear. "But for now, I kind of want her all to myself. There will be plenty of time for that later."

My eyes trail up my big alpha, taking in the way he fills out his shirt and how he looks like he could easily break me in two... That last thought tempts me to see if he'd be willing to try.

It's so goddamn warm in here.

"Fuck. Her eyes are glassy, and her pupils are dilated." Chance's finger hooks under my chin, forcing my eyes up to his. "She's never going to make it through the show. Someone needs to take the edge off until we can get to the hotel."

"If I fuck her, I'll bite her." Felix's hands drop from my waist, fisting at his sides.

The whine that leaves my lips is slow and deep.

"I've got her," Anson growls, picking me up.

My legs wrap around his waist, my slick no doubt making a mess of his outfit, but I don't give a damn. He carries me away down the hallway, and I can't help but run my nose through his hair, inhaling his deep scent that reminds me of summer rain.

"Think *he'll* bite her?" I hear Chance ask as we move farther away.

"Probably. I know I wouldn't be able to stop myself," Wren mutters.

"Dammit. I should've just said fuck it and snatched her up," Felix grumbles. "If he bites her, I'm next."

Anson growls. "Not gonna bite." Though I'm not sure whether it's to reassure me or himself. With his scent in my nose and desire sparking in my core, I can't think of a single reason why accepting his bite would be a bad idea. In fact, I can think of a whole slew of reasons why it's a fan-fucking-tastic one.

"But what if I *need* your bite, alpha?"

His footsteps falter, but he makes it to an inconspicuous door, opening it and walking in before he turns on the light. The soft click of the lock sounds ridiculously loud in the utter silence of the space, and I lift my head long enough to see a small dressing room. A long mirror runs along one wall with a small counter beneath it and two director's chairs facing it. A leather sofa sits on the wall behind them.

He sets me down, big hands gripping my hips and spinning me around. I take in my reflection. Flushed cheeks, lips slightly swollen from Wren's kiss, and need flashing in my blue eyes. His larger body dwarfs mine from behind, somehow making me feel vulnerable and safe at the same time.

"I'm not gonna bite you while you're in heat."

"I'm not delirious yet, Ans. I still know my own mind." My eyes meet his in the mirror, and suddenly I've never wanted anything more in my whole life. "Please. Just another first to add to our list, big guy."

"Baby girl." His moan is guttural. "You're going to shred every last ounce of my willpower if you keep that up."

Feeling bold, I raise my hand to the thin strap of the dress and slide it over my shoulder, then move to the other one. The thin material slips down to my waist, my bare breasts heaving as I take in the way his eyes narrow. I shimmy it all the way off until it's puddled around my feet. My hand skims up my belly, circling around one of my hard nipples.

"Would you bite me here?" I whisper, my fingertips wandering over to the other breast. "Or maybe here?"

"Fallon…"

"Or maybe my throat?" I tilt my head in an unmistakable offer and slowly run my fingers up the long line of my neck and across my jaw until I'm tugging on my lower lip. "What about right here, so whenever you kiss me, I come on the spot?"

"Fuccckkk," he growls, roughly unbuckling his belt and undoing the button and zipper. "Hands on the counter. Hold on tight."

Leaning forward, my hands grip the laminate, and I jut my ass out, an open invitation to fuck me. His fingers swipe through the insane amount of wetness between my thighs, and when he steps into me, his dick poised at my opening, I can feel the steady rumble in his chest.

"Tell me how you want it, baby girl."

"Hard and fast, Ans. Fuck me. Knot me. Bite me."

"Son of a bitch," he groans, gripping my hips as he thrusts in all the way to the knot.

The stretch is fucking insane, forcing my body up on tiptoes to ease the pressure of his huge fucking dick filling me up.

"You still want it hard?"

"Yes," I rasp.

"You got it, baby."

With effort, he slides back even though my body is doing its damndest to keep him right where he is. When he slams his hips forward, I scream, an orgasm ripping through me faster than a brushfire. I can't breathe. Can't think. But he continues to fuck me right through it, using his grip to pull my body back onto his dick just as he thrusts forward, the force allowing him to go incredibly deep, with his knot teasing my pussy each and every time but never sliding all the way in.

The second I can draw in enough air, I beg, "Fuck, Anson. Please. *Please*."

"Please what, Fallon? Ya gotta be more specific."

"I need your knot, alpha. I—" I whimper when he grinds against me, his knot so damn close to where I need it, but he holds back. "For fuck's sake. I *need* you, Ans."

"You've got me, baby girl. Always."

Our eyes meet again in the mirror. "Then bite me."

His eyes flash. I can see his tight grip on his control faltering with each plunge into my pussy.

"Not gonna fucking bite."

"Make me yours, Anson. Make me *pack*."

His snarl is practically feral, his thrusts becoming erratic.

"Not. Gonna. Bite." He emphasizes each word with a thrust.

Frustration edges my voice. "Fine. Then maybe I should go find Felix. He'll fucking bite me."

"What did you just say?" he growls.

"I said..." His next thrust is so hard, I squeal, but it doesn't stop me. "Felix would do it."

"You want my fucking bite, baby girl? Want me to sink my teeth into you and never let you go?"

"That's what I fucking said. Do it!"

With a roar, he pulls out, spins me around, and lifts me into his arms. His breathing is ragged, nostrils flared, and he's looking incredibly animalistic right now. I've never been more turned on in my life.

"Anson?"

"Mine."

My eyes search his as the head of his cock prods at my cunt.

"Yours."

With one last growl, he slams me down on his dick, sinking that fat knot inside me. I come so fucking hard, my pussy locking around him as his mouth crashes down on mine. My hips roll against him, dragging out our releases with every tug on his knot.

It isn't until I feel a sharp prick of pain in the soft skin of my lower lip that I gasp, and blood floods my mouth as he sucks on the bite.

The orgasm that was starting to ebb soars with each long pull he draws from the wound, his tongue flicking against it.

Suddenly, a bright spark of connection opens up between us. Relief. Joy. Euphoria. A carousel of emotions floods through me, and I feel the first tear roll down my cheek as he pulls back, licking, kissing, and sucking on the two puncture marks. His attention sends a matching tug straight to my pussy, making my body contract around him.

Whoa! I was exaggerating earlier when I said I'd come on the spot if he marked me here, but it turns out it's not really all that far from the truth. My lip is swollen and throbbing, and I reach up, letting my fingertips trail over it. Once he's tended the bite, it should go down and be almost unnoticeable.

A hint of worry slips through everything else he's feeling right now.

"I love you, Anson."

His purr is immediate, rumbling against me as he holds me close. "I love you too. So fucking much, Fallon."

He did it. He claimed me. *I'm. His.*

Chapter 22

The water is running in the background as I help Fallon out of her dress. Not that she *needs* the help, but I'll be damned if I haven't been dying to do this since I saw her step backstage wearing it. The way it hugs her curves and makes her legs seem impossibly long is somehow even better than I imagined when I picked it out. The same could be said for the woman.

The Syndicate handed me a stack of folders, complete with pictures and backgrounds, including their connections to the potential suspects, and told me to pick one for this particular mission. I'd take the lead, be the handler on the project, and would be responsible for coordinating all the moving parts. I went through four folders before I flipped open Fallon's in frustration, expecting another dead end. Instead, a pair of blue eyes stared back at me with keen intelligence, along with a heaping load of pain. I was hooked. I should've known right then it was a horribly awful idea. Professionally anyways. Personally? Best decision of my goddamn life.

Steam fills the room, and a large tub big enough for two or three is almost ready with a few candles and a honey vanilla bath bomb I dropped in. There was a basket on the counter when we arrived, along with a card and a note for her to relax and enjoy, from the guys.

"You're unusually quiet. Should I be worried?" she whispers.

My eyes snap up to hers. "Worried? Why in the hell would you be worried?"

She licks her bottom lip as she carefully avoids my curious stare, and I can't help but focus on the slight swell there. Lifting my thumb, I brush it along the skin, noting her swift intake of breath at the contact.

"Is it sore?" I ask softly.

"Not really. Just...sensitive." Her voice drops an octave on that last word, and my thumb sweeps over it again.

"Sensitive, you say?"

Leaning forward, I can't stop myself from kissing her. She makes this soft hum in the back of her throat, and I want to lose myself in her.

"We're going to flood the room," she murmurs, her lips never leaving mine.

"The guys will pay for it."

I go in for another kiss as she chuckles, pushing lightly on my chest.

"I could pay for it too, but that doesn't mean I want to."

She shoots me a playful look over her shoulder.

"Loaded, are you, pussycat?"

"I don't have to worry about work if that's what you mean." She bends over, plump ass on full display, to twist the knob.

"Have you gotten any requests for jobs while you've been here?"

Her lips part, surprise flashing across her face.

"Huh. I haven't even checked. Normally, I'd be chomping at the bit for something to occupy my time by now. You'd be surprised how much research and planning goes into a single job." When she sees my raised brow, she laughs. "Or maybe not."

She tests the water with her fingers, then turns back to me with a searching look in her eyes.

"What is it?"

"Will you join me?"

My dick throbs in my pants at the same time my heart twinges. I barely avoid putting my hand on my chest at the odd sensation.

"If you want company—"

"I do," she replies before I can finish.

To be wanted by her, without hesitation or uncertainty, is unlike anything I've ever experienced. For the boy whose parents didn't want him, the man whose friends betrayed him, and the professional who has never trusted anyone, it's an entirely foreign feeling.

I clear my throat. "Then hop in, and I'll join you in just a minute."

She pulls her hair up, twisting it into a messy bun on the top of her head. Stepping into the warm water, she sinks into the bubbles all the way up to her chest. She's seductive even when she isn't trying, a temptress that has no idea just how tempting she is. I don't deserve her, but there's no fucking way I could walk away now. In a short time, she's become as necessary as water and air—more important than the work that has always taken the top slot in my list of priorities.

"Chance, you're starting to freak me out."

My head comes up, finding her leaning over the side of the tub, resting her chin on her hands. I can't stop the way my lips curve at the sight of her looking so damn innocent...because I know better.

"Why am I freaking you out, love?"

Her eyes flash at the endearment just like they have the other times I've used it. To be honest, I just like catching her off guard and watching the pretty blush that always follows.

"You're quiet. Subdued. Not throwing out sexual innuendos left and right or being snarky on any level. I was just naked in front of you, yet you didn't even try to cop a feel. Do you have a fever?"

I slowly start to undress, first the vest, then the tie. Starting the tedious process of undoing the buttons on the dress shirt, I notice her eyes tracking my movement.

"No fever. I just—"

"Are you upset that Anson bonded me?" she blurts out.

Letting my pants fall to the floor, I stalk to the tub and kneel in front of her. Brushing a wisp of hair behind her ear, I trace the features of her face.

"I know I can be an annoying pain in the ass, and I know that I don't do serious well, but I would never, I repeat, *never* begrudge you happiness and love. You deserve all that and more, Fallon."

"I just don't want it to change what we're growing between us."

"It won't. You've got me for as long as you want me."

Her eyes study mine as she sucks her bottom lip in between her teeth. I'm not even sure she's aware she's doing it, soothing Anson's bite in his absence.

"And if I said I wanted you forever?" she whispers, staring up at me from behind her thick lashes.

"Then I'm yours."

"But we can't make it official—"

"You have my word, Fallon, and that's worth just as much as a bite coming from someone like me." People like her and me, our word is sacred—the only part of ourselves we're willing to give, and even then, it's doled out so rarely that it's worth its weight in gold.

She regards me quietly before one of her breathtaking smirks begins to turn her expression mischievous.

"I don't know. After all that, I'd say you do serious *marginally* well."

When I boop her nose, her laugh echoes through the tiled room, filling my soul up to the brim.

"Slide over, smartass, unless you don't want my *marginal* company after all."

She scooches forward, giving me just enough room to slide in behind her. My hands grip her hips, pulling her back against my chest. If she notices the hard sword between my legs, she doesn't comment on it. With a sigh, she leans into me, tipping her head back to rest on my shoulder.

With the scent of vanilla mixing with her tart peach scent, I'm struggling to keep my hands on neutral territory. Sure, she's in heat, but she needs to know her beta is capable of more than just pawing at her all the time. I can be the gentleman I claimed to be even if it kills me.

"Did you ever see yourself all packed up?" she asks, tilting her head to look back at me.

"Honestly? I don't think I ever saw myself living long enough to have to worry about it. In my line of work, old age isn't really a thing."

Too many of my colleagues have gone out in a blaze of glory or at the hand of someone they trusted. When you've done the sort of things I have, you quickly learn to trust no one, and always make sure to have a weapon on you at all times. The fact that I ignored both rules with her, then with the guys, tells me that maybe, against all odds, I've found where I was always meant to be.

She nods knowingly. "I think I was almost tempting fate, daring it to try to take me out. I mean, what did I have to live for? A shitty apartment and a cactus that defies all laws of nature because fuck knows I haven't watered the damn thing...ever."

"That cactus is resilient, just like you." I kiss the top of her head.

Her fingers thread into mine from under my palms, using her hands to carry my arms across her waist until I'm hugging her from behind. We barely know each other, but I could swear I've known her my whole life. Is that biology's work? Forging this connection hot and fast to mold it into what it needs to be—solid and strong? I have no fucking idea, but I'll take it. I'll gladly accept the gift I've been given because she's so goddamn precious I know I'll never find another treasure like her.

"Chance?"

"Yeah, pussycat?"

Her face burrows into my arm. "I'd bite you if I could."

Those simple words are like fire in my veins. "I'd let you."

I feel the warm wetness of her tongue along my bicep before her teeth scrape along the tanned skin. Goosebumps break out along my body, my dick throbbing with the simple pleasure of having her mouth on me...anywhere.

When her teeth sink in, there's this bite of barely there pain, followed by her hum of satisfaction, I nearly come against her back. Drawing back, she licks at the little drops of blood, tending her mark. There isn't a physical connection surging between us, but most definitely an emotional one. All of the loneliness, all of the hurt, all of the pain I've lived with my entire life, gone. All because this woman decided she wanted to keep me. *Me*. A man I always assumed wasn't worthy of a connection like this. I'm utterly and truly speechless.

She drops one last kiss on the mark, then rests her head back against my chest and closes her eyes. The silence between us is comfortable, like two matched souls finally able to just *be*.

Leaning my head back against the tub, we lay in peaceful solitude, soaking up the other's presence, letting our pasts be just that...in the *past,* as we both no doubt contemplate our future. I feel her body resting heavier against mine, her breathing evening out, and look down to find her eyes closed. Then I glance at the small bite mark she left on my arm, the claim that will slowly heal and fade away, and decide that no matter what happens from here, I'm having that mark tattooed right in that spot as a reminder of the woman who has fucked up all my carefully laid plans.

I'm not sure how long I lay there, watching her sleep. I just know that at some point, I fall asleep too—trusting a woman more than I've ever trusted another human being—unprotected, yet completely and utterly at peace.

Chapter 23

Walking off stage, I'm eager to get over to the hotel. Through our new bond, I can feel Fallon's contentment and love, as well as her exhaustion, and the connection has been alive in my senses all night. I could feel slight tugs on the bond, the hints of arousal that had me packing an uncomfortable bulge in my jeans while I played for a crowd of thousands, but it was always followed by this warmth and affection that I knew meant she and Chance were talking about the events of the day. Now, she's settled and quiet in the bond. Our girl has been going nonstop since the night we found her, and she deserves a little break from the chaos that is tour life.

"So you fucking bit her?" Felix asks, catching up to me and grabbing my arm to draw me around to face him.

There was no time to have a talk after Chance came to grab Fallon and told me the guys were waiting to walk out on stage. I made it just in time for Felix and Wren to get a good whiff of what went down, for a roadie to hand me my guitar, and for Sebastian to push me out into the darkness. I can't tell from the look on his face whether Felix is upset or just wants all the details because at the first opportunity, he's going to bite her too.

"I didn't fucking plan on it," I grumble, earning a chuckle from Wren. "But our little omega is persistent when there's something she wants. How the fuck was I supposed to deny her when she was begging for my bite?"

"You did the right thing," Wren murmurs, clapping a hand on my shoulder. "It actually makes me feel a little better knowing one of us has that connection. With everything going on and all."

"Think she's ready for the rest of us, or was it a heat thing?" Felix asks, a hopeful look in his eye.

"She's ready. Even if she's in heat and begging for it, don't hesitate. She's made it clear she wants to be pack, and that includes both of you. And let me tell you, there is nothing better than feeling our girl through the bond after all these years."

Felix raises an eyebrow. "Not even the bond sex?"

I smirk. "Bond sex is a close second."

His groan is long and deep, catching the eye of the crews hustling around us.

"So...can you tell how she's feeling right now?" Wren asks nervously.

I check in on the bond, feeling this deep sense of peace wash over me. The connection is quiet, which can only mean one thing.

"I think she's actually asleep."

Felix gets this wicked glint in his eye. "Good, because she's going to need rest for the things I plan on doing to her."

Out of all of us, Felix's tastes have always run a little bit darker, so Fallon is no doubt in for a wild ride. Before he can go into detail, Roland walks up.

"Great show tonight, guys. You're in the best form I've seen in quite a while. Pretty sure we have Fallon to thank for that." He looks around, eyes scanning the area backstage. "Where is your pretty omega, anyways?"

I share a look with my brothers. This was one thing we all agreed on this morning, even without a plan in place to find the traitor. *Trust. No one.* But we're Feral Lyrics, which means we can't exactly go M.I.A., so we handpicked a select few people to stay updated with the bare minimum of information until we have time to clear them officially.

"We planned a last-minute holiday before the show tonight, spending the next couple of days at the Regent Hotel and Suites before we head to Miami. She's waiting for us there."

"Okay, I'll send a small contingency of plainclothes guards, just in case. Do you plan on leaving the hotel at all?"

Felix snorts. "Highly doubtful."

Roland smirks. "Got it. I'll make sure to let Sebastian know in case he needs to find you. I've also got a pass for Chance Donovan. Know where I can find him?"

"He's with Fallon."

The hefty beta's expression reveals his shock, but he doesn't ask. His discretion and loyalty is one of the reasons he's included in the small number of people allowed to be in the know. Our Head of Security was one of the first people we brought on staff, right after Sebastian. Even as inexperienced as we were, we recognized the need to have people around us that we could trust. Knowing that one of those people is potentially abusing that trust makes me sick to my stomach.

"Do you need a ride to the hotel, or is that already arranged as well?"

I glance at Wren, who shakes his head. "If you have someone who can drive us over, that would be great. We've been given clearance to use the back entrance."

"I've got time right now if that works?"

I nod, reaching a hand out. He grasps mine in a firm shake.

"Thanks, Roland."

Securing one of the label's SUVs, Roland drives us the two miles to an upscale hotel catering to famous clientele and parks in the secure garage. He demands that he walk us up to the room to ensure our safety because he always goes above and beyond. We already have the room number and the combo to the keypad, so we don't have to stop by the front desk.

"So, this Donovan character... You trust him with your omega?" Roland asks as the elevator doors shut quietly.

"Yes. He's going to be pack."

At Wren's announcement, Roland's brows shoot up.

"Pack?"

Felix leans back into the elevator wall, crossing his arms over his chest. "He's a package deal with Fallon, and considering big guy over here already claimed *her*, well, Chance will be one of us soon enough."

Roland looks at me. "You claimed her already?"

I chuckle. "I know, I know, Roland. As Head of Security, you have a natural aversion to trusting people, but in this case, there was no doubt in my mind that Fallon was mine. Now, I'm hers too."

"If you trust her, man, I'm good. But this Donovan guy... I don't know. Guess I need to get to know him first."

The elevator dings at the top floor, the penthouse heat suite, and we walk into the private foyer. Roland stays on the elevator, holding the door.

"You have my number. Reach out if anything comes up. Otherwise, enjoy your time off."

We nod, then turn to the suite door. Wren enters the code, and the lock snicks softly as the elevator doors begin to close. The suite is quiet when we enter, with only a low light coming from the direction of the bedroom.

"If Chance is this quiet, he must be sleeping too," I murmur.

Felix snorts. "Considering the man never shuts up, I'd say that's probably accurate."

I laugh softly, making my way toward the room, eager to see my girl. The bed is empty, the comforter untouched. We all share a look before heading into the bathroom.

There, in the tub, is Fallon, curled in the beta's arms, both fast asleep. We stand there for a moment, looking down at the girl who stole our hearts years ago before we ever even realized it.

"Looks like your plans might have to wait, loverboy," I whisper.

Felix glances at me, a rueful look on his face.

"Don't just stand there. This water's fucking freezing," Chance rasps, his eyes popping open.

Chuckling, I step forward and dip my hands into the cool water. Chance lifts Fallon's languid body into my waiting arms, and she snuggles into me as I stand. Wren's ready with a towel, wrapping it around her as best he can. Her heavy lids open, a smile gracing her beautiful face.

"Hey, alpha."

"Hey, baby girl."

I kiss her, my lips skimming along my mark, and she gasps. There's a quick rush of red-hot heat through the bond, and my dick has never gotten so hard, so fast. She doesn't come, but it's awfully damn close.

"Mmm, I'm so glad you're here."

"Me too."

"The nest is through those double doors." Chance points toward the far end of the bathroom as he stands and accepts another towel from Wren. "We haven't been in there yet. She wanted to wait until everyone was here."

Fuck. The nest.

Fallon deserves an *actual* nest, not some makeshift room in a random hotel suite, but we all live out of an apartment—albeit a luxury one—having never considered the logistics of what would happen after we found our girl. Things like what an omega might need, a nest, a home to call our own, were never concerns we had. Now that I've taken the step to claim her, this pushing demand to put down roots, create a place we can call our own, strikes hard and fast. Part of our lives revolves around a tour bus, but the other part deserves somewhere we can settle in and enjoy what we've only recently found.

Her fingers play over the lines creasing my forehead as her eyes study mine. I kiss her forehead, trying to soothe the panic I'm sure is filtering through to her in our new bond.

Carrying her over to the nest, Felix slides one of the pocket doors open, showing off a room full of soft grays and creams. There's a bed that spans from one wall to the other and a built-in shelf behind the bed with piles of pillows and blankets. There are two softly glowing indented lights that cast shadows over her body as I lay her down. Her arms wrap around my neck.

"Don't go."

"Wouldn't dream of it. Just have to get out of these clothes first, then I'll climb in with you."

"Now you're talking." She looks over my shoulder. "You guys aren't off the hook either."

She's laid out on the plush gray comforter, naked, hair damp, looking like a wish I never thought would come true.

"Fuck, sunshine." Felix crawls up on the bed on his knees, his jeans puddled on the floor and his shirt slipping off his shoulders. "Look at you."

She rolls flat onto her back, legs sliding open in invitation. Her eyes are barely opened, but as soon as Felix settles into the apex of her thighs, she hums, wrapping her arms around him and drawing him down for a slow kiss.

It doesn't have the same powerful draw as when I kiss the mark, but its effects are definitely felt all the way to my toes.

He lifts his head, his thumb brushing over my mark, and her body goes still.

"Are you mad?" she whispers.

Felix shakes his head. "Not a chance, sunshine. Maybe a little jealous is all."

Her smile is big and bright. "Don't be. It can be your turn whenever you're ready."

His purr is loud. "And if I said I was ready right now?"

"I'd ask where you wanted your bite," she replies without hesitation.

"Sunshine..." Felix drags out the word in a moan. "You have no idea how badly I want to take you up on that offer, but I know we're all exhausted, and your heat seems to be at a low simmer. Maybe we should rest up now and prepare for the fun to begin?"

"Since when did you grow up?" Wren snarks from the door.

"Since we found our fucking omega, smartass," Felix gripes, shooting the other alpha a glare over his shoulder.

There's this feeling of rightness flooding the small room—a sense that everything will be okay despite the obstacles we face. Chance walks in, naked and unashamed, crawling onto the bed to rest beside Fallon and Felix.

"Hey, pussycat," Chance murmurs when her face turns to his, accepting his tender kiss.

"Hey, beta boy. Thanks for the bath."

"You're welcome."

I share a look with Wren.

"Chance being chill?" Wren tilts his head. "I think we've entered the Twilight Zone."

"Right?" Fallon chuckles.

"Geesh. Can't a guy just be nice once in a while?"

"Dude, I've known you less than forty-eight hours, and nice is not a word I'd use to describe you," Felix mutters.

"Well, get used to it. Fallon claimed me, so now you're stuck with me."

The silence in the room is absolute as he holds up his arm, showing off a shallow bite.

Fallon is grinning so damn big, this effortless sort of love seeping through our connection, and I know that one of us is going to have to bite him for real. Give them that connection because the way they look at each other tells me they've made their decision, and there's nothing we can do to stop it—not that we'd want to at this point.

"Welcome to the club," Felix murmurs, balancing his arm on his elbow and offering his hand.

Chance's hand clasps around the alpha's, and this shadow of a tether begins to form within our pack bond with hardly any effort at all. I'm not sure if either of them even realize it.

When I glance over, Wren has undressed. He's sliding up on the bed beside the others, whispering something to Fallon that has a lovely blush rising along her cheeks. I shrug out of my shirt, slip off my pants, and turn to close the pocket door, letting only the soft glow from the lamps play across the group on the bed.

My pack. My life. All together in one place. Fuck. I've never been happier.

Chapter 24

There's this incredible fullness, warmth, and growing arousal as I slowly come out of a deep sleep. I can feel the heat churning in my belly, the desperate urge for a knot making my perfume pungent and thick in the small room when my slick floods the space between my thighs.

The scent of sweet chocolate tickles my nose, and when I start to turn in my alpha's arms, I realize that his dick is nestled deep inside my pussy, but he's not moving, or even awake. Sometime during the night, Felix decided his dick needed a place to sleep, and it just so happened my pussy had a vacancy.

His lack of personal spatial awareness might've been a problem except I'm an omega in heat, so he honestly did me a favor. To be honest, even if I weren't in heat, I'd welcome them to share my life and my body any time, anywhere, for as long as they want it. Taking advantage of the situation, I slowly lift my leg and slide it back, softly placing it down on his, which effectively opens me up wide. I let my finger trail through the wetness at my core, my fingertip rubbing circles around my clit. My hungry cunt contracts around him, aching for more, and my hips begin to roll. Lust unfurls inside me like the petals of a flower in bloom.

It isn't until his hand flexes on my naked belly, his nose nuzzling up my neck, that I realize he's awake.

"Good morning, sunshine." His voice is deep and raspy from sleep. "Thanks for keeping my cock warm for me."

My whimper is my only response. I'm too busy silently praying he'll fuck me for real now.

"Mmm. Good morning, indeed," he purrs. His hand slides down my belly, finding my fumbling fingers, then he tsks. "You should've woke me up sooner."

His much larger hand and thicker fingers begin to play me like a fine instrument while his hips start to pull back and thrust forward the slightest bit, causing this fabulous friction to begin to build between us.

"Just like that. Fuck, you're so goddamn wet."

"Felix..." I can't think straight. I just know that I need more.

Sensing Anson in the bond, there's a rush of desire, followed by a hint of impatience, and I'd totally fucking grin if I wasn't drowning in my own fucking lust.

"Come on my dick like a good girl, sunshine. Then I'll fuck you for real."

Sliding his other hand under me, he grips my throat and forces my head back onto his shoulder as he squeezes lightly. His purr rumbles between us, and my body begins to buck against his dick, searching for more. He doesn't care. He's hard and throbbing inside me, but he continues his shallow thrusts that bring me right up to the edge without tipping me over.

"Oh god. I need—"

The hand clasping my throat moves up to my mouth, silencing me.

"You'll take what I give you and do as you're told. Now. Come. On. My. Goddamn. Dick."

The command is no more than a harsh whisper against my ear, but my body responds to it nonetheless. My release rolls over me, my moan stifled by the hand still covering my mouth.

"Good girl," is all he says before he pulls out and rolls me onto my back.

Covering my body with his, he lines himself up and slams home before I've fully come down from the high of my release. He sends me soaring again with every hard thrust into my body, his knot edging my opening again and again. His arm snags under my knee and pulls my leg up, which changes the angle, allowing him to hit impossibly deeper. He fucks like a man possessed, drilling into me like he can make up for every one of those ten years we were apart.

"One more. Come once more for your alpha, then I'll fill you up with my knot."

My groan echoes through the space as he drops my leg, sliding his hands up and lacing his fingers with mine. He drags my arms up, forcing them above my head. With a tight hold on my wrists, he locks me in place, using the position as leverage to plunge into me in long hard strokes that have my back bowing off the bed. He looks so fucking primal right now, with sweat dampening his brow and his teeth bared, his ab muscles flexing with the movement.

"That's it. *Fuck.* Your tits bounce so damn pretty when I fuck you like this."

With every slide of him inside me, my body coils tighter and tighter. It needs release almost as much as it needs a knot. Right now, it would gladly take either.

"Holy shit, pussycat. You're fucking stunning right now." Chance murmurs.

The sound of Chance's voice reminds me that my beta has no problem watching me with my alphas. He saunters in, practically licking his lips.

"Isn't she, though? As soon as she comes again, you can have her mouth while I knot her pretty pussy."

"Hell yes."

When I glance over, my beta is still unabashedly naked, stroking his cock while watching Felix fuck me.

"Hurry up, love. I want to see my dick slipping between those plump lips of yours, right over your alpha's mark."

The whine that escapes has Felix's hands tightening their grip on mine.

"You heard him, sunshine. Your beta needs your mouth. Let's show him how sexy you are when you come."

This time, when he pulls back, he hesitates—I can practically see him counting in his head—before he slams forward so hard I scream. He hits deep, touching this spot that has me bucking beneath him. My body attempts to lock around his dick, needing a knot, as fire streaks through me. It's hot and it's intense, but there's still this sort of emptiness that has my body releasing a long whine when I come.

"So fucking good." Felix pulls out despite my cunt trying to clench around him.

Grabbing my hips, he flips me over, his hands tugging me up until I'm presenting for him like a proper omega should.

"Put that pretty ass out for your alpha, sunshine, and lift that filthy mouth for your beta."

When my chin comes up, Chance is kneeling in front of me, cock hard and ready.

I lick my lips, feeling the slight tug on the bond. Anson's hunger fuels my own as Felix slides up behind me, the fat head of his cock playing at my entrance.

"You ready to suck me off, pussycat?"

Spit roasted by my two dirty talkers is going to be the death of me. I'm already a panting mess, with sweat rolling down the side of my face—two orgasms yet my body still demands more.

My head tilts up, finding Chance's blue eyes staring down at me, and I open my mouth wide.

"Fucking hell," he mutters. He runs the tip around my lips, pausing over my mark and sliding it back and forth.

"Holy shit! She's squeezing my head so fucking good right now," Felix groans.

"Her mark is *really* sensitive," the beta says just before he pushes between my lips.

His hands bracket my face, then he starts off with a slow and sensual roll of his hips. My lips close around him, my tongue flicking against the underside of his cock. He's being exceedingly gentle with me...until Felix slams home, sending Chance's dick deep into my throat. His fingers roughly grip the back of my neck, holding me down on him.

"Fuck. Yes."

It's like the alpha freed the beast. Both men take my long groan as an invitation to fuck me like they hate me. I'm gagging around Chance while the sound of Felix's pounding echoes through the space.

"Her mouth is something fucking else."

"So is this pussy. Wet and warm, ripe for fucking."

Chance moves one hand below my chin, the other cradling my head from behind as he fucks my throat, thrusting deep over and over again. He tries to hold me down on his dick, but Felix is a relentless machine, plunging in and out of me, using my body for his pleasure.

"Jesus Christ, you two," Anson growls. "Best hurry it up because she's flooded the bond with so much lust that if I don't get a release soon, I'll be shooting my load in my shorts."

"Fine," Chance grinds out, then he taps my chin. "You heard your alpha, love. I'm going deep. You swallow me down like a good fucking girl, you hear me?"

I hum my agreement, taking a deep breath before he thrusts in hard, my throat swallowing the head of his dick. He's so fucking fat that I can't breathe, and he grinds against my lips when I instinctively try to swallow.

"Oh, fucking fuck. Do that again."

I oblige him.

"I'm gonna come, pussycat."

As Felix continues to pump into me from behind, Chance comes with a groan, sending thick spurts of release sliding down my throat. I suck on him, hearing him hiss as his hands drop and he pulls out. I gasp for air, and it turns into a whimper.

"Felix, stop torturing our omega," Anson barks as he takes Chance's place. Instead of kneeling, he sits back against the headboard, legs spread wide, and strokes his fat dick. "Scoot up a little, bro."

With a grunt, Felix stops thrusting long enough to follow me when I crawl toward my other alpha.

"Hey, baby girl." His hand brushes stray hair out of my face.

"Hey, alpha," I pant.

Anson's eyes turn sharp, his head whipping up to glare at Felix. "She's fucking suffering, dickhead. She needs your knot."

"And she'll get it." His hand trails down my back, his fingertips leaving a path of fire along my heated skin. "Right after I figure out where I want to bite her."

The whine that leaves my mouth is low and needy.

"Make it fast, yeah?" Deep brown eyes search mine. "You don't have to—"

I don't give him the chance to finish that sentence. My lips close around him, sucking his tip and letting my tongue play with the sensitive underside. His hands grab the back of my head to guide the bobbing of my mouth as his dick slides in and out, right over his bond mark.

"Hell, I can't even describe how fucking good this feels."

"Probably as good as her soaking cunt feels around my dick."

There's a bubbling heat in my veins, and I start to feel a little lightheaded. My body is worked up to the point of overload without the knot I'm so desperately craving. Anson must sense something in the bond because his anger spikes.

"Felix, this is your last warning. She's *hurting* right now."

"That true, sunshine?"

I whine around Anson's dick.

"Fuck. Okay. One knot and one bite coming right up."

His body drops down, his chest laying along my back as his arms come down to rest alongside mine. The position makes his thrusts a little less deep, but a whole lot more potent with the way he's engulfing me in his pheromones. I'm burning up, taking Anson in deeper and sucking harder with every second Felix's knot grinds into my pussy.

"Ready to be mine, Fallon?" Felix asks, his tone a hint anxious.

"Mmhmm," I hum around Anson's dick.

"Bro, she's so beyond ready."

Felix's lips brush along my ear, moving to my earlobe, and his breath is hot on my sweat-soaked skin.

"I love you, Fallon."

His hips slam forward, his knot finally stretching my pussy. The second he slides in, my body locks around him so fucking tightly I hear him grunt. Anson roars as I impale myself on his cock, then without warning, he's coming in my mouth. I try to swallow it down, but considering I can't breathe, I end up with a mouthful of my big alpha, drops spilling out the side of my mouth. He manages to pull out so that I can swallow, and our eyes meet as his thumb runs along his mark.

"Fuck," Felix curses just before he gently bites down on my earlobe. A bright spark of pain floods through me until he pulls back, sucking and licking his mark. The result is immediate and overwhelming me. I try to scream, but it's silent. My entire body locks up tight in pleasure so intense, my vision goes black and I think I might literally pass out.

"Breathe, baby girl. Breathe," Anson murmurs in the darkness, waiting for me, his thumbs gently brushing my jaw until light begins to penetrate the fog. "Holy fuck. There you are. You had me worried for a second."

"Holy fuck is right. She's strangling my dick so fucking good, I'm *still* coming. You were right. Bond sex is no fucking joke," he groans, his voice deep and hoarse.

That's when I finally notice the onslaught of emotions flooding through me. Love, relief, an overwhelming sense of completion, and a hint of smug satisfaction.

"You okay, sunshine?"

Glancing over my shoulder, I send him an exhausted smile. "More than okay, babe. I can't even explain…"

My throat closes up as tears flood my eyes. I'm so goddamn happy right now. I've claimed two of my three guys, my beta is fitting into our new pack seamlessly, and I know without a doubt that whatever obstacles stand in our path, they have no chance of ruining what we're building here as long as we stick together.

"We know, baby girl. We know." Anson drops a kiss on my lip, sending a jolt of desire and love through the bond.

"Fuck, man. You're a masochist," Felix grunts when my lock squeezes him tighter.

Anson and I chuckle together, even as tears roll down my cheeks.

Chapter 25

Fallon

"For fuck's sake, is no one going to tag me out?" Chance whines.

He's lounging back in one of the armless chairs in the corner of the nesting suite, his hands limply gripping my hips. I've been riding my beta for close to thirty minutes now. I've come three times, but I *still* need a knot.

Insatiable bitch!

It's been over two days of practically nonstop sex. With this being my first heat with my alphas, my body is making up for lost time. In other words, I've worn them all out.

"You wankers! She needs a fucking knot!" he shouts.

Wren's chuckle echoes in the bathroom before he appears in the nest door. He's shirtless, wearing only a loose pair of sport shorts, his hair disheveled and cheeks flushed. The bracelets that he never takes off jingle on his wrist as he leans against the door jamb.

Anson and Felix are passed out on the nest's bed after a massive group session earlier this morning. The heat is still burning hot, though I'm pretty sure I'm on the tail end of the worst of it.

Poor Chance...about to be Poor Wren.

"Give her to me," the alpha says, and I feel Chance's body sag with relief. His head drops back, and his hands unclench from my hips.

"Honestly, I'm not sure my arms are strong enough to lift her."

My hips still while my eyes narrow on my beta.

"Are you saying I'm too heavy?" My voice cracks, and this stupid flood of self-consciousness hits me.

He groans. "That's not what I meant, pussycat. You're *perfect*."

I look up at him through damp lashes. "Yeah?"

His hands limply slide along my ass until he's tugging me in closer and dropping a soft kiss on my lips. "Yeah."

"Come on, sweetheart. I've got you," Wren murmurs, lifting me out of Chance's lap and carrying me out of the nest and through the bathroom.

The actual bedroom is still mostly untouched and thankfully blissfully dark. He lays me down on the bed and doesn't waste any time, pulling off his shorts and settling in between my thighs. His dick unerringly finds my center, sliding in with this exquisite sort of tightness that has my head tipping back to bare my throat.

His purr is loud in the utter silence of the room, the vibration against my breasts driving me crazy.

"You have no idea what you do to me, sweetheart," he whispers just before his tongue licks up the curve of my neck.

My head dips, eyes meeting his.

"Then why haven't you claimed me yet?" I ask, trying—and failing—to keep the hurt out of my voice. "Have you changed your mind?"

His eyes narrow. "Fuck no. I was just waiting for you to ask. I... I didn't want to assume anything. It's not like you have to bond me just because you bonded the others."

"Wren..." My hands reach up, dragging his face down to mine. He's resting on his forearms, his head hanging low so our foreheads can touch. "Do you remember that time we snuck out and walked miles to the carnival in town? I wanted to go on the Ferris Wheel, but Felix wanted to check out the duck shooting game, and Anson wasn't the biggest fan of heights."

He chuckles. "He was shaking like a leaf but was trying to hide it from you."

"You were the one that grabbed my hand, helped me get situated on the seat, and slipped your arm around my shoulder so I could rest my head there while we took in the lights of the city from the top of the ride." His thumb is brushing away tears on my cheek, clueing me in that I'd apparently started to cry. "We sat there in silence, this comfortable quiet settling around us because we didn't need to fill it with words."

"That was the first time I kissed you," he whispers. "Just as the wheel started to come down, I leaned over and pressed my lips against yours. That was when I first realized I loved you."

"You always steadied me, Wren, giving me this sort of safety that was always there to shore me up when I was feeling unsteady."

His hips roll back, and the slide of him inside me is the perfect complement to the feelings simmering in my blood.

"You've always been this wild storm I've chased, watching in awe because you just draw in those around you. I used to wish I was brave enough to get closer, brave enough to stand in your path and let you swallow me whole. Then I did, and it was fucking amazingly terrifying. I was never the same."

I kiss him then, slow and sensual, my hips grinding against his.

"This life—this pack—wouldn't be the same without you, Wren. I need your stability as much as I need Anson's warmth and Felix's chaos. I..." I find his eyes, needing to explain to him how much he means to me. "I love you so fucking much, alpha. I need your bite."

He studies me intently, his jaw muscles clenched tight. For a second, I worry that he's going to turn me down.

"It's been ten years since I told you I love you, Fallon." He wipes another tear from my cheek. "But I'm so fucking lucky I finally get to tell you again."

He drops a kiss on each cheek, then one on my forehead, his hips moving in a constant push and tug in and out of my pussy.

"I love you, Fallon. I want to be your alpha if you'll have me."

I swallow down my joy and relief, looking him straight in the eye.

"You've always been my alpha, but I'm ready for you to make it official."

His hips begin to pump harder, making my desire burn brighter in my soul. He doesn't slam forward or even thrust particularly hard, but his knot sinks into me so incredibly slowly that I feel the stretch and the exact moment he sinks into me. My body, as if understanding the intensity of the moment, locks around him gradually. We both gasp, maintaining eye contact while we come, long and hard, wave after wave of sensation rolling over us while we grind into each other.

His hand gently cups my jaw, his thumb carefully tilting my head back to expose that sensitive spot at the base of my neck. He kisses it first, sucking on it and giving it one quick lick before his teeth sink in deep. My pussy contracts almost painfully around his knot with each drag he takes off the bite, long hard pulls that have me whimpering his name. Then he's finally pulling his teeth out, with the first lick along the sore skin firing up the bond. He's steady, even there—comfort, joy, an incredible well of love and acceptance that I can't even begin to describe.

"This feels..."

"Incredible," we both whisper, then grin.

Wren rolls us over, carefully pulling my leg over his hip so he stays locked inside me. We kiss like two teenagers discovering each other for the first time, and my heart is so incredibly full that the tears start up again.

"Shhh. You've got us now, sweetheart. You'll never be alone again."

"Don't forget me," Chance whispers. "You've got me too, honey."

He crawls in behind me, nuzzling into my neck.

"So...cuddle pile then?" Felix murmurs sleepily, dropping onto the mattress behind Wren. His arm lands across Wren's body until his hand hits my waist.

"Fucking really, Felix?"

"What? We used to do this all the time. What's the big deal?"

"How about your erection in my ass?" Wren grumbles.

I bury my face in his chest to contain my laughter.

"Don't worry. It's not for you."

"Doesn't make me feel any better."

"What the hell are you all arguing about in here?" Anson asks, running a hand through his long hair as he takes us all in.

"Wren is no longer a fan of our old cuddle pile," Felix mumbles, his eyes already closing.

Anson trails his eyes over their position. "Yeah, I can see why."

We share an amused look before he glances at Chance.

"We're pack," he says, this strange look on his face,

"We are," I agree with a tilt of my head.

"We're all bonded."

Chance's hand flexes on my belly, but I know what he's thinking. *Everyone except him.*

Anson kneels at the bottom of the mattress, staring at the beta until Chance finally glances up at the giant man at our feet.

"What's your point, alpha?" Chance mutters.

"Do you want to be?" Anson asks.

Chance goes still behind me. Glancing over my shoulder, our eyes connect. I can feel surprise and the anticipation in my bonds with Felix and Wren, then they both send their agreement through our connection.

"You said you were mine."

"I did. And I am."

"This would make that official if that's what you want."

"Is that what *you* want?" Chance whispers.

"I'd love to have you forever, Chance."

Chance glances up at Anson, an open expression on his face. "I'd really, really like that. How do we do this, big guy?"

"Where would you like the mark?"

"I..." Chance faces me, brushing his thumb along my lip, then turns back to the alpha. "I want a matching one. But I assure you, this will be the one and only time you'll get a taste of these lips."

Anson grins. "Come here then."

Chance sits up, scooting down to the end of the bed. The two are chest to chest, with Anson easily dwarfing the beta, who isn't exactly small. When his large hand wraps around the back of Chance's neck, pulling his lips to his, I suck in a breath. Watching the intimacy of their position sends a rush of desire through me. Wren groans.

"Fuck, sweetheart. You squeeze me much harder, I might be out of service for a while."

I struggle to relax in his arms. "That would be a pity."

Chance gasps, and Anson's teeth bury into the tender skin of his lower lip before withdrawing so he can lick across the wound. When the alpha draws in his new beta's lower lip, sucking gently, I hear the loud moan followed by a choked sound.

Anson chuckles. His amusement rushes through the bond, then all of a sudden, there's this new connection—not as bright, but brimming with emotions that I can't catalog fast enough.

"Did he just come?" Felix murmurs.

"Shut the fuck up," Chance grumbles around Anson's mouth. "We'll never talk about this again."

"Ha! Fat chance, bro."

"Go lay next to your omega, brother. I'll be behind you in case the bite needs more tending."

Chance comes up behind me, his affection and something that feels a lot like love flowing between us. He kisses the back of my neck, causing peace to wash over me, as Anson settles in behind him.

"I feel something poking into me, alpha, and I'm shoving you off the bed."

"Noted."

My smile is so fucking wide that I can't contain the utter happiness I'm experiencing in this moment, then a hint of desire flickers to life when I think about my alpha and my beta kissing.

Four groans echo through the room, but I just laugh.

Chapter 26

Knocking on the bedroom door, silence greets me. Slowly twisting the knob, I enter and find the bed empty. Soft humming reaches me over the sound of the running shower, and the grin spreads before I can stop it. I walk into the steamy bathroom and lean against the door jamb, listening to her soft voice sing one of our songs—one that I happened to have written.

"I knew I'd found forever when I looked into your eyes."

I sing the next line. "Then they tried to tempt me away with all their beautiful lies."

Her bright eyes peek out of the shower. "Even when they offered me the moon and stars."

"Nothing else could touch what was already ours." I stalk toward the shower, seeing her flushed cheeks and wet hair, tracing the water drops trailing over her tanned skin. "I didn't know you knew that one. It's a little older."

She shrugs like it's no big deal, but it hits me for the first time that she sat back and listened to our music, heard the words that expressed everything we were feeling, and still never reached out to us. A little hurt bubbles up but also understanding because we were all so damn young and helpless. But it doesn't stop me from asking the one question that's been left unanswered.

"If you know our music and heard the stories in the media, why didn't you ever come to us, sweetheart?"

The water shuts off, so I reach over to grab the towel, holding it open as she pushes back the curtain. She steps into my arms, regret and a little bit of hurt filtering through the bond while I hold her, my hands doing shit work of drying her off.

"A lot of reasons. I was angry. Hurt. Fully believed you were using our love, our experience as a ploy to draw in fans. I was too mired in my own misery to step back and look at it objectively. To see that they were all siren calls, hoping to lure me back to you."

Spinning her around, I pull her in close.

"I like that. A siren's call. I'm just sorry it didn't work."

"I think it did...subconsciously. Without that, I don't think what we've built now would've happened as effortlessly. Your music planted the seed, and seeing you all again watered it and helped it grow."

"When did you become such a romantic?" I drop a kiss on her forehead.

"When I fell in love with three rock stars and a snarky beta."

I laugh, seemingly the first whole-hearted laugh I've felt in years.

"We have a meeting with Sebastian in fifteen minutes. Chance refused to let us go on our own, not that I think Seb would be stupid enough to do anything considering we're his bread and butter."

She nods. "Good. I would've asked him to join you anyways. If he's the insider, he's not going to give a damn about anything other than saving his own ass if he knows we might be onto him."

"You really think it's him?"

"I don't know, and that gives me enough pause to be cautious. But don't worry about me. I'll be fine here until you get back."

"Roland is actually on his way. The bus will roll out for Miami right after the meeting, so finish getting ready. He should be here to pick you up."

"Okay. You all be careful, you hear me?"

"Yes, ma'am." I grin as her brow furrows, then let my lips fall to hers just because I can. What a novel concept. She's *mine*. No longer just in name alone, but through an actual connection that ties her to me forever. *Fuck*.

The kiss is slow and sweet, without all the urgency of the last few days. Don't get me wrong, heat sex is fucking phenomenal, but this is much more my style. I'm a romantic at heart, and there's so much more I want to do for her now that she's mine. Things like buying her flowers just because, or taking her out to an expensive dinner, or cuddling on the sofa and watching our favorite movies. All of the things we never got to experience, I want to make them happen for her.

"Don't give Roland any trouble, okay, sweetheart?"

"Who? Me?"

When our eyes meet, the wicked heat there is nearly my undoing. The growl sneaks out before I can stop it. This primal urge is an automatic reaction when it comes to her.

I let a hint of my alpha bark into the command. "Be. Good."

"Yes, sir," she whispers, her scent rushing over me, and I nearly toss the towel on the floor and say fuck the meeting.

"Wren, let's go!" Anson shouts.

"Fuck. Gotta go, sweetheart."

"I'll see you soon." She gives me one last kiss and steps back.

Leaving her standing before me, dripping wet and practically naked, is probably one of the hardest things I've ever had to do.

When I make it back to the living room, three sets of eyes are watching me.

"What?" I bark, frustration nipping at my toes.

"We had a bet going on as to whether or not you'd be able to walk out of there without fucking her," Chance replies matter-of-factly.

I snort, some of the tension in my body easing.

"Who won?"

The beta shakes his head. "None of us. We were all sure she'd break you down and you'd succumb to her charms, so we changed the bet to how long it would take."

"C'mon, shitheads. Let's get this meeting over with."

We all walk out of the suite and head down the elevator, meeting Roland and one of the other guards in the foyer.

"Perfect timing. She's getting ready. You can wait out here, and we'll let her know to come out when she's done."

Chance pulls out his phone, no doubt sending her a text.

"Jonathan will drive you back to the bus. Sebastian should be there waiting."

"Thanks, Roland. Watch over our girl."

"Of course," he replies with a nod, taking his post outside the door.

We follow Jonathan down to the car and make the short drive back to the bus. The lot is mostly empty, with only a few SUVs left that will follow us on the drive to Florida. It feels almost odd to be back here without her now, her presence already ingrained in our routine in such a short amount of time.

"Anyone else fucking antsy without Fallon here?" Felix asks.

"Yeah. Something doesn't feel right." Anson opens the door, and we all trail in after him.

"Do you think we should check in with Roland and make sure everything is okay?" I fight the urge to grab my phone and do exactly that.

"No. I'm sure it's just a strain on the new bonds now that we're away from her. It should settle down soon." Anson checks his phone, telling me he's not as calm about this as he appears, but I try to settle myself by going with his logic. "If we don't hear anything by the time the meeting is over, then we'll call Roland."

"Hey," Chance calls up the stairs, "I've got a few calls to make. I'll be right outside, so holler if you need me."

"Wait, we haven't exchanged phone numbers. I need to make sure we can get a hold of you if something were to ever happen," I suggest.

My phone dings, and I pull it out, showing a text from an unknown number. Looking up in shock, I find Chance's cocky grin staring up the stairs at me.

"I mean, are you really that surprised?"

Anson chuckles when his and Felix's phones ding practically in unison.

"Be back in a bit," the beta says, blowing me a kiss before he shuts the door.

"You bonded him," I point out unnecessarily.

"I did. He's a fucking livewire in the bond. You never know what's going to come through next."

"What do you think Sebastian wants to talk to us about?" I ask my brothers.

The cryptic message didn't give us a whole lot to go off of, which is another reason Chance wanted to tag along. He didn't trust it, and now I'm starting to understand why. In the years he's been our manager, we've never been called in for a last-minute meeting. Of course, we've never spent two and a half days at a hotel with our new omega and our beta packmate either.

"I honestly don't know," Anson replies, drawing me out of my head. "Maybe it's to handle the growing media storm surrounding Fallon?"

"Could be. I know #FightingFallon was trending on social media. They're spinning it like she purposely avoided us all these years while we fought to get her back. A second-chance romance kind of thing. Now they're speculating on what we could've done to drive her away."

"I mean, that's exactly what happened, isn't it?" Felix pours himself a drink and makes his way over to the sofa.

"Yeah. It's just... I don't know. Seeing it simplified like that makes me angry for some reason, especially when I read headlines like 'Which Feral Lyrics member cheated and drove her out of their lives?'"

"They don't know the whole story, and that's how it should be. Let them spin it however they want. We know what really happened." Anson sits down in one of the spinning recliners. "Something new will come along and take over the headlines, then the drama around it will die down."

Felix takes a sip of his drink. "We need to start writing some new music. Use it as a way to spin our take on what happened. Think Fallon would be down to help?"

"I heard her singing in the shower before we left. Her voice is actually pretty good."

"Hmmm. Maybe we could bring her on stage. Let her sing a little duet with us. Remind me to talk to Sebastian about that in case she's down."

"Where the hell is Sebastian anyways?" I ask, brow furrowed. "It's unlike him to be late."

"I'll text him now," Anson offers.

"I texted him too. If he doesn't show up in fifteen minutes, I'm calling Roland."

Within a few minutes, we hear the sound of breaking glass and jump to our feet.

"What the fuck was that?" Felix growls.

"Maybe Chance threw something or kicked a bottle?"

The sinking feeling in my gut tells me that's ridiculous, then we hear Chance's worried shout.

"Guys! You better get out here, quick!"

Chapter 27

Dread begins to pool in my belly while I dial the number, making the tones sound excessively loud. I've purposely avoided all calls and messages the last couple of days, and now it's time to face the music. With my phone up to my ear, I pace around the exterior of the bus, trying to walk off the nervous energy plaguing me. My alpha and my omega check in through the bond, but I quickly reassure them. Just me...freaking the fuck out. My bad.

"Donovan!" the harsh voice growls. "Where the fuck have you been?"

"Fallon went into heat," I respond, as if that answers the question.

"And?"

"And...we're pack now, so I kind of had to help my omega out."

Silence. I can practically count the angry breaths as my faceless, nameless boss attempts to take in what I just blurted out.

"You're a smart man, Donovan, so you know that a beta and an omega can't be a pack alone."

"True. But they can if they're bonded by a pack of rock stars."

"Please tell me you didn't."

"Didn't what? Get claimed by a member of Feral Lyrics? Or didn't become a pack with the band and their new omega, Fallon Parker? For the record, the bond between Anson and me is not at *all* sexual, by the way."

There's cursing through the line, so I pull the phone away from my ear to save my eardrum.

"This was supposed to be the mission that saw you climbing our ranks, Donovan, your biggest solo mission to date, and you just shit the bed."

My brow furrows. "That's a really fucking gross figure of speech."

"Have you even tried to get any additional evidence on who might be leading things from the inside? You know, the primary objective you were *supposed* to be focusing on."

"Unfortunately, no. Our most likely suspect is still Sebastian Fuller, but we haven't been able to find any evidence to support that."

"You need to get your head in the game. There are rumblings on the dark web that there is an omega auction in the works. We believe it's being organized by Raphael Montoya, with potentially a half dozen omegas up for grabs. They're always invite only and take place solely online. Bids are submitted in real time and the winner announced before the close of each auction. Pick-up instructions are then provided, with the omegas being handed off to the winning bidder within twenty-four hours."

I lean back against the bus. Fuck. We're failing spectacularly if they managed to sneak six omegas out right from under our noses.

"How much time do we have?"

"Roughly forty-eight hours. We managed to secure an invite, but with this latest development, I think the conflict of interest might—"

"You know I can still do this. *We* can still do this."

They clear their throat. "There's something else you need to know."

The dire tone makes my stomach churn. "What is it?"

"Yesterday, they began to promote a special *high-value* auction in addition to the others, with bidders needing to be vetted in order to participate."

"Okay. What am I missing?"

"We have reason to believe that they may be targeting Fallon after the failed abduction attempt."

My entire world goes still, this deadly sort of anger beginning to slither through my veins at the threat to my woman. Anson's worry sneaks through the bond once again, and I do my best to calm myself down, but it's a struggle. I can only hope he waits patiently for my explanation. I don't need anyone else's anger affecting mine right now. That's a disaster waiting to happen. Fallon seems distracted, otherwise I'm sure she'd be hounding me for answers already.

"There's no way they can get to her, and even if they could, she's more than capable of taking care of herself."

"Don't underestimate them, Donovan. They're anticipating bids of upwards of five million on that auction alone. It's drawing incredible interest. They wouldn't be promoting this if they weren't confident of the outcome."

Fury simmers in my blood at the same time fear becomes a living thing inside me. I can't lose her. I won't.

"Time is of the essence. You need to find the insider and figure out what they're planning."

"Got it."

"I don't need to tell you this, Donovan, but the stakes just increased ten-fold. We've never lost one of our projects, and I don't want this to be the first. Set your feelings aside and utilize the deadly skills you were hired for in order to save the integrity of this organization, as well as yourself."

The threat hits its mark. If anything happens to Fallon, not only will I lose the woman I've only just found, but I'll have lost any favor I had with the Syndicate, and termination protocol will likely be activated.

"Ten-four."

"Good luck, and keep us updated."

The line goes dead, leaving me staring out at the empty lot, hearing the sounds of cars whizzing by on the busy downtown street. This last week has been a whirlwind, one that has left my entire life up-ended. I've gained a pack—a band of brothers that have my back and a woman who does insane things to my head, along with other parts of my anatomy—and the thought of life without any of them is as unimaginable as a black hole swallowing up the planet earth. I've got a to-go bag ready with a new passport and cash stashed away. The Syndicate would likely never find me, but I hadn't counted on a pack. Hadn't counted on leaving behind the only people who have ever given a damn about me. That changes everything.

I straighten and start to make my way back to the bus's door...to my alpha and my pack. If only Fallon were here.

My loyalty is now divided. Part of me is dedicated to the cause I've spent years fighting for. The other to my pack. With the information I now have, I have to decide how much I divulge to the people who are only just starting to trust me. If I keep it to myself, and the worst happens, they may never forgive me. If I tell them, and the Syndicate finds out, it could mean my life. I'm damned if I do, damned if I don't, which is not a good fucking position to be in.

Passing between the black SUV and the bus, I hear a soft chime, like the notification of a phone. Pulling mine out, I don't have any new notifications, and my brow furrows. That's when I hear it again.

Glancing at the black SUV, I realize the driver and passenger seats are empty and all the windows rolled up. The doors are locked, and since I can't really see through the back windows because they're tinted, I peek in through the front.

I don't notice anything unusual, but then I hear the chime again. Walking around to the back of the SUV, I peer through the rear window but can't see anything. Rustling the handle gets me nowhere since the car is locked and I don't have the fob. I'm about to walk away, see if one of the guys might have a spare key, when a low groan halts me in my tracks. Then I hear it again. Rushing over to the driver side door, I pull back my elbow and let it smash into the glass. The sound is incredibly loud as it shatters into thousands of tiny pieces. Carefully leaning in and unlocking the door, I swing it open and press the button for the rear hatch, sending up a silent prayer that it works without the fob. The tell-tale beep of the door lifting is music to my ears.

The groan is louder now, and I rush to the back, only to freeze in shock. There, on the floorboard of the cargo space, with his hands and feet hogtied and a piece of duct tape across his mouth, is Sebastian Fuller.

"Guys! You better get out here, quick!" I shout, praying I was loud enough for them to hear me.

The alpha's eyes open slowly, their dazed look making them glassy. When he sees me, he starts to struggle against the bindings.

"Hey, easy," I say, stepping forward and grabbing my knife out of the sheath at my ankle. "I'm gonna get you out of these, but I need you to stop moving so I don't accidentally hurt you."

He goes still, eyes wide and terrified.

The sound of boots running across the pavement reaches me as Anson, Felix, and Wren run up. Their faces pale when they take in the sight of their manager.

"What the fuck happened to him?" Wren whispers.

My hand grips the knife, slicing it through one of the thick ropes. "I don't know yet. I heard his cell phone and started searching the car. Had to break the fucking window to get to him back here."

Anson steps closer. "You're bleeding."

I glance down at my arm, noticing the cut through my shirt sleeve and the blood beginning to spread out along the fabric, either from when I broke the window or when I stuck my arm through the broken glass.

"I'll be fine. Let's worry about him first."

In seconds, the ropes are all loose and I help Sebastian sit up. He's weak, sweaty, smells like piss, and he's most likely dehydrated. I try to remember the last time any of the guys had mentioned talking with him, but I can only come up with the call they received the night we checked into the hotel. That was over forty-eight hours ago, wasn't it?

When my fingers go to the duct tape across his mouth, I grimace.

"There's no easy way to do this, so I'll try to make it quick."

My fingers grip the corner, the other hand pulling the skin taut as I rip the tape away from his lips. He moans, and I can sense the alphas behind me losing their struggle with their patience.

When the last of it comes free, Sebastian sags, a limp hand raising up to his mouth to rub the irritated skin. His eyes lift to mine, then shift over my shoulder to where the guys are waiting. I step aside when tears start to fall, giving them their first glimpse of the broken alpha.

Felix steps forward. "Holy shit, Seb. What the fuck happened?"

He tries to talk, but it comes out as more of a croak.

"He needs some water."

"I'll get it," Wren offers, running over to the bus. He's back in less than a minute, removing the cap on the bottle of water and offering it to his manager. "Here. Let me help you."

Wren gently tips the bottle, slowly letting the water spill into Sebastian's mouth.

"Not too much. It could make him sick," I say softly.

Wren nods, never taking his eyes off the man.

Once he's had a few small sips, he tries to clear his throat.

"I'm not sure what fucking happened. Roland came to find me. I was with two...no, three omegas who had tried to talk their way onto the bus. You know how they are. He offered to take care of them and make sure they got a ride home, but I assured him I had it under control. I noticed two of his security guards flanking me from behind, and the next thing I knew, it was lights out. I came to in the back of this SUV. I'm not entirely sure how long I've been stuck back here, but I thought I..." His voice breaks. "I thought I was going to die."

"It's been almost seventy-two hours, Seb. We need to get you some medical help."

There's dread building in my gut. *Security guards.* My mind zips back to the night of Fallon's attempted abduction. Three security guards, all under Raphael Montoya's payroll, but who's in charge of those security guards when Raphael isn't around?

Roland Hayes. Head of Security.

Holy fucking shit. How did we not see it sooner?

And we just left him alone with Fallon.

Son of a bitch!

My eyes meet Anson's, noting the dawning horror flashing across his face as he no doubt starts to put the pieces together himself. Whipping my phone out of my pocket, I frantically start dialing Fallon's number. Each ring takes years off my life.

When her voicemail picks up, I search the bond, but there are so many emotions blasting me right now, I'm struggling to separate them all. It's hard to tell which are even mine.

"Do any of you feel her in the bond?"

"What's going on?" Felix asks.

"It's Roland. He's the insider on Raphael's payroll," I grind out.

"Son of a bitch!"

"She's—" Wren begins.

We feel it at the same time. Even through the secondary bond, I catalog every single emotion that comes rapidfire along our connection. The panic, anger, and irritation, followed by a sharp stabbing pain. The alphas have gone very still, overwhelmed with the feelings they're getting first hand.

Suddenly, the connection goes eerily quiet. Anson's chest is rising and falling rapidly. Felix curses as he stalks over to the bus and punches it hard with his fist. Wren is pacing with both hands on top of his head.

"Is she...?" Anson's voice cracks at the end.

I shake my head, taking deep breaths in and exhaling slowly, trying to get my mind to calm enough that I can think clearly, but that's fucking impossible. Someone stole my fucking girl. Someone responsible for managing an omega sex trafficking ring. The implications have my stomach churning.

"She's okay. She's strong and smart and can handle herself. She'll be *okay*."

I'm not sure if I'm trying to convince them or myself.

"What do we do?" Anson rasps.

Wren is staring out at nothing, his fists clenching and unclenching at his sides. "We have to find her."

"But how the fuck do we do that if the bond is dark?" Felix shouts. "The motherfucker pretended to be our *friend*. Sat right under our noses while he kidnapped innocent women and sold them. Now, he's got our fucking girl." His voice breaks. "We practically handed her right to him. It's our fault."

"Okay. Everyone calm down. We're going to find her, and we're going to get her back. I just need quiet for a minute so I can work out my plan."

Pulling out my phone, I dial a number I know by heart, realizing that by doing so, I could very well be signing my own death warrant. The Syndicate was very specific about the consequences if I failed, and I have...spectacularly. The only way to save my girl now is to call the very people that will likely kill me when they have to come clean up my mess. But I'll do it if it means Fallon is found and safely delivered back into the arms of the men who love her. Even if that can't include me.

Chapter 28

Applying my lip gloss, I risk a quick glance in the mirror. I've never been concerned with the way I look or the clothes I wear, but dating a rock band and knowing there will be paparazzi flashing their lights everywhere we go changes a girl's perspective. The blush pink pleated skirt hits mid-thigh, my white sleeveless v-neck shows off a healthy amount of cleavage, and the blush pink thigh-high boots make my legs look stupid long. I feel girlie and playful and ready to take on the world.

Chance's text said Roland would be waiting in the foyer, so when I walk out, I'm surprised to find him in the living room, kicked back on one of the sofas we christened sometime around hour thirty-six of my heat. I'm pretty sure there's not a flat surface in this place that doesn't need a little extra sanitization once we're gone, but I won't tell the man what he's probably sitting in.

"Hey! Sorry to keep you waiting."

"No rush. Figured I'd let you doll yourself up, then we could hit the road."

His choice of words seems a little condescending, but I shrug it off. I'm in too good a mood to let anything dull my shine at the moment.

"I'm ready if you are."

"I see why they were so into you." He stands, his eyes raking over me. "Searching for six years and singing their hearts out to you every night."

Placing a hand on my hip, I tilt my head. "Personally, I'd like to think it has more to do with my bubbly personality than my looks."

He shrugs. "But looks sure don't hurt."

I roll my eyes, masking my unease when this little tingly sensation in my brain tells me that something feels off. "Such a dude thing to say."

He smirks. "C'mon. I'm parked in the garage."

"Sure." I grab my clutch off the table, pretending to look for something. "Shoot. I forgot my lip gloss. One sec."

Trusting my instincts, I head back through the bedroom and into the bathroom. Thankfully, I strapped my knife sheath on just inside my leather boot. Quickly debating my options—also wondering if I'm being overly paranoid—I'm reaching for my knife when I hear his footsteps approaching.

"Find it?" he asks, right behind me.

Nope. Not paranoid. I turn, eyes wide and innocent and my lip gloss in my hand.

"Yup. Right here." I make a show of putting it back in.

He takes a step forward, closing the distance between us. "I'm sorry, Fallon."

My belly flips, my hand slowly making its way to the top of my thigh. Definitely should've gone for the knife in the first place. The pieces are starting to come together in my head. All the clues I shouldn't have missed but did because I wasn't given enough time to research my targets. And I was just a *teensy* bit distracted.

Fucking hell.

"For?" I play dumb, hoping he drops his guard.

"They warned me that you're not as helpless as you seem. You'll understand why I need to do this here, not in the car."

"Do what?"

He steps forward, pulling a needle out of his pocket. "If you play nice, I'll make sure this is painless."

I drop the innocent act because, to be frank, fury is building up inside, and it's going to need an outlet soon. My fingers slip into my boot and slide out my back-up knife since the Syndicate still hasn't returned my favorite switchblade.

"If you hurt my guys, you'll pay for that."

"Don't worry. They're fine."

"They *trusted* you!"

Now, I realize the meeting was a diversion to get me alone. I should've fucking known better. This is like...*How not to fall for stupid shit 101. Shame on you, Fallon.*

"And I failed them. I'll have to live with that." He shakes his head. " But it didn't start out this way. I was loyal in the beginning."

"What changed?"

"Money. A lot of it. I couldn't turn it down." He shrugs like it's no big deal.

"You tossed away a legitimate job and good friends, for what? A fat bank account? You're fucking pathetic."

He ignores me. "I'm guessing they've all bonded you now?"

I stare at him in silence, carefully watching his movements.

"We'll find out either way. That will create some issues, but nothing they won't know how to deal with."

"My bonds are not something anyone is going to *deal with*," I snarl.

He moves faster than I gave him credit for, a big hand darting out to grab me. Barely managing to dodge him, I slip under his arm, then we spin at the same time, facing off again.

"It doesn't have to be like this, Fallon."

"Oh, it really does. If you think I'm just going to hand myself over, you're dumber than you look."

His eyes narrow. "Fine. But don't say I didn't warn you."

He charges, and I spin with the blade in a reverse grip, letting my momentum add a little extra force so it slices through the front of his shirt, shallowly digging into his chest. It's not deep enough to do much damage but painful nonetheless. A hiss leaves his lips, but it doesn't stop him. With a roar of fury, he lunges, his much longer reach giving him the advantage he needs to snag a handful of my hair.

"You fight like a girl!" I shout as he tugs me back, forcing a sharp cry from my lips.

His meaty arm wraps around my throat and squeezes until oxygen becomes scarce.

"I told you it didn't have to be this way," he growls.

"I was right," I manage to rasp out. "You're dumber than you look."

I thrust the knife back, feeling the blade sink into his side, and his howl of pain echoes off the bathroom tile. It's not a lethal hit, but it does its job. He releases me, the hilt sticking out of his side. He glances down, then yanks it out, his blood dripping from the blade. Fury is written over the tense features of his face, and that's when I realize my mistake. Now, he's got a size advantage *and* my motherfucking knife.

Son of a bitch!

We're both breathing heavily, eyes focused on each other as we try to anticipate the other's next move. With my options fading, I spin on my heel and run, making it all the way through the bedroom. I attempt to slam the door behind me in order to buy myself as many precious seconds as I can, but he catches it with his foot.

I don't have anywhere to go. The foyer leads to the elevator, and he'll be on my heels before the doors even open. The window is locked—not to mention I'm fuck-knows how many stories up, and since I can't fly, it wouldn't be a viable option anyway. I can sense the guys tugging on our bonds, frantically trying to reach out to me, but I can't afford to spare even a second of my attention right now.

"You're cornered, Fallon."

Turning, I face him with my shoulders straight and chest heaving. "You're going to have to kill me. I'll never go with you willingly."

"The guys—"

"The guys will survive."

Even as I say it, my heart's already breaking. We came so close to getting our happily ever after, but I should've known better. Those aren't meant for a girl like me.

"I don't want to kill you. They want you alive. This is your last chance."

"Fuck you, Roland."

"So be it."

He throws the knife with a form I'd be impressed with if it wasn't aimed at me. It flies through the air, and despite my agility, I'm not fast enough. It plunges into the side of my abdomen, sending fiery pain through my body that makes me stumble back.

"Motherfucker!" I cry out, watching red bleed through my stark white shirt.

Using my distraction to his advantage, his meaty fist plows into my face, sending me tumbling backward to the ground. My head hits the tile of the entryway, and for a second, everything goes black. I fight through the pain, knowing I can't give in to the darkness. I'm staring up at the ceiling with a knife protruding from my belly, blood dribbling down my chin from my mouth and my head pounding. Everything fucking hurts, and I can feel the first tear roll down the side of my face. Roland appears above me, his form becoming distorted as the world seems to tilt. My stomach pitches.

Taking deep breaths in and exhaling, I try to get the room to stop spinning. When I'm finally able to focus, it gives me a little satisfaction to see the big beta winded, his hand clasping his side with blood dripping through his fingers. At least he's not getting off completely unscathed.

"I'm sorry, Fallon," he says before he leans down, jabbing the needle into my neck with his free hand.

Oh, how the tides have turned. I don't even struggle. It's no use. I have to hope that wherever he's taking me, I'll get an opportunity to escape. I'll bide my time, no matter how long it takes or what I have to endure, then I'll run. Just like I did all those years ago. Except this time, I have something to run back to.

Thoughts of my guys play through my mind as the world begins to dim. I'll get back to them. I have to. For their sakes and mine.

Chapter 29

I thought we'd experienced the worst pain imaginable when we were forced to walk away from the girl we loved ten years ago.

I was wrong.

Knowing she's out there somewhere, in the hands of ruthless, despicable men, is a hundred times worse. My thoughts become increasingly dark as all the gruesome possibilities play through my mind. The only solace I can find is that she's still alive. The bond gives me that much. After the intense pain we experienced, it's been suspiciously silent. Like a door has been shut and we're locked out.

It's been hours—I stopped keeping track at hour six—and the wait is killing me inside. The bus door opens, and Wren steps up with Chance right behind him. The beta runs his hands down his face. He's been on the phone, planning and pacing outside since we found Sebastian, doing everything he can, calling in every favor, in order to save our girl. I'm not sure how to take the grim look plastered on his face.

"How's Sebastian?" Anson asks Wren.

"He had a minor concussion and some minor scrapes and bruises. They hooked him up to an IV, and he'll need some rest, but other than that, he should be fine." Wren walks over and practically crashes into one of the chairs. "He told me I should come back here and be with you guys."

The tension in the room is thick, and helplessness sits heavy in my gut. I feel like I need to be doing something, anything to find my omega, but what could I possibly do? I'm a fucking *musician*. Not an operative like Chance or a hired killer like my girl. I sing pretty lyrics and wear fucking bow ties. Fuck, I'm pathetic.

Wren turns to Chance. "Did you get a hold of your contacts?"

He nods. "They've agreed to pool all available resources and have them focus on our case. I'm expecting another call back shortly."

"That's fucking good news," Anson declares, then pauses. "So, why do you look gutted?"

Chance straightens, putting him at damn near my height. "By allowing Fallon to get taken, I've put the organization in jeopardy. They don't look too kindly on that. We have a set of rules that are to be followed, and I... Fuck, I broke damn near every one. There will be *repercussions.*"

I share a look with my brothers. "Repercussions? Like what?"

"By now, you've probably ascertained that the organization I work for isn't exactly a public entity. We operate in the shadows, under the radar, with the knowledge that every project we take could be our last. If we're captured, we're on our own. There's no one to save you if shit hits the fan. Imagine what an organization like that would do to someone who broke the rules and put their main objective in jeopardy." He sighs, one born of defeat. It's so unlike the snarky beta we've only just begun to know that a spike of alarm runs through me.

"The second I got involved with Fallon personally, it divided my focus. I wasn't able to protect her like I should have been able to, and my weakness is what got us into this mess."

"Chance, if anyone is to blame, it would be us. We hired a man we thought was one of the best, and he became a friend, only to find out too late that he's been kidnapping innocent women behind our backs for years. We served Fallon up on a silver platter, for fuck's sake! How naive can we fucking be?" Wren's head drops to his hands.

I throw back the whiskey I've been swirling around inside my glass. "Pointing the blame isn't doing any of us any good right now. We need to come up with a plan to get her back."

"The organization believes she's been taken for a live auction organized by Raphael Montoya."

"Auction?" Anson's horrified voice cracks. "They're going to sell her off?"

Chance nods. "It's only a matter of time until they confirm she's been bonded."

"And when they find the marks?" I ask, knowing I'm not going to like the answer.

The beta's serious eyes collide with mine. "They'll come after you guys. With you out of the way, your bonds won't be an issue."

They'll kill us to sever the bonds. *Fucking hell. This just keeps getting worse.*

Chance's phone rings, and we all sit up a little straighter, preparing ourselves for an update.

"Donovan," he says. "Is she—"

My breath catches, anxiety flooding through me as I wait for him to finish that thought. His eyes dart between all of ours, and I'm not sure how to read his expression. I wish like hell I had bonded him so I would know what he's feeling right now. Maybe it would give me some sort of idea just how bad the news is. Emotions are too high right now, and the shadow of his bond within the pack is overwhelmed by that pressure.

"I'm not sure it's a good idea they—" He closes his eyes and exhales harshly. "Yes, I realize I don't have a say in this. I just think that it would be particularly cruel to—"

Fuck, whatever this is, it's worse than I thought.

"Fine. Send me the link. I'll see if they have a laptop we can use." He listens for another minute, with all of us waiting in anticipation. "Got it. I'll wait for another update."

He hangs up the phone, staring at it like it's poison in his hands.

"Chance," Anson murmurs, desperation clear in his voice.

"They've taken her to an undisclosed location. Her auction link went live roughly thirty minutes ago."

"Auction link?" I ask.

"Bidders are given links to the auctions. The link directs them to a live video feed of each omega up for bid. The feed lets them observe the girls, using it as a way to confirm their interest in a particular auction."

My mind plays his words through my head over and over again in an effort to comprehend the level of depravity involved with this operation.

"You're telling me we have access to a live video feed of Fallon...right now?"

He nods. "As soon as I receive the link, yes."

"How is that cruel?" Wren asks, bringing the conversation back to that nausea-inducing word.

Chance walks over to the kitchen, grabs a glass, and pours way more than two fingers of whiskey before slamming it back. He pours another, walks back over, and sits on the arm of the sofa.

"She's bound, naked, and apparently injured. The auction link promotes her as a special *high value auction*, perfect for an alpha or pack of alphas with..." He clears his throat. "...*rougher tastes* because she likes to fight back."

Horror floods through me. "You're telling me your organization has already been watching her?"

He nods. "I'm not sure this is something you guys need to see. That image..." He closes his eyes, nostrils flaring. "That image is not something you'll want to live with. Especially if the worst happens."

My heart is in my throat when I turn toward my brothers. We've been together long enough that I can read them without words. There's no way we're going to let her suffer through this alone. Even if the image is burned into our retinas, we'll be with her every step of the way until we can get her the hell out of there.

"We need to see her." My voice is hoarse, dread rushing through my veins.

Chance's phone dings with a notification. He looks up at me, blue eyes swimming in regret. "Grab a laptop."

Wren rushes over to the bunks, riffling through his shit until he comes back with his computer. He places it on the small dining table, opens it up, and enters his passcode. Chance sits down beside him while Anson and I move to stand behind them. My hands are fisted in the pockets of my sweatpants, my jaw tight, as I wait to see my girl.

Chance's fingers fly across the keyboard, and a website pops up, requiring a username and password. He types in both, hits enter, and we wait while a loading window appears on the screen.

When the screen flashes and the image comes into focus, I think I'm going to get sick. Fallon is laid out on a bed, cushioned by a blood-red silk comforter. Her hair is neatly brushed and positioned around her head. Her breasts are bare, legs parted enough that the viewer is given a perfect view of her shaved pussy. Her hands and feet are bound to the posts, allowing her very little slack to move. Not that she's even trying. No, she's still passed out cold. An inset window gives us a close-up glimpse of her face, and unbridled fury races through me. Her lip is split, and the entire side of her jaw is bruised. When my eyes move back over to the main feed, scanning the rest of her naked body, I see the bright red, jagged wound on her belly and have to close my eyes to get myself under control.

"She was fucking *stabbed*?" Anson whispers in horror.

"It looks that way. They've stitched her up, but it was a rush job because it's still bleeding."

I force my eyes to open. Force them to take in my omega, lying helpless and alone on a strange bed, while vile men view the feed of her unconscious and bleeding. How fucked up is this world?

"What do we do?" I rasp.

"My team is trying to trace the video feed. It's randomly bouncing between IP addresses, so it's damn near impossible, but we've got our best working on it. If they can track the location, I've asked that I be allowed to be part of the team that attempts the extraction. I'm waiting to see if they approve that request."

"We're going with you," Anson declares.

"You know as well as I do that you're not trained for this. Fallon needs you alive, *here*, waiting for her to return in case…"

"In case you don't make it." Wren looks over at the beta beside him.

Chance nods. "I'll get her out of there. I promise you."

I feel her before I see her come awake on screen. Pain floods through me, but I stifle my groan.

"Fuck. She's starting to wake up." Anson plants his hands on the back of the bench seat, steadying himself.

If he's feeling what I am, it's a wonder we're still on our feet at all. We watch, waiting for her to open her eyes. When she does, her low whine nearly sends me to my knees.

"Fuck, sunshine," I murmur.

Every instinct I have demands I fix this, that I save the woman who owns my soul, but I can't. She's locked away somewhere I can't reach her, and I've never felt so worthless in my entire life.

As if on cue, the door to her tiny room opens, the sound of footsteps loud in the otherwise silent room. It isn't until his face appears in the corner when he skirts around her bed that I recognize him. Raphael Montoya. The sleazy son of a bitch.

"You're finally awake, Ms. Parker."

I watch with unbridled fury as he steps up to the side of the bed, staring down at my woman. His eyes lazily trail over her exposed body, and I swear on everything I have that if I ever see him again, I'll fucking kill him.

Chapter 30

J esus Christ. I feel like I've been hit by a truck. No, worse than that. Like I've been flung off a cliff and tumbled down head over foot, hitting every rock and branch along the way until I landed in the hot summer sun without water for days. My head is pounding out a rhythm like I'm backstage at the band's show, only the room is quiet. My side is throbbing, and if I move even the slightest bit, white-hot fire rushes over me. I'm pretty sure I have a fever, or my head must have hit the floor a little harder than I thought because everything seems a little wonky.

"You're finally awake, Ms. Parker."

At the sound of a voice, my head tilts, and I immediately regret it. Everything begins to spin, and I'm forced to close my eyes while I slowly inhale, then exhale, praying I don't get sick. That would just be a cherry on an already shit-tastic sundae.

When I'm fairly certain my stomach is under control, my eyes open to find Raphael Montoya beside the bed I'm currently in. Glancing down, I realize I'm naked, spread out and bound to each bedpost, leaving me spread eagle and fully at his mercy. Anger and fear jockey for first position, and I find myself praying anger comes out on top.

"Mr. Montoya, to what do I owe the honor?" My voice is hoarse but steady, downplaying my complete misery right now.

"You, Ms. Parker, are a difficult woman to obtain. Roland is currently recovering from surgery for a punctured spleen. It seems that he sustained the injury in the fight...with *you*. Now, my most trusted man is in the hospital, which leaves me short handed."

Anger it is.

"Do you honestly expect me to apologize for stabbing that lying son of a bitch when I'm tied up to a fucking bed, with a knife wound of my own? Eye for an eye and all that."

I'd like to think I'm being brave in this moment, rather than falling apart, but more realistically, I'm being too fucking reckless for my own good.

Raphael's eyes narrow, then his fingers trail up from my toe, over my leg, and across my hip until they reach the wound in my side. He presses down...*hard*...until I scream in pain. I can't stop the flood of tears or the way my chest heaves. My stomach churns as the reality of my precarious situation becomes frighteningly clear. I'm usually the one with the upper hand. Having those tables turned is a hard fucking pill to swallow.

"You'll be fucking grateful that I kept you alive, allowing my doctor to stitch you up. Omegas like you need a firm hand and a powerful alpha to bring them to heel. Lucky for you, that's just what we've got planned."

I'm not stupid. The man runs a trafficking ring, which means I'm being sold to the highest bidder. It's humiliating but a welcome reprieve considering it will hopefully provide me with the chance to escape.

Bide your time, Fallon. Wait for the perfect moment. Then run!

Softening his touch, he plays his hand up my rib cage until his palm cups my breast, squeezing it gently.

"Unless, of course, I decide to keep you for myself, though that would disappoint all of the interested parties watching this feed right now."

His words have my heart pounding for multiple reasons. The thought of being his is enough to make any woman want to chew off her own arm to get away. Then there's the tiny mention of parties watching me.

"Feed?" I ask innocently.

He turns, pointing to the cameras in the room—one beside the bed and another pointing down from the ceiling at the end of the bed.

"Say hello to your lovely viewers."

An *online* auction. This is somehow so much worse. There's no way for me to know who's bidding or who wins the auction until they arrive to claim their purchase. I'll be going in blind, and there's nothing I can do about that.

But if I'm here, that means that the other omegas must be somewhere nearby. If I can figure out a way to get out of this bed, maybe I can save us all.

That's assuming I don't pass out the second I stand up.

"You're drawing quite the crowd, I must say. Feral Lyrics' Mystery Girl up for auction!"

"They've already claimed me, you know. I'll never belong to anyone else. I'll always be theirs."

"Oh, we have ways of getting around that. I have an associate that has recently acquired a new pharmaceutical breakthrough that miraculously dissolves an omega's bonds, and I eagerly agreed to let you be one of the first to try it out. Before your buyer arrives to claim you, you'll watch your connections to those alphas disappear. Just increases your price, is all, considering you require extra maintenance to prepare you for delivery."

My soul roars at the possibility of our bonds being removed as if they were no more than an unwanted parasite. This alpha truly believes omegas are nothing but a piece of furniture or some appliance—a possession rather than a human being with her own wants and dreams. Fucking selfish. He's the reason I do what I do, fighting for those who aren't able to fight for themselves in a system that gives an advantage to those who are the strongest.

"What? Nothing to say to that? Did I finally render Fallon Parker speechless?" he goads as he leans down over me, placing one hand on either side of my head.

His eyes track my features, his face mere inches above mine.

"You really are gorgeous, you know," he whispers quietly, so low the cameras can't hear him. "It's a shame to let that beauty go to waste without getting a taste of it myself first."

His head descends, eyes on my lips as he goes in for a kiss.

Doesn't this asshole ever learn? My arms and legs may be bound, but my head is not. With all the strength I can muster, I fling my head forward, smashing my forehead into his nose. He screams, the sound of bones breaking followed by blood gushing...everywhere. He stumbles back, both hands holding his nose.

"You fucking bitch!" he growls, though it's muffled by his fingers. "You'll pay for that."

I spit out his blood, unable to wipe it from my eyes. I probably look psychotic, eyes wild and glassy, a manic smile curving my lips, covered in his blood, but I'm glorying in the fact that I mussed up his fucking face.

"If I ever see your face again, I'll fucking kill you," I growl, fully aware that it's a slight exaggeration considering I'm tied up and at his mercy. But from the expression he's wearing, I know he understands that won't always be the case. One day, I'll be free, and I *will* hunt him down and put an end to his brand of evil once and for all.

His eyes narrow. "I'm adding a new caveat to your sale. I get to be witness to all sexual acts within the first thirty days of your purchase. I'm going to enjoy watching them break you, Fallon. Enjoy watching them fuck you raw until you bleed, then fuck you some more. I'll enjoy watching as they stuff every hole you have so fucking full you're screaming in pain. By the time they're through with you, you'll pray for death because only then will your suffering cease. Think of *that* while you lie here waiting for what the future has in store for an omega who didn't know her place. You will soon enough."

He stalks out, leaving me in the quiet of the room. I want to break down so badly, to give in to the pain and suffering I'm experiencing, but I refuse. Not while unseen eyes are watching. No, there will come a moment when I'll allow myself that freedom. But not here. Not now.

Instead, I think of Anson's warm hugs. Wren's steady comfort. Felix's naughty mouth. Chance's confidence and snark. Let my mind skim over all the good times throughout this last week, all the moments that melted the ice around my heart until I was a puddle of mush in their arms. Looking back at it now, I can't believe I wasted ten years on all the hate and anger. So much time we'll never get back.

Not that things are looking all that bright for our future at the moment. Part of me wonders if I should've let them go. Told them that I no longer felt anything for them so they could start over with someone new. Why did I decide dragging them into my hell was a smart plan? My life isn't all sunshine and roses. I wouldn't know the first thing about building a nest or what to do with a baby or...

Thoughts of the guys' words from a few days ago hit me. They wanted to start a family. They wanted to see me round with our child. They wanted the picture-perfect pack. Could I have given them that? Is that what I would've wanted? It's so far off anything I ever saw for myself that I can't even picture it clearly.

My mind circles back to our future, if we ever manage to have one. Will I be able to pick up where we left off? Slide into the role of happy omega with a wealthy pack? Let them pamper and coddle me? Lie around rearranging pillows and picking up after my three alphas and my beta? Carry their babies? That's what an omega's role is, right? They sure as hell aren't hired killers, that's for damn sure.

My heart pangs. For them, I'd try. I'd give up everything I was if it meant being theirs forever. Now, I just have to hope that I can find my way back to them, that they'll accept me with open arms, even if I'm half the woman I once was.

Now that Raphael is gone, I finally take note of the rush of worry and anger in the bond. I try to block my anguish, my pain, my uncertainty, but it's useless. As if sensing my turmoil, they each send an almost overwhelming amount of love back, and suddenly I don't feel quite so alone.

A single tear slips out, rolling down my temple. That's all I'll allow myself for now.

Chapter 31

Leaning against the outside of the bus, I revel in the sounds of the night surrounding me. Watching that screen, seeing my girl helplessly lying there in pain is simply more than I can bear. The guys stoically stood by, watching her scream when the jackass dug his fingers into her wound. Watching her smash that smug fucker's face in. Watching the slow rise and fall of her chest as she awaits her fate. Watching the single tear trail down her face before she packaged it all back up, burying it deep inside so she could continue to be strong.

Fuck, I'm not sure how they can watch her hour after hour. I had to step away to clear my head of all the voices demanding pain and suffering for every single person aiding in Raphael's fucking plot, so I don't risk losing my mind completely.

I've never known a woman as strong as Fallon. One who would bite back at those who try to pin her down even when she's suffering on the inside. She's a fighter, and I'm so fucking proud of her.

My phone rings, and for a second, I consider not answering it because my mind is too fucked up right now to try to fake general niceties. But this is probably an update on her situation, and I'm not selfish enough to risk missing it.

Pulling out my phone, I hit the button. "Donovan."

"We got it. We've confirmed the location of the warehouse where they're housing the omegas for the auction. I've got a helicopter on its way to you right now. Be ready. It's time to get your girl back."

The line goes dead. Everything inside me has gone still while I begin to compartmentalize all of the feelings consuming me. I have to if I want any hope of being successful, and I will be. I'll make sure she gets home, no matter what.

Straightening, I run my hands over my face and prepare to tell the guys the news. My mind starts running through scenarios as I open the bus door and climb the steps into the living room. The guys are gathered around the table, where the screen still shows Fallon covered in Raphael's blood in the middle of the bed. She hasn't moved, not that she really can, and I know—without a doubt—she's shoring up her energy in case an opportunity presents itself.

My girl is so fucking smart. Have I mentioned she's a badass?

"How's she doing?" I ask, not that I can't see it for myself, but I have no idea if I missed anything while I was outside.

"No change," Felix replies, sitting back against the bench and stretching his arms over his head.

"I've got news."

All three of them turn, worry and a hint of hope staring back at me.

"Tell me they've found her," Anson pleads, his desperation a living thing in our bond.

"They've located the warehouse where all the omegas are being kept. A chopper is on its way to pick me up. I'm going after her."

Wren sits forward. "Can't we come with you? We need to be there when—"

I shake my head. "My organization's involvement in special operations is kept under strict lock and key. It's associates only. I'll let you guys know as soon as I have her, I promise."

Anson stands, stepping toward me. "We trust you. Just…" He clears his throat. "Just tell her that we love her and make sure you both make it back safely, yeah?"

I nod, afraid my voice isn't steady enough to reply. This will be the first mission I've been a part of where I have a reason to make it back safely. I refuse to let them down.

I glance at the screen, taking in our girl. She's so fucking small on that giant bed. I wish I could tell her that I was coming for her. Give her that little bit of hope to cling to while she endures the remaining hours alone.

The sound of the helicopter's blades is loud, even inside the bus.

"Guess it's go time," I whisper.

Felix holds out his hand, and I clasp mine around his. "Be safe, you hear me? We want you both back in one piece."

Wren steps forward. "Get in, get her out, then get the hell out of there. No playing hero, or I'll let her beat your ass when she gets back."

I smile for the first time in hours. "Don't worry. She's my only priority."

He gives me a quick bro hug before I turn to Anson. My alpha.

"I can't lose my omega and my beta," he says, voice low and husky. "So make sure you both come home to me, okay?"

Fuck. Even though our connection is new and born of a budding friendship and respect, I can sense the responsibility he feels for Fallon, and for me, and it blows me away. I never knew something like this could exist in a bond, and now I can only hope that I get to watch it grow for years to come.

"You got it. The next time you see me, I'll have our girl, and we'll live happily ever fucking after."

"Hell yes, we will," Felix agrees.

I make my way toward the door. With one last look over my shoulder, I head out into the muggy Atlanta night. The helicopter is waiting in the middle of the vacant lot, its blades still spinning. Rushing over, I duck, moving toward the cabin. A hand reaches out to help me up, and within seconds, we're airborne.

"Glad they allowed you to tag along," Nixon shouts over the sound of the engine.

When I turn to the man beside me, I can't see his face through the mask, but he can see mine.

"We have to get her out of there, Nixon. No matter what. You hear me?"

For a few beats, he's quiet, then he nods.

"You have my word, brother."

I know so few people within the organization, but Nixon and I have worked side by side on numerous projects. He's one of a handful of people I'd trust with my life. And Fallon's. I hold out my hand, and he takes mine, a show of solidarity.

"If I help save her, think the alphas would let me join the pack, too? She's a hot little—"

Releasing his hand, I punch him hard in the arm, and his laughter roars over the sounds around us.

"You're lucky I like you, Nixon."

"I'm pretty sure she and I have a thing. I'll have to ask her."

"You fucking try it, and I'll shank you, got it?"

He chuckles, but it dies off as he briefs me on the intel they've received, preparing me for what might lie ahead. By the time the helicopter lands just shy of two hours later, Nixon is all business. He tosses me a bag with my gear. Moving out from the helicopter's blades, I suit up. Black tactical pants. Black long-sleeved shirt with a black tactical vest. I set the mask aside, filling up the numerous pockets with knives and extra clips, strapping holsters on my thighs and slipping guns into all of them.

"You ready?" Nixon asks, with a team of twelve behind him.

"Yeah. You running point?"

He nods. "Our goal is to clear out everyone in your path. Your sole objective is Fallon. We are not to hunt for Raphael Montoya, but if an opportunity presents itself, we are to bring him in *alive.*"

He says that last bit with added emphasis, knowing damn well I want to kill that motherfucker.

"Ten-four." Then another thought occurs to me. "What about Roland Hayes?"

"We've been alerted that Roland is onsite in the medical ward. Should you find yourself along that corridor, he can be handled as you see fit."

My eyes narrow. *Fucking right he'll be handled...by my knife in his gut.*

I slip the mask on, cracking my neck to each side, gearing up for the fight of my life.

"Alright, team. Four SUVs. Split up. Each one will take an entrance. North, East, and West teams will enter first. Camera feeds should be down by then. Know your routes and stay together. First priority is clearing out as many unfriendlies as possible. South team will hit last. This team will consist of myself, Chance, and Diego. Our primary objective will be the omegas. When your section is clear, secure any

P.O.W.s and call in for transport. Then make your way to the south entrance and provide back-up as necessary. Any questions?"

The men are silent.

"I don't need to remind you that Chance's omega is in there, and she's injured. We don't allow our projects to be harmed during their time with us, so this mission is especially important."

"We've got your back, Chance."

"We'll get her out of there, brother."

Brief words of support flood the night, and I'm not ashamed to admit I get a little choked up. In the bond, I feel Anson providing extra reassurance, so much fucking love for a man who always thought he wasn't worthy of it. It's damn near enough to bring me to tears.

"Now, let's head out. Everyone meet back here by twenty-two-hundred hours, got it?"

With everyone's shouts, we load up and take off for the warehouse. It's in a mostly abandoned industrial section of Houston, full of empty buildings that are on the verge of collapse. There's a spattering of businesses that are still operational, but for the most part, this part of the city is dead.

Nixon gives the green light to the first three teams while we're parked a block away, waiting for the all-clear. It feels like hours go by, but in reality, it's less than ten minutes until we receive the signal.

In seconds, we're at the south entrance to the warehouse, blasting through the door and making our way to the section of the building where our source tells us the omegas are being held. You can hear the rapid gunfire randomly breaking out in other portions of the building, but my sole focus is finding my woman.

There are men in gear similar to ours, and we happily take them out. By their fumbling efforts, it's obvious they're scrambling to secure their assets. Every once in a while, we'll come across a staff member in scrubs. They're given the option to lead us to the omegas, and if they refuse, they meet the same fate as the others. We have no sympathy for anyone who supports a man like Raphael Montoya.

Rounding the corner, I put a bullet into three heads before I start to get frustrated. This place is a giant maze of corridors, and we've yet to find the girls.

"Where the fuck are they?" I growl just as another woman in scrubs rounds the corner and runs straight into my chest.

Gripping her by the shirt, I shake her. "Where are they holding the omegas?"

Fear pours off her in waves as she points the way she came. "Down that hall, then take a right."

I pass her off to Diego to handle, but right before I take off running, I stop.

"What about the medical wing?"

"From the omega hall, it's a right and two lefts."

Nodding, I rush forward, intent on reaching Fallon. I'm in a blind panic, knowing I'm this close and needing to make sure she's okay. Taking the last right, a loud blast has my ears ringing. A door halfway down the hall flings open, and I know in my heart that it has to be Fallon's room.

Sliding to a stop in front of the mangled door, my breath catches in my throat.

"Take another step closer, and I swear to fucking Christ I'll pull the trigger."

Chapter 32

Fallon

I'm not sure how long I've laid in this bed, covered in Raphael's blood, needing to pee so badly that I finally just pissed myself rather than risk a serious UTI—as if I don't have a million other more pressing concerns rushing through my head right now. Like the fact that I'm burning up with a fever, probably from an infection in the knife wound. The least they could've done was provide some antibiotics before handing me over to my new owners, for fuck's sake. What kind of show are they running here?

A nurse finally comes in with a warm bucket of water and fresh sheets. I'm assuming she's here to finally clean me up, but the logistics appear to be sorely lacking.

"I'm going to get you all washed up, okay? I'm not here to hurt you." Her voice is whisper-soft, gentle, and most decidedly getting on my damn nerves, but I don't give that away.

I nod, letting her think I'll be a good little omega who will do exactly as she asks...at least until she releases one of these fucking bindings and I can strangle her with it. Unfortunately, they must've warned her about me because she injects me with something that turns my muscles to mush.

"Don't worry. It's a mild muscle relaxer. It should wear off in ten minutes. Just enough time to get you out of this mess."

She unties one of the bindings, dragging it over to the other wrist, then she does the same thing with my foot. The movement causes a piercing pain in my abdomen that makes me cry out. She softly whispers soothing words while she does something beneath me. When she comes to the other side of the bed, she uses the warm water to wash off my face and clean my hair as best she can with what she's been given.

"Why do you help them?" I slur, both the pain and the medication making it hard to talk.

"Because I have no choice. It's do what they say, or they threaten my entire family. I'm not an omega. They can't sell me off for money, but they can force me to do their dirty work."

Her brow is furrowed, anger clear in her voice, and I suddenly feel just a little bit of sympathy for the woman. By the time she's done, she switches the bindings to the opposite side one by one—giving me a brief warning this time before she rolls me over and once again shifts the bedding beneath me. She must be a wizard because she has the entire bedding set changed and the mess that was my face cleaned in just enough time that I start to regain a little bit of control in my limbs.

"There you go. I bet that feels better."

"It does, thank you."

I'm a little bit delirious, a whole lotta crazy, and barely lucid when I hear the first shots being fired. At first, I'm pretty sure I'm hallucinating the whole thing, but an eager sort of anticipation builds inside me as I watch her straighten, her face paling. For a brief moment, I sense

Chance in the bond, and I wonder if he's come to save me. But then more gunfire erupts, and I wonder if I imagined it in my pain-induced haze.

"What is that?" she whispers.

"Sounds like gunshots to me."

Her hand raises to her chest. "Gunshots?"

"Yes. If you untie me, I'll make sure to get us both out of here alive."

"I can't—"

"You can. Help me, and I'll help you. I promise."

She studies me, then another round of rapid gunfire rings through the hall, a lot closer this time. Making a split-second decision, she unties all the bindings, helping me to my feet as I bite my lip hard enough to reopen the split and draw blood. My side is on fire, and I'm significantly unsteady, swaying until she steadies me beneath one arm.

"Can you walk?" she whispers, like the gunmen can hear her from here.

"Let's give it a shot."

She slowly steps away, her hands at the ready. I shuffle more than walk, but I just barely manage to stay up on my own. Looking over at her, then around the room, I don't see anything I can use to protect us.

"Do you have a weapon or anything on you I can use as one?"

She regards me carefully for a second before she pulls out a small utility knife.

"That'll work."

She hands it over, and I test it in my hand. A gun would be better, but it'll do. Carefully hiding it in my grip, with the blade resting flat against my arm, I'm as ready as I'm going to be. In my current condition, I've got a couple good swipes in me. Anything beyond that, and we're screwed.

"Go over to that corner and duck down. You'll be safest there."

She does as she's told, curling herself into a ball in the far corner of the room. Just as she's out of the way, the sound of the lock disengaging hits my ears, then the door swings open. Raphael Montoya stands there with his hair sticking up in all directions, his eyes wild.

"Who the fuck let you loose?" he growls, stepping toward me while pulling a nine millimeter from behind his back. With a steady hand, he aims it at my head.

"You should know by now, Raphael, that you should never, *ever* underestimate me."

I'm about seventy-five percent certain I didn't even slur that time.

His eyes narrow, and with one hand, he shuts the door behind him. From watching him leave the first time, I know they lock and unlock with a key. I'm not sure if my new friend in the corner has one, or if someone let her in, but I do know Raphael has one, and it's about to be mine.

"Get the fuck over here, little omega." His alpha bark rings through my body, and even though I desperately try to deny its call, my feet start to move in his direction. "You are nothing, do you hear me? *Nothing* without an alpha. And I'm about to make you mine."

He pulls out a needle and removes the cap with his teeth. Panic tries to crawl up my spine, but I refuse to let it influence me. When I'm a foot away, a smirk tilts his lips.

"See? You can't even deny a direct order. You are ours to do with as we see fit. Just accept that, and things will be so much better for you."

Tilting my chin up and making sure my eyes are wide in order to keep his attention on my face, I shift the knife in my hand. Taking a deep breath, I exhale, preparing to put all my strength into my one chance at getting out of this alive.

"Never!" I shout, letting my hand swing through the air, aiming for the hand with the gun.

It slices through his wrist, deep into the tendons. With a roar of pain and fury, his hand instinctively releases its grip on the weapon, and it slides across the floor. He charges at me, backing me up until I'm slammed against the wall. The wind is knocked out of me, and I'm pretty sure I've got blood pouring out of my freshly opened wound, but I don't give a damn. With everything I've got left, I grab his wrist with both hands when he tries to jab the needle into my arm. I'm weak, and he's an alpha, so I know I'm in a losing battle, but then a small voice shouts my name.

"Fallon!"

When I glance over, the woman has Raphael's gun. She tosses it to me, and I release one hand just in time to catch the gun around the barrel. I feel the needle prick into my shoulder, but it doesn't stop me from pushing Raphael back, flipping the gun around in my hand, and aiming it at the delusional alpha's head.

The needle falls to the floor with a clink, but I've got more pressing problems. Namely, the man in front of me who's looking a little shell shocked.

"Now, who needs to learn their place?" I snap.

Raphael holds up his hands in a show of surrender. He's such a fucking pussy now that the *little omega* is armed and no longer tied up. And he claims to be an alpha.

Pathetic.

"Fallon, we can work this out. I can let you walk out of here and right back into your alphas' arms. Just let me get a head start."

"You can *let* me?" I growl. "More like I can *make* you considering I'm the one with the goddamn gun. Now, give me the key."

"I can't do that."

"Do it, *now,* or I'll put a bullet through your knee."

My hands are shaking, but I'm hoping he doesn't notice. Guns are fucking heavy, and I'm barely coming off a muscle relaxer and hours of being tied to a bed with no food or water. Cut me some fucking slack.

"Fallon—"

I pull the trigger, and the bullet zips through the air, hitting him right in the thigh. *Close enough.* He wails, clutching his leg as blood pours from the hole.

"Key. Now."

One hand raises to his pocket, pulling out the material to show me it's empty. "I... I don't have it."

"You're lying!" I shoot his hand.

He cries out, stumbling forward a few steps.

I sigh. When you want something done right, you might as well do it yourself.

"Fuck it."

Stalking over to him, I spin the blubbering man around by the shoulders, using him as a shield for whatever lies in wait in the hallway. I'm getting a little lightheaded, probably from the blood loss and the bass drum pounding inside my skull, but I know if I don't get out of here soon, I'll lose any chance I have of getting free.

Taking aim, I lift the gun and pray to all that is holy as I pull the trigger. The bullet hits the lock, shattering through the metal. The door swings open, and before I can tell Raphael to fucking start walking, a figure in full tactical gear appears in the doorway with an assault rifle aimed at my head. I'm pretty sure at some point, there are two, either that or I'm starting to see double.

"Take another step closer, and I swear to fucking Christ I'll pull the trigger." I lift the gun and aim it right at Raphael's head.

"Fucking hell, pussycat. You're a sight for sore eyes."

The voice strikes a nerve, making my hand begin to shake in earnest. "Chance?"

He whips his mask off, blond hair falling down around his flushed face, and I've never seen anything as sexy in my entire life.

"Fallon, I...."

His eyes are glassy, and so help me, if he loses it right now, I'll collapse in a heap at Raphael's feet. I'm running on pure adrenaline, so I do the only thing I can think of.

"Bout time you showed up. I thought I was going to have to do all the heavy lifting by myself."

His eyes spark, that wicked smirk twisting his lips. "Decided I couldn't let you have all the fun."

"Fun. Right. Then you might as well come take this fucker off my hands..."

Before he can move, another man appears beside him, gun aimed and at the ready. He clears his throat.

"Ms. Parker, another mess for us to clean up, I see."

Chance growls. "Nixon, do *not* stare at my girl's naked body, or I'll fucking dick punch you."

Nixon just laughs, and I can't help but grin in response.

"You know me. All in a day's work." I feel Raphael twitch and get a little worried he's going to try something stupid, so I hit him upside the head with the butt of the gun, and he collapses at *my* feet. "And considering I caught this one on my own, I feel like someone owes me hazard pay or something."

The guy—Nixon, if I remember correctly—laughs out loud. "I'll make sure to put it in the report with a personal recommendation."

"Thank you."

"You're welcome."

"Now, can one of you come grab this asshole since he kind of landed on my feet and I don't have the energy to kick him off?"

"Fuck! Sorry, pussycat. Seeing you all GI Jane has me a little hot under the collar."

"Well, keep it in your pants, beta boy. I'm not in my best form right now."

Nixon walks forward, chuckling, as he pulls out a pair of handcuffs. Grabbing Raphael by the collar, he tugs him off to the side. Before he can do anything more, Chance walks up, takes aim, and shoots him right in the dick.

Nixon looks up at his partner. "Really?"

The beta just shrugs. "I feel better now. Proceed."

The other man shakes his head, making quick work of securing the monster who will no longer hurt innocent omegas.

Chance is suddenly in front of me, his eyes trailing down my naked body. When he reaches the knife wound, his worry whips through the bond.

"Fuck. We need to get you to the hospital."

"You're right. But first, I need you to hold me."

"Oh, love."

He steps forward, gently wrapping his arms around me as he pulls me into his chest. He smells like fresh laundry and gun smoke, and the combination immediately soothes my nerves. Everything is going to be okay because he's here.

"You came for me."

"I'll always come for you."

I snort. "I read that in a book once. The girl was too injured to point out the joke."

"I've got something pointing out, but it's definitely not a joke."

I laugh, burying my face into his chest to hide my wince of pain. I can feel my emotions bubbling to the surface, but I fight them back.

Not yet. Soon.

"Um. Ms. Parker?"

"Yes?"

"What are we doing with her?"

Nixon points to the woman who helped me.

"Make sure she and her family are safe and taken care of. Can you do that for me?"

"You've got it." He glances at Chance. "Donovan, you gonna ask her if I can join—"

"Fuck no. Like I said, get your own fucking omega. This badass is mine."

I'm grinning when Chance gently slips his arm around my shoulders, starting to guide me out of the room. My toe kicks something, and I look down to see the syringe Raphael had jabbed into my shoulder. Suddenly, I think I'm going to be sick.

"Chance, wait."

He looks down at me, concern furrowing his brow.

"What is it, honey?"

"My bonds. He injected me with something he said would dissolve them."

Pain shoots through me, having nothing to do with the stab wound. He walks over, picking up the syringe and studying it before he turns back to me with a smile.

"You mean he *tried* to inject you with something. Look."

He brings it over, and I see the liquid still sloshing around inside the plastic.

"You mean—"

"He never pushed the plunger. Your bonds are safe."

He drops the syringe to the ground, crunching it under his boot. Tension eases from my body, and I sag against him. "Thank fuck for that."

"Come on, pussycat. Let's get you out of here." We head down the hall, but he suddenly stops.

"What is it?"

"You think you have enough juice left to make one last stop?" he asks, a mischievous twinkle in his eye.

"If it's got you grinning like the cat who got the cream, definitely."

"Don't say the word cream."

"Why?"

"Because then I get this image of you covered in our cream, and I just want to shove you against the wall and—"

My hand grips my side as I grit my teeth. "For fuck's sake, Chance, I'm fucking bleeding here, and you have my pussy clenching, which makes my abs tighten and—"

"Sorry, love. No more talk about railing you against the wall. My bad."

I groan, and he tugs me into him, tilting my face up to his with gunfire still echoing through the building. I barely hear it because I'm with my beta. I know he won't let anyone hurt me.

He stares down at me, looking almost angry.

"I've never said these words to anyone in my life, but I need to say them to you now in case I never get another chance." He swallows roughly, his hand cupping my jaw. "I love you, Fallon. Thank you for making me yours."

Tears fill my eyes as I look up at the man who has saved me in so many ways, all because he drugged and kidnapped me. The irony is not lost on me.

"I love you too."

His lips are gentle when they touch mine, the brief kiss full of shared love that passes through our bond. Anson wraps us both in his love from afar, his eagerness a living thing flowing between us.

"I need to call them, but we've got one last stop to make."

"Wait! What about the other omegas? I can't leave them here."

He points down the hall, opposite the way we were headed. I see other men in tactical gear leading shaken women out of door after door, their bodies wrapped in blankets.

"I'm going to fuck you so hard for that."

He grunts. "I thought we agreed no talking about fucking until you're healed?"

I shrug. "Meh. I changed my mind."

He rubs his dick through his pants. "God, I fucking love you, pussycat."

I laugh, letting my beta pull me down hall after hall. Despite my blood loss, despite the pain, I give him this because I can tell whatever it is, it's important. After this, we're getting the hell out of here. I require some stitches, a heavy pain med, and a cuddle pile. Stat.

Chapter 33

Watching the woman tend to Fallon was like needles poking into my skin. I longed to be the one there with her, not some fucking random woman with who knows what kind of agenda. Then we heard the gunfire and started praying that it was from Chance and his men. When we lost the feed, we were forced to sit and wait, worrying about what was happening and if they'd make it out alive.

Thanks to the bond, we knew Fallon was alive, and I was able to confirm Chance was okay too. Our omega was still in a lot of pain, but sensing her through our connection, having her respond with a rush of love, was enough to keep my instincts at bay. That is until I felt a jolt of panic from Chance right as Fallon's tether to me went dark.

That was over an hour ago, and I've been pacing the floor of the fucking bus ever since, waiting for word.

"He would've called if—"

"Don't even talk like that!" I bark. "She's fine. She has to be."

At least twice, I felt our connection wink out almost completely before it reappeared just as fast. It was enough to give me a heart attack.

"You're gonna wear out the fucking carpet, brother."

I whirl on Felix. "How can you sit there being all calm and shit? I'm losing my goddamn mind over here."

He lifts his glass, then tips back the last swallow of whiskey. Great. He's completely snockered. Should be interesting when we get the call that we can finally see our girl.

There's a loud whirring sound that has me freezing in my tracks. I recognize that noise.

"Helicopter's here!" I shout as I rush for the door, making my way outside and stopping when I see a man in all black, from head to toe, making his way over to me.

"You Anson?"

I nod.

"Where are the others?"

I glance over my shoulder and see Wren helping Felix out of the bus, holding him up with his arm under Felix's shoulder.

"You all are to come with me. Chance is waiting for you at the hospital."

My gut sinks, but I don't argue. We duck under the blades and follow him into the helicopter. In seconds, we're lifting off and flying through the night sky.

"Where are we going?"

"A hospital near Houston."

"Is Fallon okay?" Wren asks.

"I'll leave the details for Chance. The last update I had was that she was heading into surgery."

"Surgery," Felix whispers.

We don't ask any questions after that. My mind is a mess by the time we make it to Houston. We land on the helipad at the hospital and are quickly ushered down to a waiting room where we're told to wait.

I don't know how long we sit there before the double doors open, and Chance walks out looking ragged and exhausted. He's wearing the same tactical outfit as the other guy, but the vest is missing and he's sporting significantly less weaponry.

We jump to our feet, meeting him halfway.

"Chance, what the hell's going on?" I ask.

He runs his hands through his hair. "Turns out, shit was more serious than we expected. Fallon passed out on the way here. Her blood pressure dropped, and she went into septic shock. The infection was bad, and we almost lost her twice."

"Holy shit!" Wren gasps. "Is she okay?"

"She's stable. They had to take her in for surgery because they had to stop a bleed in her large intestine. With that fixed, and assuming they can get the infection under control, her prognosis is good."

"What took so fucking long? We've been worried sick."

"Fuck! I'm sorry. I was with her until they wheeled her into surgery, then I was on the phone calling in some favors. This is a specialized emergency room, vetted by...my employer. I had to get approval for you to come here just in case."

I glance at Wren and Felix, my stomach sinking at his unspoken words.

Just in case we lose her.

"When can we see her?"

"I can take you back now. She was just assigned a private room." He heads back through the double doors into the ICU. We follow him, and the steady beeping of the monitors and the smell of antiseptic has my nerves on edge.

He pauses just outside a door. When he glances at us, I can feel his tension and worry through the bond.

"I'm just going to warn you, she looks bad. Her face is swollen from where Roland punched her. Her lip is puffy, and she's got bruises pretty much everywhere."

We nod, steeling ourselves for whatever we're about to see. He pushes the door open to a room that's mostly dark, with only a couple small lights glowing softly. She's laying in the hospital bed, looking so fucking small. Chance was right. She's battered and bruised, appearing more fragile than I've ever seen her. I look away to watch the steady drip of the IV as it flows down the tube attached to her arm, trying to steady my emotions. I don't want my internal chaos to add to her distress.

"I want to kill him," I whisper, fury and helplessness rushing through me.

"If it's any consolation, she handled Raphael herself. Even while injured and practically dying, she fucking owned his ass and knocked him out with his own damn gun."

"Good!" Felix growls. "I just wish we had been there to see it."

"Is he dead?" Wren asks, his voice deeper than I've ever heard it.

"No. The Syndicate took him for questioning. But don't worry, he'll get what's coming to him. They don't play around. Once he's been drained of his usefulness, they'll make sure he's removed from this earth for good."

"The Syndicate?" I ask, watching Chance stiffen, his eyes going wide.

"Don't ever repeat that. Promise me."

I nod, nudging Felix's arm until I see both of my brothers do the same.

"Fuck. It's been a long ass day."

Walking over and pulling a chair up to the side of the bed, I sit, taking Fallon's tiny hand in mine.

"We're here, baby girl. You get your rest, and we'll see you when you wake up."

Wren walks up beside me and drops his hand to her leg, gently rubbing up and down along her knee.

"We love you, Fallon," he whispers, his voice breaking.

Felix walks over to the other side, grabbing her free hand. "We need you, sunshine. Stay with us, okay?"

Chance watches from the foot of the bed, exhaustion weighing his lids down.

"Hey, man. Go get some rest. We're all here now, and we'll let you know if anything happens."

He nods, running his hands down his face. "It's my fault," he whispers.

"What's your fault?"

"We would've left sooner, but I dragged her along for one last task. She said she was up for it, but I should've known better. I could've lost her. We *all* could've lost her."

"Fallon's tough as nails, Chance. If she thought she could make it, she would've tried...for any of us. Don't beat yourself up over that. You got her out of there and brought us here. Now we're all together, and that's how we're going to stay."

He nods, glancing at the small sofa behind him.

"I think I'm just going to crash there for a bit. I don't think I can be too far away from her right now."

"We've got you, brother. Go sleep."

With one last look at Fallon, he walks over to the ridiculously small sofa, lays down with his feet hanging over the edge, and is fast asleep within minutes.

My thumb brushes back and forth across the back of her limp hand, willing her to open her beautiful blue eyes so I can see them staring back at me again. I tell myself it will happen. I just have to be patient.

A week later, we're still gathered around Fallon's hospital bed, using her lap as a table while we play asshole. The hospital staff pretty much hates us, but once Chance threatened to have their funding pulled, their tune changed dramatically.

"Alright. Beat a pair of nines," Chance declares, setting his cards on Fallon's legs.

Wren smirks. "I'll see your nines and raise you two queens."

"I've got nothin'." I throw back a swallow of my soda since alcohol isn't exactly allowed here.

Felix whoops out loud, dropping two kings. "Take that, suckers! I'm president."

"How the hell did you get rid of all your cards that fast?" I slam the rest of mine down on the bed.

Wren's eyes narrow. "He totally fucking cheated."

"Check his pockets," Chance suggests. "Maybe he's hiding cards in there."

"Or you can check under my hand," Fallon rasps, her eyes suddenly open.

We all jump to our feet.

"Fuck, baby girl. You're awake." My hand grips the one closest to me, and having her fingers squeeze mine is the best thing I've ever felt in my life.

"Yeah, and giving away my secrets," Felix mutters, but he's looking down at her with so much fucking love in his eyes that it's hard not to get choked up.

He drops a lingering kiss on her forehead. Relief floods through the bond, quickly followed by intense love. Having our connection come alive again after being dark for a week is a welcome change, even with the hints of pain it includes. It means she's here, and she's safe.

"How are you feeling, sweetheart?" Wren asks.

"Like I was gutted by a knife." She attempts to move, then whines. "Fuck, that hurts."

"Here, let me help you."

I slide my arm behind her back, taking the brunt of her weight as I shift her up along the mattress. She settles back with a groan, cheeks flushed but eyes bright. Wren pours her a small cup of water, and she takes a few sips.

"Thank you. That's so much better." She sighs. "How long was I out?"

"Longest seven days of my life," Felix groans.

"Seven days? Holy shit." When her gaze turns to the beta, I sense his nervousness through the bond. "Alright. What gives? You're making me itchy."

His brows raise. "That sounds like a personal problem."

Her eyes narrow. "Chance, I swear to Christ—"

"I'm so fucking sorry, pussycat." His head drops, and his fists clench at his sides. "If I hadn't forced you to go after—"

"Okay, first of all, you didn't force me to do anything. Second of all, I wouldn't change a goddamn thing."

"You almost fucking died," he growls.

"But I *didn't*. I'm here. Because of *you*."

They're staring at each other with angry glares, but Chance has been pretty tight lipped about what he's been punishing himself for since we got here.

"What the hell did you two do, anyways?" I finally ask.

Fallon turns to me with a wicked smile on her face, and for a second, it takes my breath away. I'd gotten so used to seeing her face peaceful in sleep, that seeing her not only alive, but full of *life* makes me so goddamn happy.

"Roland was being kept in the medical wing, so Chance suggested we pay him a visit."

"Why should the fucker get an easy pass when Raphael is being tortured twenty-four-seven?" he mutters.

"Oh, he's being tortured? Can I watch?" Fallon asks eagerly.

"No," all of us say in unison, not even flinching at this new blood-thirsty side of her.

I'd be lying if I said there wasn't something incredibly alluring about the sparkle that lights up in her eyes when she goes into badass killer mode.

"Y'all are no fun."

Felix crosses his arms over his chest. "Sunshine, you were just abducted, stabbed, held hostage, and almost died. We're not letting you out of our sight for even a second."

She pouts. "Fine."

"Roland...?" I prompt.

"Oh. Right." She takes another sip of her water, trying to hide her grimace, but I see it, and it tears me in two. "I don't think he was very happy to see us."

"You should've seen the look on his face when we walked in. He was scared shitless."

Her eyes meet ours. "I'm sorry someone you trusted betrayed you. It was all for money. It wasn't anything personal if that makes a difference."

"I wanna hear what you did," Felix murmurs.

"Babe, I don't think..."

"No. We need to hear it, Fallon. Need to hear that he's no longer a threat to you anymore."

She sighs. "It's kinda gruesome if I'm honest, and I don't want you to look at me weird."

"For fuck's sake. Just spit it out. We're not going to look at you any differently. I swear on my life," Felix pledges.

"Fine. But don't say I didn't warn you."

She glances at Chance, who gives her a brief nod.

"I cut out his tongue for lying to you guys for years, then carved the word traitor into his forehead. All while he screamed in pain because no way was I going to give him the easy out and kill him first. He deserved to suffer for hurting god knows how many innocent souls." Her brow furrows, and her cheeks flush. I can sense her pain spiking through the bond. "I'll admit I was a little selfish when I had Chance cut off the hand that he punched me with so I could shove his fingers down his throat."

"Fuck." Felix looks a little green, but his hand is softly brushing through our girl's hair.

"She was spectacular," Chance whispers, and if he could have hearts in his eyes, he totally fucking would. As it is, I can see the erection straining against his shorts and feel his desire lighting up our bond, but I decide not to mention it. "In the end, she didn't have the strength to kill him, so I took care of that for us by slicing his throat. Good fucking riddance."

"Thank you," I whisper, earning a wide-eyed look of surprise. "We all wanted to kill him for what he did to you, but you did it so we wouldn't have to."

"I'd do anything for you guys," she whispers, her eyes going glassy.

"Right back at ya, babe." Felix drops another kiss on her forehead.

"What happened with your tour?"

"It's been postponed while they question everyone, from the label to the roadies, in order to filter out anyone who was on Raphael's payroll. It'll be months before we get back on the road."

"So what does that mean for us? Where will we go from here?"

I share a look with the guys and can't stop the huge smile from lighting up my face.

"It's a surprise. You focus on getting better, and as soon as you're released, we'll show you."

"You're such a tease."

"You haven't even begun to see my teasing yet, baby girl," I growl.

Her lips part, and her eyes get that heated look I've missed so fucking much. I can't resist. I drop a gentle kiss on her lips, needing that tart peach on my tongue to remind myself that she's okay. She's here, and she's ours.

Chapter 34

F eeling the sunshine through the window is the best fucking
feeling on earth. After almost two weeks in the hospital, I was
finally released this morning. The Syndicate offered to provide a ride to
wherever we wanted to go. The guys were tight lipped, but the second
I started to see the mountains in the distance and the huge saguaro
cacti popping up along the dry desert landscape, I knew we were in
Arizona.

I have no idea what they have planned, and to be honest, I don't
care. Everything I need, everything that *matters* is right here with me.

Looking out over the gorgeous Arizona landscape, I let the warmth
and the desert air fill me with a peace I'm still barely coming to terms
with. It's hard to reconcile the girl from the slums of Chicago with
the woman surrounded by four men who keep looking at her as if she
hung the moon and stars. All I really did was cut out a man's tongue
and knock another unconscious, but they don't seem to care about
the details.

We begin to descend onto a private helipad set into the back corner of someone's gorgeous mountain property. Built into the rock, the home sits nestled against the rugged stone—a beautiful backdrop with an obstructed view of the entire Valley spread out below it. It's breathtaking.

The guys help me out of the helicopter, carefully avoiding the spinning blades. Nixon follows us until we're clear, and I turn to him with a smile.

"Thank you. For everything."

"The Syndicate appreciates your hard work and dedication, Ms. Parker. They'll be reaching out soon for a final debriefing."

"I'll be waiting."

"Donovan," he says, turning to my beta. "It's been my pleasure to serve with you on this mission. Protect our girl, you hear me?"

Four growls sound off around me, and I laugh.

"How about you protect your dick so I don't cut it off?" Chance snarls.

Nixon just laughs and heads back to the helicopter. It takes off the second his foot is off the ground, and I watch it fly away. When I look back at the guys, they're all staring at me in anxious anticipation.

"Alright. So who's going to let me in on the secret?"

They all share a look, then Felix grabs my hand and drags me to the front door. Without ringing the doorbell, he twists the knob, walking right into a gorgeous foyer.

"Felix, you can't just walk into someone else's house!" I growl, attempting to tug him to a stop, but the effort sends a twinge through my side that has me sucking in a harsh breath.

"Knock that off, sunshine. You're going to hurt yourself!" he snaps, brow furrowed.

"What do you think, sweetheart?" Wren asks, watching me expectantly.

"About what?"

"This house," Anson replies nervously.

My eyes scan the open, airy interior, decorated in warm creams and browns. The huge floor-to-ceiling windows give an amazing view of the Valley, even from here.

"It's stunning. Whose is it?" All four of them are lined up and staring at me with wide smiles.

"It's ours," Felix murmurs softly, and it's then I notice the nerves twitching through the bond.

"Ours?" I whisper, my hand reaching for my side as my heart begins to pound in my chest.

"Our home. A place where we can just *be* together when the band isn't on tour," Chance offers. "A place to call our own, to build a life in. Memories in."

His voice is so full of wonder and hope that a tear rolls down my cheek.

"It's..." I hiccup, then a soft sob escapes my lips as I slowly spin in a circle, taking it all in with a more keen eye, "perfect."

I almost crumble to the ground when overwhelming emotion floods through me. All those pent-up feelings I bottled up inside, all the hurt and hope and fear, come exploding out of me. Wren catches me, lifting me into his arms and holding me tight. His caramel apple scent has a bitter edge when he hugs me, letting me release everything I've been keeping to myself for so long.

As the sobs begin to ebb, the tears drying up, he kisses my forehead.

"You're here." He nuzzles into me, marking me with his scent. "You're safe."

"We're with you now, and no one is going to hurt you again." Anson brushes my hair off my tear-stained cheeks.

"We love you, sunshine," Felix declares.

"I love you all too. So fucking much."

Chance walks up to Wren, taking me from his arms. "We have one more thing to show you."

"There's more?" I whisper.

He carries me out the huge sliding door, walking across the patio of the infinity edge pool to a smaller casita on the edge of the property. When he opens the door, twinkle lights spark to life, illuminating the room in a soft glow. The entire front wall is a floor-to-ceiling window, giving off the same amazing views as the house. He's standing on a landing that leads to a small desk and office set up to the left, the horizontal railings giving an unobstructed view of the space sunken into the ground just beyond it. Taking the four steps down, we land on a soft mattress that makes up the entire floor. In carefully placed shelves cut into the walls are pillows and blankets, all in blush pink, gold, and cream. There are two ginormous loveseat-sized bean bags placed in the corner that look cozy, with built-in bookshelves above them holding more books than I can count. Running along the side walls of the space are two large cylinder-shaped pillows that could be used for a back rest.

"This is..." I'm speechless. "It's gorgeous."

"It's your nest." Chance's arms squeeze me a little tighter, giving away his nervousness.

I gasp. *A nest?* My *nest?*

"I've never had a nest before," I rasp, already feeling the tears starting to fall again.

"You do now."

I turn toward the voice. Anson is walking down the steps with Felix and Wren behind him.

"This is your space," Felix adds. "You can add to it, change the colors, make it however you want it."

"Do you like it?" Wren asks, anxiously awaiting my answer.

"Guys, I didn't need all of this. I only needed you."

The alphas' purrs echo through the space.

"But you deserve this and so much more, baby girl."

Chance sets me down, and my feet sink into the softest mattress I've ever felt in my life. I can't stop the groan from slipping between my lips.

Felix adjusts his dick. "Sunshine, you can't make noises like that yet."

"Why not?"

"You're not healed enough for what we want to do to you when we hear it," Wren replies responsibly.

"Look, I may not be healed enough for any kinky shit…" I pointedly shoot a look at Felix, whose eyes narrow in challenge. "But I'm pretty sure I can lay on my back while you all hop on the Fallon train. All in favor…?"

Chance raises his hand, immediately followed by Felix.

"Son of a bitch," Anson mutters before raising his hand too. Then he shoots a look at Wren.

He shrugs, a smirk curving one side of his mouth. "When in Rome, I guess."

The words are no sooner out of his mouth than Chance carefully raises my shirt above my head. The wound is still angry and red, but the infection is gone. My body has slowly begun to heal. He slides my leggings down my legs, helping me balance when I step out of them.

Then he's on his knees, staring up at me with pure unadulterated appreciation in his eyes.

My hand skims along his jaw, feeling the stubble scraping against my skin. I look up to watch the others shrug out of their clothes.

"A couple of ground rules. This is a sprint, not a marathon. Be kind to the next man in line—in other words, mind your knots. That should be all. Please keep your hands inside the train at all times, and thank you for riding the Fallon Express. All aboard!"

Chance chuckles into my pussy, taking a long lick up the center with a groan. "Fuck, you taste good, pussycat."

My hands grip his head, letting my fingers play through his long hair while he gently eats me out. When he pulls back, he does this crazy maneuver showcasing his incredible strength, lifting me up and carefully setting me down on the mattress in front of him. His body immediately comes down onto mine, covering me with his warmth, and my arms slide around his neck.

"Hi, love," he whispers, dropping his lips to mine for a sweet kiss.

His hard dick prods at my hole until I feel his hips roll, then the head of his cock slips inside me. It feels so fucking good to have this connection, this intimacy, with my guys again. He's intently watching my face—for signs of pain, I realize. When I smile up at him, he finally pushes in so slowly I can feel every inch of his dick dragging against my walls.

"God, that feels good," I murmur.

He drops to his forearms, hands bracketing my head, and we just stare into each other's eyes as he makes love to me. Our connection has grown impossibly stronger this last week. Not only through our mutual bonds with Anson, but also because we're two humans connecting on a level few ever experience.

"Come for me, love." He sucks on my bottom lip until I can feel my pussy clenching around him, then he licks over my mark.

My orgasm unfurls softly, slowly, rolling over me until I'm consumed by the intensity of it. His hips still against mine, and when he finds his release, the pulse of his dick prolongs my own. With a groan, he pulls out, dropping one last kiss on my mouth before he rolls onto his back next to me.

"Who's up next?" he asks, voice hoarse.

The smell of chocolate has me licking my lips as the lead singer of Feral Lyrics positions himself between my legs. He stares down at me with that cocky smirk of his, one hand lining his dick up with my dripping pussy hole.

"No kinky stuff, eh?" he asks just as his hips thrust forward. It's not gentle, but I know it's not as rough as he'd normally be, and it feels fucking amazing.

"Later, I promise. Let me heal a little more, then I'll have you tie me up and fuck me at your leisure."

He groans, pulling out and thrusting forward again with these long, steady strokes that have my breath catching in my throat. His knot is there, pressing against my sex, and I bite back a whimper because if I give him that inch, he'll take a mile. I know my alpha.

My hand reaches between our bodies; the position is a little awkward and a hint uncomfortable, but it's worth it once I see my alpha's face when my fingers wrap around his knot as he thrusts into me. Each time, I squeeze just a little harder.

"Fuck, sunshine. *Harder*. Squeeze me as you come undone."

One, two, three more thrusts, and I can feel the tingling sensation shooting up from my toes. A rush of pleasure floods through my veins, and I tip my head back with a groan as my hand squeezes Felix's knot...hard. He shouts, grinding into my hand, and we both soar into oblivion.

His lips touch mine, his tongue sweeping in with a last show of aggression, before he pulls out and rolls off to the other side.

"Fuck me. Vanilla isn't so bad after all."

I snort just as Anson crawls over to me on all fours. There's something incredibly sexy about a man his size prowling toward you like a wild animal ready to eat you whole.

"Baby girl, that look in your eyes is going to get us both into trouble."

"I don't know. I like a little trouble now and then."

He looms over me, hair loose and falling around my face like a curtain as he kisses me, then he licks along his mark on my lip. My hips buck, and I can't hide the grimace fast enough. Placing one large palm against my hip, he holds me to the mattress.

"None of that. Lay back and let us love you."

I swoon, for real this time, feeling so fucking special and loved that I'm damn near bursting with it.

"Then love me, alpha. Show me what you got."

His purr rumbles between us as his body drops to mine. It's then I realize he's humming one of their songs in this deep soulful tone.

My hand runs along his face, watching his eyes when the fat head of his cock finds my opening.

"What song is that?" I murmur.

"A new one I wrote," he whispers.

"Sing it to me."

He slides in, all the way to his knot, then stops as he meets my eyes. For a second, I think he's going to deny me—he's not the singer of the group after all—but then his deep voice pierces my soul.

"I've never needed perfection..."

Another tear falls, and love floods through our bonds.

"Just one woman's heart."

His thumb brushes the tears off my cheek. His dick is thrusting in and out, building our pleasure with each word he sings until I feel like I'll simply detonate beneath him.

"Would walk a hundred miles in the wrong direction..."

He kisses me swiftly, sucking on his mark. When he pushes up, his body shifts so that he's roughly grinding his knot into my clit, and that's all it takes. I'm coming on one long, continuous loop while he continues to serenade me with both his body and his words.

"If it meant we'd never be apart..." His voice cracks on a groan, his body going taut as he fills me up.

His forehead rests on mine, his breathing uneven, and we both float back down to earth.

"The fuck?" Felix is lying on his back beside us, staring up at the other alpha like he's an alien. "Since when can you fucking sing?"

"Since forever, asswipe," Anson grumbles.

I'm not sure if the pink on his cheeks is from exertion or if the big guy is blushing. He pulls out of me, kneeling between my legs, glaring down at Felix.

"Why the fuck have you never sang with us on stage before?"

"Because I only sing for Fallon."

Yup. Total swoon.

Chance scooches over, making room for him, and Anson collapses beside me.

Wren's staring at me and stroking his cock while the other two alphas bicker back and forth. Lifting my hand, I curl my finger and motion him forward. His crooked grin has a matching one spreading across my face.

As he settles over me, I wrap my arms around him.

"I love you, Fallon," he whispers.

"I love you, too."

His dick slides through the insane amount of wetness dripping out of my pussy, naturally lubing himself up with our combined cum. There's something seriously hot about knowing his dick is coated in his brothers' releases. Not gonna lie.

When he slides into me, my eyes close, and I take in the moment, savoring the rush of affection I can feel through the bond and the overall contentment of the men in the room.

"Sweetheart," he whispers in my ear.

"Yeah, baby?"

His hips haven't stopped pumping into me, my body strung tight even after three orgasms.

"Don't tell them, okay?"

"Tell them wha—"

With one perfectly rough thrust, his knot slips into my cunt, stealing my breath. The world around us goes still for mere seconds until I'm blasting outward into rays of colors and lights. My release is so potent, I'm pretty sure I leave my body at one point, and when I come crashing back to reality, Wren's face is nuzzling my neck while he giggles like a little kid caught with his hand in the cookie jar.

"You dirty cheat!" Felix barks playfully.

"What?" Wren laughs. "I don't have to mind my knot if no one's going after me."

"And what if I wanted another go, eh?"

The two argue over just how soon Felix would be able to get it up again, to which the alpha responds he's always able to get it up with me, how that's never been an issue, and how dare Wren call his manhood into question. I'm laughing so hard my side is beginning to ache.

"Okay. Fuck. That hurts," I cry out, still laughing despite the pain.

"See what you two did?" Anson mutters.

"This is why a beta is perfect in a pack. Easy in and out. Nothing to hold anyone up. Just sayin'."

As the guys bicker around me, I let my soul just...*feel*. I'm here, I survived, and I'm surrounded by four men who love me. Sure, they're not perfect, but neither am I. Guess that makes us perfect for each other.

Epilogue

One Year Later

I'm pacing the foyer, waiting for the text to come through. My nerves are making my belly pitch, and I'm worried I'm about to be sick. Remembering the guys can sense my turmoil through the bond, I take a deep breath, exhaling the negative energy and focusing on the positive.

Then my phone chimes, and I rush out the door, over to the helipad. The helicopter's blades are spinning when Nixon steps out in full tactical gear, holding the brown paper sack in his hand like it's a bomb that's about to detonate.

I can't stop the giggle that rushes out of me any more than I can stop my raucous laughter at the evident distress he's under as he hustles toward me.

"Parker, explain to me why one of the Syndicate's most decorated handlers can't go and buy this shit herself?"

"Nixon, have you *met* my guys? I tell them I'm running to the store, and they'll insist that someone goes with me. Even almost a year later, overprotective is too loose a term as far as they're concerned."

"Point taken. But why's it a secret?"

"It's not, per se. I'm just... Well, I don't want to get their hopes up, ya know?"

He hands me the bag, and even though he's wearing a mask, I can feel the fondness he has for me in the tilt of his head and the way his shoulders relax.

"You got a sister?" he asks, and somehow I know he's smiling behind his mask. Of course, I've never seen his face, so for all I know, he's a robot under there, but I've got a feeling.

"Can you imagine two of me?" I scoff.

"Yes. Yes, I can." He laughs. "Good luck, Parker. Tell Donovan I said hello."

"Stay safe out there," I call to his back.

He gives me a thumbs up in reply.

Walking back into the house, I head for the bathroom.

Dinner is done, the table set. I even pulled out the fancy new cutlery the guys insisted we had to have, though I'm not sure why. Half the time, we order takeout, and that usually includes the nifty little plastic utensils with the napkin wrapped around them. Our favorite playlist is on low, and I hum along as I stir the risotto.

Yeah. I'm a badass *and* a regular Betty Crocker. Who knew?

I hear Chance walk in first, the sound of his boots pounding across the tile as he groans.

"Fuck. Something smells delicious."

He walks into the kitchen, coming up behind me at the stove and wrapping his arms around my waist. I can feel the tension ease from his body. I wasn't joking. The guys' anxiety any time they've had to be apart from me is something we've had to work through over the last year. PTSD, the doctor called it. Some days are better than others, and I just know, with my latest news, it's about to get worse.

"Beef Wellington and mushroom risotto. It just sounded yummy."

"I'll need to add an extra workout to my routine if you keep this up."

I turn, wrapping my arms around his waist. "I can help with that."

"Now, are we talking workout or *workout*?" He wags his eyebrows.

Beneath my laughter, I hear the garage door open and the sound of the guys' voices trailing in.

"Damn. What's the occasion?" Felix asks when he struts into the room with Anson and Wren on his heels.

"No occasion. Just because," I lie, reciting the recipe in my head, step by step, just to keep my emotions level so I don't give anything away.

"She's softening us up for something." Anson leans his hip against the counter, crossing his arms over his massive chest.

"I most certainly am *not*."

"Oh, she definitely is." Wren chuckles. "You two have a new job coming up or something? Last time you were going to be away for a few days, she distracted us with so much sex we couldn't say no."

"I haven't been told of any upcoming projects..." Chance's eyes narrow. "You wouldn't take a job without me, would you, pussycat?"

Needing just a little bit of time to shore up my courage, I spin around, grab the mitts, and pull the meat out of the oven. With finesse I didn't know I possessed, I carefully place it on the serving plate and set it on the large granite island.

"Now she's avoiding us," Anson murmurs.

"I just don't want dinner to burn." Accurate. But also a lie.

"Sunshine, so help me God, I will throw you over my knee and spank your ass if you don't tell us what the fuck is going on."

My thighs clench and my perfume leaks out, but I manage to hold it together.

"Fine. I've taken on a new job. And before you get upset, you should know that the training will take roughly nine months."

The room is in an uproar, the guys shouting over each other as they freak the fuck out. Okay, yeah, I did it this way on purpose. I'm mean. Sue me.

Placing my hands on my hips, I wait for them to wear themselves down.

Wren runs his hands down his face. "Sweetheart, we talked about this. We were okay with you joining the Syndicate because they agreed you and Chance would be partners, and that was only after you had to con them into keeping him alive by offering to go to work for them. We all agreed that the contract work was no longer a viable option. Your face is plastered on the tabloids at every supermarket. Your anonymity is gone."

"But this job is important, and I've already committed to it."

"Why would you do that without consulting us first?" Felix growls.

"I mean, technically speaking, I did."

They all stare at me dumbfounded.

"Pussycat, I can assure you, there was no conversation had about a new job."

"I beg to differ. I specifically recall Felix saying he was, and I quote, a little bit excited about the possibility." Felix's deep brown brows are furrowed so tightly I'm starting to wonder if they'll be stuck like that forever. "And Wren even said he saw the appeal."

Now it's Wren's turn to look confused as fuck. God, I'm a horrible omega.

I watch, noting the exact moment Anson figures it out. He straightens, his arms falling to his side as his eyes begin to widen.

"Son of a bitch!" he exclaims, practically bulldozing me over in his haste to get to me.

He sweeps me off my feet, hugging me so damn tightly that I can barely breathe, but that's okay. Who needs oxygen anyways?

"What the hell did we miss?" Chance mutters.

"I, for one, fully support this new job," Anson declares, sliding his arm around my waist and setting me back on my feet with a quick kiss on my lips.

"The fuck?" is all Felix gets out before the metaphorical lightbulb appears over Wren's head.

"No fucking way!" He stalks toward me, pulls me right out of Anson's hold, and kisses me like he hasn't seen me in ten years. I mean, it's identical to that very first kiss on the bus when he was damn near feral. "Me too. I am one hundred percent here for this job."

Chance and Felix are both struggling with confusion and growing irritation, and I sigh. Guess I'll take pity on them.

"The last one to figure it out gets diaper duty for the first month."

Or maybe not. Fuck, I'm evil.

The two men share a look then literally *whoop* in unison, crashing into me while they whisper their full and total support for my new job.

From contract killer to rogue mercenary to mother.

Just another day in the life of an omega finally living her happily ever after.

WANT MORE OF THE UNDERGROUND OMEGA SYNDICATE?

https://geni.us/UOSSeries

About the Author

Sinclair Kelly is a paranormal & contemporary romance author who writes to give all of the feral characters in her head a voice. She's fluent in sarcasm and dry humor. She lives in sunny Arizona with her loving husband, three adorably exhausting kids, and a feisty Australian shepherd puppy named Havoc. She loves reading, writing, coffee, vodka, tattoos, wine, donuts, broody asshole book boyfriends, badass FMCs, sangria, and all of the friendships she's made since she began her writing journey.

Want more Sin?

www.sinclairkelly.com
https://linktr.ee/SinclairKellyAuthor

Other Books by Sinclair Kelly

Knot Yours Omegaverse Series

I Think Knot

Knot A Chance

Knot My Problem

Sinner's Mark MC Series

Saint

Rogue

Ace (Coming Soon)

Trip (Coming Soon)

Squire (Coming Soon)

The Ghost Girl Series

A Fate Unknown

Twist of Fate

It Must Be Fate

Land of Legend Series

If The Broom Fits

If The Wand Sparkles

If The Throne Calls

Made in the USA
Las Vegas, NV
12 April 2024

88293067R00174